# BREAK LINE

SARAH E. GREEN

Edited by: Jessica DeWulf & Jennifer Davis
Proofread by: Bex Harper, Morelia Garcia, Lacey Thach
Book Cover Design by Letitia Hasser, Romantic Book Affairs
Cover image © Shutterstock
Back image © Shutterstock

Interior Formatting by Stacey Blake,

ISBN-13: 978-1548146535
ISBN-10: 1548146536

*To my mom and dad—for always believing in me.*

*Also, sorry about making you read that one scene, Mom. It won't happen again lol*

# CHAPTER ONE

## Emery

A LINE IS TETHERED TO ME, KEEPING ME ALIVE.
*My eyes are heavy, like sandbags.*
*Everything is muted. Everything is dark.*
*I feel so tired. So light.*
*Someone is whispering to hold on. To fight.*
*Fighting sounds so hard right now. Why am I fighting? Why can't I open my eyes?*
*The line tugs at my core, making my body jolt, but I'm sinking, sinking back into myself.*
*There's only so much they can do until the line breaks and I flatline.*

≈

Buzzbuzzbuzz.
The alarm drags me from dreaming.

Sweat coats my skin in a fine film. The scenes of my dream already fading. Some people remember their dreams and for some, the images disappear the instant their eyes open. For me, even if the moments fade, the images stay, imprinting on my memory. Impossible to shake.

That's what happens when your brain decides to reminisce on an actual nightmare. One you will never be able to shake. One that you lived.

*Buzzbuzzbuzzbuzz.*

My body protests as I reach over to turn off the annoying alarm. When silence descends, I throw the gray comforter over my head, moaning into my pillow.

There is something unnatural about being up before the sun. But even as I grumble, talking incoherencies, and my body fights to go back to sleep, I roll out of bed, hitting the floor with a soft *thump.*

"Hmph," I groan as I try to rub the sleep out of my eyes. Little yellow eye crust sticks to my fingers. "*Mhhh.*"

Getting up early has been my reality for the last two years. Nothing new about the moaning, the heavy eyes, or the exhaustion fighting my body as it silently screams to go back to sleep.

I made a promise, a commitment, to myself. A promise I refuse to break.

Two years and my body hasn't adapted to this schedule. Waking up early every morning is a choice I make, but I am never going to be a morning person—unless copious amounts of coffee can be consumed first.

Through a sleepy haze, I grab the essentials: a change of clothes, a bathing suit, and a bottle of water from the mini fridge in my room—a fridge that was originally bought for my dorm. Unbeknownst to my parents, I withdrew from school, taking everything from the room with me under the guise of winter break.

Most of the belongings sit untouched in my walk-in closet, but the fridge is by my desk, in the corner. The best place to hide it while still using it. My parents hardly come into my room, so it isn't a pressing issue to stress about.

What *is* an issue is finding a way to tell my parents their child is no longer in college. I did three semesters, three more than I ever wanted to do. And in those three semesters I discovered what I always knew to be true.

School isn't for me.

I'm smart, a fact my parents like to remind me of, but I'm not a classroom type of girl. Never have been. Learning in a classroom, to me, is boring. There isn't enough stimulation to hold my interest. I prefer hands-on learning to sitting at a desk in a lecture room getting hand cramps from taking pages of notes.

I used to argue that my dad didn't go to college. Back in the 80s, Dad was too busy catching waves and entering every surfing competition he could. Too busy going pro and becoming the best. Sure, school was probably something he could've done, but he became a surf legend. A household name.

Mom went to college, though. She has a degree in coastal environmental science and works in a lab.

They are both pro-school, pro-education. So am I, but going to college isn't for everyone. There's nothing wrong with that.

Nothing wrong with being different and going against the social norm.

So after three semesters of being miserable, I decided I was done. It was time to go after the life I wanted, instead of following the path that others had laid out for me.

The decision wasn't scary when I went to the administration building and withdrew. It was freeing. My steps lighter when I left than when I had entered.

I'm happier now.

But the minute I tell my parents, the happy bubble I've been in for the past week will pop.

I took my finals, packed up my car, and came home. The only reason I waited until the end of the semester to leave was because my parents like to see my final grades. Not just hearing them, but physically, with their own eyes, seeing them. On my computer screen.

My parents aren't the earliest of risers. They both take winter break off every year so we can have family time. Which translates to vacation time, which translates to more time for me to sneak out and get back before they wake up.

They think I gave up surfing. They think I'm enrolled in college for the spring semester. They think a lot about me that isn't true.

Like how I'm happy with the life they built for me a few years ago, a different life than the one we had always talked about.

The life they want me to live is a lie. The hastily built wall around the façade has been cracked.

Broken.

Destroyed.

Smashed into a thousand, impossible-to-rebuild pieces.

My life is full of secrets, secrets I never thought I had to keep from my parents.

Secrets destroy relationships, but so does resentment.

For the past three years, I've been festering in a pool of resentment toward my parents. I love them wholeheartedly but there comes a time when their choices for my life get quieter and mine get louder.

Which is why I've slowly started to take back control.

In secret.

As bad as it sounds, my parents pay for everything. While in school, I'm not allowed to have a job. My entire focus has to be on education. So in order to make sure I'm taken care of, they gave me a stipend of my trust fund last year.

On my eighteenth birthday.

A trust fund.

One I had no idea existed. Yet, here I am, with a trust fund. I'm a trust fund baby.

I've always known my family was well off. Well, *well* off. But still. I didn't know we were at the level of having trust funds.

I'm not the only one keeping secrets in this household.

Leaving the house quietly, I text my best friend's brother, Geer, letting him know I'm heading to his house.

He lives right on the water, with the beach as his back-yard. It's a two-minute drive to his place from mine. We both live off Ocean Avenue in a small Florida beach town, but while Geer lives on the beach, I live in a gated community full of extravagant homes.

Parking my car next to his huge-ass truck, I get out to punch in the code to the garage door and walk inside, where I keep my surfboards and wetsuits. I grab my stuff, do a quick change, and head out to the beach.

Growing up, the beach was my home. I spent more time rolling around in the sand and swimming in the ocean than I spent at my actual house.

The ocean is my heart. My first love. A part of who I am.

That doesn't mean I trust it. It's too vast, too wild, and full of too many creatures to not be wary. Off the coast alone, there are thousands of sharks and fish that sometimes stray too close to shore.

I used to love the ocean blindly. An all-consuming feeling, taking over all my thoughts. Thinking it loved me as much as I loved it.

I know better now.

Going surfing alone, when the sun isn't up yet, is extremely dangerous. Between rip currents and not being able to see much of what's in the ocean, the water turns into a danger zone.

I text Geer every day for this reason. He worries if I don't and it gives me peace of mind knowing at least *someone* is aware of where I am.

The texts are predictable by now. Part of the routine. But if I miss a day, I'll have an angry Geer on my hands. And nobody wants an angry Geer.

Throwing my board onto the sand, I gather my hair up before letting it fall against my back. Light brown with blonde strands bleached from the sun. Perks of living in South Florida. Summer almost year round.

I fish around in my bag for the circular block of pink, fruity smelling surf wax. After applying a healthy amount to the board, I throw the wax back in my bag and tuck the board under my arm, heading toward the water.

As I get closer, my steps slow.

Cold water brushes my toes as I stand on the edge, where the sand meets the surf.

No matter how much time passes, hesitation is now a part of my sport. A consequence from years before that has turned into an unbreakable habit. Subconsciously, my fingers dance along my neoprene-clad thigh. A hidden reminder.

With a deep exhale, one last grab of courage, I run into the water.

The sun has started to break over the horizon, casting orange-yellowish rays in the sky, a painting-picturesque scene just as I'm almost done with my morning surf sesh. On the beach I catch a tall, muscular silhouette standing with his hands on his hips by my pile of stuff. Watching me.

After I ride out my last wave, I paddle to shore, a weight presses down on my chest as I chant, *please be Geer. Please be Geer.*

He comes out to check on me some days when he's up early enough but every time he does, a little zing of panic shoots through my veins, igniting my fears.

As I get closer to the beach, picking my board up, the pressure in my chest subsides.

Geer Jackson looks mean, with hard eyes and harder angles.

He shares similar features with my best friend, Brit. They have the same hair, the same eyes, except Geer's built like a dude. His bone structure is sharper, like chiseled ice along his jaw and has corded muscles on his arms with tree trunks as legs and a long torso. He loves the gym, making him a six-foot-three wall of pure muscle. And his black hair is always kept closely shaved to his skull, with just a layer of fuzz covering his head.

His face is set in a permanent scowl, one that doesn't intimidate me as I approach him.

My favorite part about Geer has always been his eyes. They are this gray color that is reminiscent of melted silver. While his face is always set in that scowl, his eyes contain all the emotions. Smiling at him, I see the melted silver of his eyes harden.

Geer doesn't speak until I sit my butt on the towel, grab the water, and chug that sucker down. He pinches the bridge of his nose, dragging in a deep breath. "What am I going to do with you?"

"I don't know what you mean." I twist the cap around the plastic.

Geer looks tired, dark circles weighing under his eyes.

I scoot over, patting the towel space next to me, inviting him to sit. "Stay up late last night?" I wiggle my eyebrows.

"I'm not telling you shit, Em." He rubs his eyes, cursing under his breath. "Fucking sand."

"You never tell me," I remind him. "That doesn't mean I'm going to stop asking."

Silence cloaks us as we sit in the sand, me leaning my body into his side and head resting on his shoulder. He doesn't even protest as my wetsuit dampens his clothes. We're quiet as we watch the sun rise above the horizon, illuminating the sky, enjoying the company of not being alone as the town around us starts to wake up to begin the day.

A new day means new memories and new adventures.

New ways to lie.

The only other person that knows my secret is Brit and she is *not* a morning person. I think I'm bad, but Brit is on another level. She won't even stir when her alarm goes off.

Geer takes my board, promising to wash the salt off, and tells me to get a shower before heading home. I start to protest, he's exhausted—from his eyes to his sluggish movements—and needs sleep more than I need a shower.

I can rinse off my board and my body at the same time with the hose on the side of his place, but he pins me with a glare, cutting off my argument before I'm able to voice it. "Owe me another time, like when I see you tomorrow night. You can bring me brownies."

Oh, right.

We're having dinner at his parents' house since Brit and I are back from school. Not that our families need an excuse to get together. We probably see each other a minimum of four or five days a week. We're more like family than friends.

"Do you want special brownies or...?" I let the question hang between us as Geer just glares at me.

I grin, standing up and rubbing the sand sticking to my foot on his leg.

He grunts as he looks down at the little flecks of sand. "C'mon, let's go so I don't have to see you for the rest of my morning and can actually have a good day." He starts walking up the beach.

"You know you love me," I tease as I continue to twist the cap of my drink.

He ignores his love for me, the sister he never asked for but has always needed, and eyes my water. "Isn't your mom against plastic water bottles? She always gives me those reusable ones on birthdays."

I nod. That's exactly my mother. We have an entire cabinet full of reusable and travel friendly water bottles. "But this makes less noise than running around the kitchen, sooo she doesn't need to know."

Geer huffs, his version of swearing secrecies, as he pushes my shoulder and I stumble to the side with a smile.

We're quiet for the rest of the walk.

After taking my shower, the quickest of my life, I'm in my car, backing out of his driveway.

On the drive home, my phone buzzes with a text from my cousin, Nori.

The text has a picture, but I don't look at it until I'm parked in the bakery parking lot—another morning ritual.

When I see what she's sent, a laugh comes out. Nori's at a diving competition, but the picture is of her in the locker room, holding up her tablet, the screen showing an article written about her journey to get to the Olympics.

Her brown hair is pulled back in a messy bun that's tilted to one side of her head. She's making a face at it, her blue eyes set in a glare as her lips twist in a scowl.

Her expression is clear.

She's not a fan.

Nori wants to dive, to make it to the Olympics, but she doesn't want the attention. The press. She just wants to compete and let her athleticism speak for itself.

I send a text back.

Psh, enjoy the spotlight, girl. Before you become like my dad, spending your time talking about the golden years.

My phone vibrates with a response.

I don't want my face all over the Internet!

I don't mention that if she makes the Olympics, she's probably going to have to make public social media accounts to share her journey with the people. Not to mention her face will be on televisions around the world during the games. Instead I settle for something equally as true.

Haha, miss you. Come home soon!

I send the text as I walk into the bakery to get my usual order of cream puffs and croissants before heading home. The sweets provide a cover if my parents wake up early and wonder where I am.

I'm nineteen and still act like I'm in high school. I wonder if I'll ever be able to walk through that front door without having to lie about where I was.

After placing the blue box on the kitchen's island, I head to the coffee maker. Surfing is like my natural coffee, the adrenaline acting as a wake up call, but natural or not, I still need my caffeine fix.

The rich, earthy aroma fills the kitchen. My mouth salivates as I inhale the decadent scent.

*Caffeine, come to me.*

I begin to fill up my mug as my mother makes her morning debut. She's wearing linen sleep pants, slippers, and a plush, fuzzy robe. "Morning, sweetie."

"Morning," I mumble as she kisses my cheek. She grabs her own mug, filling it almost to the brim.

Rule number one in the Lawson household: no conversations until everyone has had their first cup of coffee.

With my drink in hand, I settle on a bar stool, bringing my knees to my chest. In front of me sits the latest edition to *Rip Current,* a popular surf magazine. The person on the cover has me rolling my eyes.

Sebastian "Bash" Cleaton is the lucky surfer of the month. Not surprising. He has graced the cover a few times already.

But that's what happens when you are the hottest surfer of the generation.

Not my words, I swear. They were the words on his first cover of *Rip Current.* It was a part of their Sexy September feature. Or something like that.

The guy has risen to fame in the surfing world because of his talent, but thanks to social media, he's become more famous for his looks. More popular than he probably thought possible.

His skin is like mine, sun-kissed from always being outside. His brown hair is artfully messy. Like instead of him running his fingers through it, he had a stylist perform the task for him. He's wearing his signature expression: a pout with hooded eyes.

Brit has dubbed it his "bedroom look".

Yeah, it's hot. He's hot.

My thumb brushes along my mouth for a drool check. It comes back dry. Good, good.

I want to be different than the rest of his admirers. I want to find him ugly, but I don't.

His arrogance, on the other hand, is enough for me to not have fantasies about him. Yet, my curiosity always wins. I flip open to the interview section, wondering what he has to say in this issue—

"It's weird."

My eyes snap to my mom, who is on the opposite side of the island, a tall coffee mug held loosely in her left hand, her wedding rings sparkling under the kitchen light. "What is?"

"You," she says before taking another sip.

"Gee, just what every girl wants to hear from their mother." Sarcasm is thick in my words.

"Don't be a smartass." She smiles, the expression full of warmth.

"Can't help it, Mom," I tell her, grinning. "It's who I am. Accept me and love me anyway."

"Always." She kisses my forehead before she shakes her head. "It's just still weird seeing you up before ten."

I bite my lip, looking down, not uttering a word. *Secrets. My head is full of secrets.*

When her gaze becomes too much, I just shrug, taking a sip of my drink. Mom stays in the kitchen for a little longer, throwing together a bowl of granola and yogurt, before she walks to the back porch.

I watch as the door closes behind her before reaching for my coffee and magazine, heading toward my room. I've got some lounging and reading to do.

My house is pretty big, a small mansion by some standards. A two-story equipped with an attic—somewhat of a rarity in Florida—and five sets of stairs, each one leading to a different section of the second floor. Perhaps it's too big for three people, but growing up it was always full of family and friends so it never felt empty.

I walk out of our kitchen to the hidden stairwell behind the pantry.

As I climb the stairs slowly, my fingers run along the bluish-gray paint that decorates the walls, with pictures of my childhood adorning them.

One of my favorites is of me sitting on a hot pink bike with a white leather seat, training wheels attached to the back tire. On my head is a matching helmet that has two braided pigtails poking out from underneath it. A smile carved between my lips, highlighting two missing front teeth. Behind me, with one arm on the handlebar and the other on the seat, is my dad. His auburn hair is shaved almost as close to the scalp as Geer's, with teeth so white I used to swear they sparkled. In the picture, he's smiling down at me, the corners of his eyes crinkling with adoration.

I was about four in that picture, and the way my father treats me now is pretty much the same. I'm his little girl.

Which is why my accident hit him so hard. No matter what is said, he can't be swayed.

One day, I know I'll have to tell him. Tell both my parents, especially if I want to go after my dreams.

But not today.

Not tomorrow.

Going after what I want won't happen until my bravery outweighs my fear of disappointment.

# CHAPTER TWO

## *Bash*

A VACATION IS SUPPOSED TO BE RELAXING, RIGHT? OR IS it only relaxing for a certain period of time? Did I max out my quota?

Twenty days.

Twenty fucking days of doing absolutely nothing.

I am about to go up the wall.

I should be in a state of bliss. My first vacation in almost a decade and I hate myself for feeling this way. Maybe I'm just too much of a workaholic to know what it's like to relax.

Surfers are known for being chill, and I like to think that, for the most part, I am. But I seriously doubt that other pros have a personal life as stressful as mine. If they do, I bet their asses wouldn't know how to unwind either.

For the first week, I tried to get up on my board every morning. But each day I felt less and less motivated. The first two days consisted of me floating on it, letting wave after wave pass me by. By day three I had to force myself to walk from the sand to the water—something I've never experienced in my life. At the end of the week, I gave up going to the beach entirely.

Ever since I was little, the water, as cheesy as it sounds, has called to me. My mother, sister, and I would log countless hours at the beach in the summer. Soaking up sun and digging in the sand.

Some of my earliest memories include my sister putting me on a bodyboard and holding on tight every time a wave carried me back to shore.

After that, it was game over. I wanted more bodyboarding, more time in the water, and eventually that lead me to surfing.

Surfing has never felt like a job. It's more than that. It's my passion. But what happens when the thing you love turns into the thing you hate? What do you do then?

For me, the answer was easy. I ran. Or rather, I flew.

One day I woke up and just had enough. Enough of the pressure. Enough of the fizzling fear that the fiery passion I once had burning inside me got snuffed out like water over a fire.

I packed a bag and two of my boards, changed my bank account records so only I had access to them, and left. Flying from one side of America to the other. I didn't regret the choice for a second while the plane was in the air, but when the wheels dropped down and the plane was at the gate, I had a huge moment of *what the fuck did I just do?*

I flew into West Palm, but I knew no one in town. I had no place to stay. I didn't even have a car to get anywhere. The rental place only had cars that were too small to fit my boards.

So while I waited for the baggage claim carousel to come to life, I tried to think of a plan. None that got very far before

I remembered I did know someone. A friend I met on the surf circuit a few years ago. One of the only guys I've kept in touch with over the years.

I found his contact and hit call, hoping he was awake at—I pulled the phone away from my ear—two-thirty in the morning. And if he was awake at this time, please let him be sober.

"Yo!" Voices in the background muffled his words. Well. He was definitely awake. It was too loud and hard to comprehend what words were shouted, but they sounded foreign. Maybe Spanish? But it was difficult to tell if he was at a party or liked to watch his movies on the highest volume.

"It's Bash." I didn't have time for small talk, but it felt wrong to just come out and ask for his help.

"Dude, I know. These funny little things we're talking on are called smartphones and they have caller I.D." I could feel him rolling his eyes. "What's up, man?"

"Are you busy?" No sooner than the question was asked, a girly scream rang in my ear and I had to pull the phone away. Oh fuck, he wasn't—he had better not be fucking a chick while on the phone.

"Shh, angel." Oh for fuck's sake. Dez whispered to the screaming girl before saying to me, "Nah man. Just chilling with family. What's up?"

Hanging out with family at two-thirty in the morning—

You know what, I didn't want to know. I got to the point of why I was calling. "I need a ride."

After telling him where I was, Dez ended the call with nothing more than a *gotcha*, arriving at the airport within an hour. He didn't ask questions. Instead, Dez brought me to his house, letting me crash in his roommate's room, who was away on vacation with his family. Still, he didn't ask questions. Not even when I asked for his help with finding a place to stay for a while.

Within the first few days of being in Florida, Dez's mom, Alma, helped me find the rental that I've been staying in for the past fifteen days. It's nice. Located on the water with a lot of space, more space than I need, and practically barren, aside from the bare minimum of furniture.

I'm sprawled out on the couch with the blinds shut and an arm thrown over my eyes, surrounded by darkness. I don't know what time it is or how long I've been out here, but today hasn't been one of my better days.

My mind is in the dark, swirling farther and farther down the abyss and all I want to do is sleep. All I want is to be alone. I haven't left the house at all today or talked to anyone in the past two.

Yesterday when I woke up, I felt off but tried to push it away, tried to ignore it. But waking up this morning, I knew today was going to be another bad day.

I've been like this my entire life, but within the past year, it's now taken another form. The bottle of pills sits unopened on the counter behind me, but I can't bring myself to take them. So I tolerate the bad days.

I groan as I hear my front door open. The downside to not picking up my phone today is that I can't text my one and only friend in this town to fuck off and not come over.

Something he likes to do more than three times a week.

Sometimes he comes by three times a day. Needy bastard.

"Dude!" Dez calls as he walks down the hallway. "Why the fuck is it so dark in here?"

I groan, not bothering to answer. Dez walks further into the house, stomping like an angry elephant brigade, until he's in the living room.

"Leave, Dez."

"Nah, bro." He's standing above me now. "Get out of this—" he gestures to my body, "—whatever the hell this is, because you and I have plans tonight."

"I'll pass." That's usually what I do when I get like this. Being around people can sometimes help, but I already planned on going to bed early, thinking of the promise I made to myself.

"Nope. No can do." He walks around me and I know what he's going for. The bottle of pills jingle as he walks over to me and shakes out the allotted amount. "You made me promise that if you send an SOS, I'm to come over and provide a distraction." He thrusts the pills at me. "Here. Take these."

"I don't remember saying I needed help."

"Your silence was the ask for help, dude. Now pills."

I vaguely remember this conversation. We were pretty drunk and I was feeling truthful. Dez knows a lot about my reasons for getting out of California. He even said that if I were looking for something more permanent here, his mom would help me find a place.

"Fine." I pop the pills into my mouth, swallowing them dry. I left one mother only to gain another.

Honestly, when I told Dez everything, I thought he would forget. He's chiller than me, always looking for fun and likes to party. I never thought he would take his promise seriously. But it's days like today that I'm glad he does.

This is the second time he's come over to find me like this.

Last time, he was so much like a parent that I joked he was hiding a kid somewhere in his house and he almost shut down on me completely. Joke was not well received.

"Good. Now get your ass up and get dressed. I'm fucking starving and need to grab something to eat before we head out."

"Where are we going?" I swing my legs to the floor, putting my elbows on my knees and rubbing my eyes roughly.

"Nope. Can't tell you that, dude." Dez chuckles as he walks back into my kitchen and starts digging around in my fridge.

Not bothering to waste time getting an answer out of him, I stalk up the stairs, into the bathroom, and hope that tonight isn't going to make me regret everything tomorrow.

Turns out, Dez wasn't planning on leaving my house. Dressed to leave in shorts, a long sleeve shirt, flip flops, and a snapback, I walk down the stairs to find Dez reclining on the couch with a plate of food on his lap.

Spread out on my coffee table are containers of wings and two large boxes of pizza. There's a game playing on the TV.

I give Dez a look as I reach for a slice of pizza.

"What?" he asks, his mouth full of food. He shakes his head, laughing before grabbing his beer. "Oh yeah. I didn't know this game was on. We're staying in."

I shake my head, not commenting on his change of plans. I sit my ass on the floor and eat the pizza.

I didn't need to go out, I just needed to not be alone, something Dez knew without me having to say anything.

Maybe calling Dez at the airport those short weeks ago gave me something besides a ride to my vacation destination.

Maybe I'm learning what it's like to have an actual friend. One that gives a damn.

# CHAPTER THREE

## *Emery*

"**D**ON'T YOU DARE EAT THAT PIECE OF STEAK, JASON!" The sound of Brit's mom yelling travels outside their house as the doors to the SUV open. Voices collide. Noises clash. A mental picture of the kitchen in disarray flashes, with dishes flying and food splattered on the walls.

My parents roll their eyes; I grin as we walk to the door.

"Heyooo!" I call, walking through their living room, towards the kitchen, with Geer's pan of brownies. I stop in the entryway and watch.

Jason and April Jackson are in an intense stare down in the middle of the kitchen. Light gray-speckled granite lines the counters with white cabinets hovering above; their kitchen makes a beautiful battlefield for a showdown. As the oven timer goes off, neither of the Jacksons blink an eye. Their laser-focus gazes are on each other.

"If Jason is sampling the steak, then I sure as hell want a

piece too." I walk further into the kitchen.

That breaks their stare down.

April turns her storm cloud colored eyes toward me, making me take an involuntary step back from the heat of her glare. Jason grins at me in victory as he bites into the piece of meat.

"Emery Lawson, why do you always take his side?" April asks as she points a big spoon at me.

I shrug as I make my way over to give her a hug. "He's the one who gives me beer when y'all get drunk. He kind of solidified my unwavering support."

"Get out of my kitchen before I whack you with my spoon!" she yells, not liking my answer.

Brit and I have been best friends since birth. Our dads grew up next to each other, practically brothers. Jason is an only child and my dad just has a younger sister. Even as my dad got famous, Jason was always right by his side. How they met our moms is a little hazy since neither of them remember either night.

Ah, young love. What a beautiful thing.

Our dads joke that Brit and I are like them when they were growing up, but worse. Which might be true. We do tend to get in a lot of trouble. Our wild fathers spawned even rowdier daughters.

Me more so than Brit, but she's always along for the ride.

One time we started a marshmallow fight in my kitchen when we were having a sleepover and my parents woke up to find our kitchen decorated with sticky lumps of fluff and we blamed the mess on the dog.

I had no dog at the time.

My trusty ole partner in crime.

I find said partner in crime in her bedroom with her eyes

glued to her laptop, her camera sitting beside it. She never goes anywhere without it and no matter where she is, or what she's doing, the thing is always an arm's length away from her.

I sneak up behind her, quietly, closing her computer screen as fast as I can.

"Hey!" she yells, yanking her fingers back to avoid getting them squished. "What if I was on the very cusp of finding the cure to cancer and now all my research is lost? Gone forever!"

"You don't even like science, brah."

She raises a brow. "I could like science, dude."

"Okay, let me rephrase." I roll my eyes. "You aren't even *good* at science."

"It's hard, okay?" She pretends to pout.

"Remember that one time you tried to bribe our chemistry teacher with twenty bucks to give you extra credit so you wouldn't get a D on your report card?"

"And how you convinced our biology teacher that you didn't believe in science?"

I laugh, remembering how high-pitched his voice got as his face grew to the shade of a dark, red cherry. "We were awful."

"You still are," she points out.

I fold my hands over my heart. "You say the sweetest things to me, friend."

Brit snorts and I walk to her bed, my mind replaying countless memories from high school. Some good and some that altered my life in ways I never could've imaged.

"Sometimes I miss it."

Brit gives me a look, her face is pinched up in what can only be described as disgust. Her tone matches. "Really?"

"Well, not all of it. Just how easy life was when we were freshman and sophomores."

She makes a new face this time, one that compresses into sympathy and my stomach curdles. "I'm fine. I swear. *You* know I am."

Before she can say anything, or worse argue how unfine she might think I am, annoying chimes chirp from her phone. Brit unlocks it, reading the message. After typing out a quick reply, she locks her phone and faces me with a knowing grin.

The conversation from before is now forgotten.

When she doesn't share, I raise a brow and cross my arms. "You going to tell me what made you so happy?"

"We're going to a party!" She claps her hands before pumping them in the air. "First one of break."

"Okay, when?"

"After we eat."

I nod. "We need a DD," I tell her, being responsible and what not, before asking, "Nose goes?"

My finger is already touching my nose while Brit has her hands in her lap. HA! I win!

She handles her loss with grace, by not acknowledging it, and glances down at her phone again.

"Are you going to charge that before we leave?" Knowing Brit, her battery is probably down to ten percent, but I need to be able to find her if we get split up.

She shrugs. Ignoring my question, she asks her own, "Aren't you going to ask where?"

"Nope." I shake my head. "As long as they have alcohol, I'm good."

"You're so predictable, Em." She rolls her eyes as she begins typing on her phone.

"Yeah, well, this is why we're friends. You're my sober sister!"

"Not tonight." She looks up at me with a smirk before

going back to her screen. I'm getting ready to ask who she's texting when Geer walks into the room, phone in hand, a glare fixed on his sister.

Aaaand I have my answer.

"So, what? I just get nominated as the driver? What if I had plans?"

"You don't have plans," Brit and I say in unison. Brit adds, "We need you to drive us."

"Yeah," I agree. "We need you to be our sober sister. Or in your case, brother."

"Gotcha." Neutral tone. Geer is great at hiding emotions. He's also great at being a big brother, and a pushover. If we need him and he has plans, he'll cancel.

We're lucky that he likes to hang around us. No matter what his friends said growing up, Geer's protective and loyal to me and Brit. He's never ashamed to be seen with his sister and her best friend.

He even offered to be my date to prom, but Brit and I decided to bail on that before it was even planned.

If Geer wasn't always so broody, we'd call him the other sister in our squad, but he'd snarl at us.

Geer is a man's man.

April's voice calls from the kitchen, putting our party planning on pause.

"We're leaving after dessert," Brit tells her brother as she walks past him. "So I hope that's what you're wearing."

I pat his chest when he doesn't move from the doorway.

He's only wearing basketball shorts.

Two hours into the party and a few beers later, I have to stifle a yawn.

It's nearing close to midnight and I have to get up early. I would have already left, but I spied Brit talking to Dez Daimon, a guy she was borderline in love with in high school, and knew I couldn't ask her to leave just yet.

Brit sees me watching them and I grimace, knowing what's coming. I'm a protective best friend and an awful third wheel. I usually make sure no making out happens—one time even going as far as putting my hand between two sets of lips—but Brit seems to have forgotten that.

She waves me over and dread settles in.

I don't know why she wants me there.

She finally has Dez all to herself.

Let me stay here, drinking my beer, while I teach myself how to sleep with my eyes open. I'm perfectly fine being alone by this wall. Especially if it means I don't have to talk to Dez.

But now she is practically landing a plane, trying to get me to come over and join them. Her arms are above her head, flapping about.

With a sigh, I push off the wall.

Dez gives me a hug when I reach them and I'm trying not to make a face as I pull away.

We're not friends.

We used to be, but not anymore.

My feet shift under me.

Dez is twenty-one, half-Hispanic, half-Irish, and built like a lean baseball player. His expressive hazel eyes shift to dark brown or amber depending on the clothes he's donning. His body has a light dusting of freckles that almost match his complexion, but when he's outside and his skin tans, the freckles are nearly invisible unless you're close enough to spy them.

Dez ruffles my hair, which causes me to scrunch my face

in annoyance again. Why does he keep touching me? "How've you been, girl?"

"Better than you." I take in his appearance some more, noting a short beard. "What is going on with all that shit on your face?"

Brit hits my shoulder, but she's trying to smother a grin.

"Doesn't it make me look good?" Dez asks.

"It makes you look like you just hit puberty." It's patchy and needs to be filled in. Do they make a beard filler powder like they do for eyebrows? 'Cause dude needs some.

He still looks like the guy from high school, with his shorts hanging low on his hips and a guy tank on. He's even wearing his old baseball hat he wore in high school backwards. Some of the rich purple color and the mascot have faded with time. Even his outfit is irritating me and reminds me of how he hasn't changed.

Well, that's not true. He's back to acknowledging Brit and me.

Brit has a softer heart towards him than I do. She always sticks up for him whenever my dislike shows. For years we've been divided on our opinions of Desmond Daimon.

We all grew up together, super close family friends who did everything from the ages of birth to the summer before Brit and I started high school. When we got there, Dez acted like he didn't know us, but I guess with him being a sophomore it was embarrassing to be seen with us freshmen.

At one point, he was almost my first kiss—until Brit threw a cumquat at us, hitting me in the eye. We were seven.

Now, he's a stranger to me.

"Aw, Emery. Don't be mean just 'cause you missed me." He runs a hand along his patchy beard. "I've had this since August. I'm keeping it until they make me shave it."

"Who makes you shave it?" Brit asks, drawing the attention back to her.

*Yes! Talk him up, girl!*

While I don't care for the dude, my best friend will always like him. He was her first crush. And what a crush it was. Spanning years and time and going against all logic.

A part of me always thought they would eventually get together, but then he grew into his dick and abandoned us.

"I got accepted into the Fire Academy."

"No way!" Brit's face breaks out in a smile and she starts bouncing. She's an excited bouncer. "Just like your dad."

"And my grandpa," Dez says, pride ringing in his words. "It's kind of a family tradition."

Speaking of his family, I love them. They are just a bunch of sweethearts and I still talk to his sister on the regular and go out to lunch with her when we're free. I miss Dez being in my life the same way his sister is, but I hold grudges and high school is still too fresh to let go.

Especially for what he put Brit through.

I raise my beer, mentally cheering Brit on. There isn't that much left in the bottle, so I drain the rest, letting the alcohol find a home in my belly. I wonder how long I have to stand here now that my contribution to this reunion is done.

"When do you start?"

"This upcoming semester, so I'm trying to soak up as much fun as I can." His words are full of suggestiveness. The way he's angling his body toward Brit, speaking to her, looking at her, I get the message. I am officially free to go as I fade into the background, forgotten. I move away, but stay close enough so that I can overhear a few more minutes of the conversation.

It's the best friend way.

"I'm here until January, so we should definitely try to see

each other before we both get busy," Brit says. There's something about the way that she says the words that have my brows pulling together. Something off.

She and Dez share a look before he nods, leaning down to whisper in her ear.

I watch them for a moment longer before leaving them alone. I walk toward the kitchen, sidestepping two guys in a serious lip lock.

I try to take a sip from my bottle, only to remember it's empty.

Too busy looking inside the bottle, hoping some liquid will magically appear, I'm not paying attention to my surroundings and I stumble into something.

Something hard.

Moving my palms to push away, I freeze.

This doesn't feel like a wall—it feels like a body.

*Shitfuckshitfuck.*

Stumbling back a few steps, I look into a set of leather brown eyes that are attached to the very face decorating the cover of this month's issue of *Rip Current*.

Sebastian Cleaton.

He is staring at me too, but probably not in the same way.

My top feels tighter than it did moments ago. Wet and pressing against my stomach like a heavy, second layer of skin.

Glancing down, I have the answer why. Beer is running down the front.

He spilled his beer on me. The fabric gets more soaked by the second and the liquid begins to seep onto my skin.

"You're not a blonde with tequila." He looks down at me, a little taken aback.

"No! I'm just the girl you practically tackled to the ground!" I yell, partially because there is so much noise around us, but mostly from the fact that I'm starting to smell like a brewery. "And you made beer go down my shirt, damn it!"

"Whoa, Cherry Pie." He holds up his hands in mock defense as a smile takes over his face. He isn't taking this seriously! Internally, I stomp my foot like a child. "Let's just take a sec—"

I look down at my outfit, at the red shirt I'm wearing.

"Did you just call me *Cherry Pie?!*" My voice suddenly sounds louder, even though the octave stayed the same.

Someone turned the music off and quiet quickly descends around us.

I inwardly groan.

Everyone in the kitchen and living room just heard me yell at the famous guy crashing the party.

Which—Why *is* he crashing the party? What is he even doing at a house party in our small town?

Or…

What if this isn't real? How much does one need to drink in order to imagine a childhood crush in their presence?

"You're right, Cherry Pie doesn't work." He regards me with a lot more clarity than I'm capable of at the moment. The world's edges are blurry. "I'm thinking Firecracker works better."

I step closer to him, finger raised to poke him in the chest.

An arm curves to fit the shape of my waist, pulling me backward. My glare darkens at my captor.

"All right, that's enough." Geer looks down at me with an unreadable expression. I try to break out of his grasp but he holds me tighter. "You're drunk and embarrassing yourself."

"I am not drunk." My feet stumble slightly and I lean into him. "And you should know by now that I don't get embarrassed easily."

"That's the problem," he grumbles.

Thinking I've calmed or something, Geer naively loosens his grip enough for me to break free. Only I end up losing my balance and stumble into another body.

*Bash's body.*

I slam into Bash's body *again.*

He puts his hands on my shoulders to steady me as I mumble, "Oh, for fuck's sake."

"Didn't anyone tell you it's unattractive when a lady curses?" His lips breathe across my ear. Turning my head, his face doesn't move and we're now sharing the same breath. If either of us shift our heads just a centimeter, our mouths would be encased in each other.

"It's a good thing I'm not a lady." If anyone has a problem with a girl cursing, they can go shove their opinions up their ass. There is no time for that.

Bash takes a step back, just enough so his eyes can wander the length of my body, honing in on my chest. When they finally settle back on my face, he's wearing a shit-eating smirk. "Look like one to me."

"You're a pug."

"A pug?"

"Yes! A mammal, often kept as pets, with curly tails. A pug."

A laugh, so rich but rusty, like he hasn't used it in a while, erupts out of Bash's mouth as he looks down at me. His eyes lighten with amusement, crinkling in the corners.

When he laughs, he looks younger than his twenty-two years, putting him more around my age. It's as if all the tension built around him gets a momentary lax, creating an opening so he's able to enjoy life. "Sweetheart, I hate to break it to you, but the animal I think you're looking for is a pig."

"Hmm." I tap my index finger against my chin. "I don't think so. I mean why would I call you a pig when pugs are so much cuter?"

The ghost of the smile he had from when he was laughing grants me its presence again and this time it is a full-blown smile, but it's broken. The corners aren't as high and it doesn't fully reach his eyes.

There's something about it that makes him more real, human, and not just a picture I used to have as a background on my phone.

"So you think I'm as cute as a pug?"

"I think that you think that you're as cute as a pug." My words come out too fast to comprehend, even by me, and from the confused, pinched up expression on Bash's face, I think I throw him off too.

If I were able to stomach the thought of being indoors all day, I'd have no problem being a lawyer. I can argue anything and win.

"I don't know what you're talking about anymore, Firecracker." Bash glances around, finally realizing that we are drawing the attention of more people. Something passes over his face before he's reaching for my hand. "C'mon."

He begins leading me through the sea of bodies, pulling me after him. I glance over my shoulder at Geer, giving a quick head shake, warning him off.

Nothing is going to happen.

Probably a stupid thought for me to have, but if Bash wants to do anything that is going to land him in prison, he's leading me to the wrong place. Instead of walking me up the stairs, we're heading toward the back of the house, to the back porch. Some of the party has carried out to the backyard.

"Where are we going?"

He peaks over his shoulder. "Taking you somewhere you can keep yelling at me."

"I'm all yelled out," I admit. It's past my bedtime and grandma-me needs sleep. "Now I'm just sleepy." To prove my point, a yawn surfaces, stretching my jaw. Bash is still looking at me, yawning himself. "Copycat."

He winks. We stop at a set of chairs in the corner of the wrap-around porch.

"So when you said somewhere for me to yell at you, you meant a stage for everyone to witness."

"Well, someone has to testify if you turn violent." He gently pushes me into one of the Adirondack chairs. I slap his arm before sitting completely. He grins. "See, the abuse has already started. I thought you loved me, Firecracker."

"No, I said you're a pug." I gesture to his face. "All scrunched up and goofy looking. Fits you."

"You think I'm goofy?"

"I don't know." I shrug. "I don't know you. All I really know is that my shirt is wet because of you. I smell like beer now."

"Well we can't have that now, can we?" He stands, reaching up, tugging at the collar of his shirt. Pulling it off.

Pretty sure my jaw detaches as I watch. His tan abs are right in my face and I'm taking in my fill.

God, his body.

Golden and ripped, but not like Geer—a body born from the gym. Bash's body looks like a surfer's. One born from putting less time in the gym and more in the water. Abs sculpting his body, each ridge looks as if it has been individually hand carved. Arms that have muscles showing without flexing.

His body should be the eighth deadly sin.

There's also some ink on his chest, but it's too dark to

make out the design.

He pulls the shirt over my head. "Take off your shirt, then put your arms through the holes."

"When I imagined a guy getting me naked, this isn't what my mind came up with." I shimmy under his shirt, wiggling around and trying keep my stomach covered while attempting to get out of my shirt. Bash watches, but not leering in a creepy, pervy way.

No, he's looking like he's trying to hold back a laugh. A fist pressing into his mouth, the corners of his eyes crinkle. "I hate you so much right now." I pull my shirt over my head, throwing it at him.

"Yeah?" He catches it without breaking eye contact. "Give me back my shirt then."

"Ha-ha," I deadpan, pushing my arms through his shirt and sitting back in the chair. I bring my legs to my chest, resting my chin on my knees. "Too late. I'm all comfy. It's mine now. If you get cold, you can put on that one."

I nod to my shirt.

Bash gives me a look. One that clearly says he's not even entertaining that idea. He holds up the red top. "This wouldn't even fit one arm."

I grin, pulling his shirt closer around me. Soft cotton warms my body. Winters down here are other states' spring. It gets a little chilly sometimes and tonight it's more cool than warm.

His shirt smells intoxicating, like laundry detergent and body wash mixed with something else. Something that is only describable as man. Masculinity. It's a distracting scent that invades my senses. I try to ignore it. "Now you're only stroking your ego. You'd be able to get it up to your shoulder. Easy."

He raises a brow, challenging me. I watch as he slips a

hand up the shirt and see the fabric fading from the force. He gets it to his bicep when I hear the material stretch. I jump up from the chair, pulling my shirt back.

With it securely cradled to my chest, I look at him. Giving him my best glare even though the alcohol and the need for sleep make it less intimidating. "You proved your point."

"I think you proved some as well." He brings his chair closer. His knees touch mine. The contact of warm skin seeps through my jeans and makes my breath hitch.

It's a jolt, like the feeling of getting shocked by a shopping cart mixed with the forgotten touch of a man.

I look up at him, but Bash is staring at my lips.

My eyes dip to his, wondering what they would feel like, taste like against mine. Just for a second—or two—before looking at his eyes.

This time his eyes are on me. They're smiling. Teasing. He totally caught me looking.

He knows where my thoughts strayed and he inches forward, one of his legs slipping between both of mine. His hands slide up my thighs, eliciting a shiver all over my body.

My breathing stops as his head comes closer to me, tilting ever so slightly. I close my eyes, moving my head towards him. Hoping to close the distance.

When his lips finally touch me, my eyes snap open.

What. The fuck. *Was that?*

Sebastian Cleaton just kissed my forehead.

# CHAPTER FOUR

*Bash*

S HE STARES AT ME WITH A BURNING FIRE IN THOSE bright green eyes of hers. The glare does nothing to deter me from what I want. She's beautiful. Gorgeous. Light hair that tumbles down her back in soft waves. A few freckles spread along her face, almost like the sun strategically placed them.

My shirt is like a shapeless sack on her, pooling down her thighs and over her jeans. The neckline shifts to one side, exposing more of her neck and collarbone.

Tan skin with a few more freckles. I wonder how many randomly placed freckles she has, and where they lead.

"Hmm," she hums in the back of her throat, her gaze darting from my lips to my eyes. Her stare is calculating. Twisting and turning. The more she stares, the more exposed I feel. She already has my shirt so why do I feel like if she looks any longer she'll strip me bare?

In the back of my mind, a small voice is straining to shout, *she knows,* but I ignore it.

"What?" Caution clouds my tone and I sit up straighter.

"Nothing." She shrugs. "Just a noise."

"A noise that means something."

"It could or it couldn't. Oh the endless possibilities of a noise."

There's one noise I want to hear from her and it's not *hmm.*

It's been a while since I've had a hook up; it's been a while since I've done anything for me. The last girl I dated was for a publicity stunt set up by her PR team and that was over a year ago. And the only affections she and I showed each other were in front of the cameras.

It's been a while and I'm wondering if Firecracker is down for more when she surprises me and straddles my lap. I huff out a breath at the sudden impact of her body on top of mine.

She looks at me, like she's expecting some protest. Some time-out. Something to put a stop to this.

She won't be hearing a no from me.

I'm about to move back in, but she surprises me again by grabbing the back of my neck, pulling me toward her.

The long strands of her hair brush against my chest as her lips touch mine. Brushing them once, twice in a soft, sweet caress before the kiss builds, like there's a clock she's racing against.

She pulls at my bottom lip with her teeth. The biting pressure causes a groan to slip out of me.

*Holy fuck.*

She might have initiated the kiss, but I'm taking it over. I've wanted to do this since she called me a pug.

I'm no stranger to physical attraction.

Hooking up at parties is something I'm also not a stranger to.

But not only do I want to have this girl, I want to hear her keep talking. She's amusing as hell. I don't think I've smiled as much in the past year as I have tonight, just from interacting with her.

I slide one hand higher up her thigh, squeezing it and getting a moan that I swallow as I dip my other hand behind her neck, tilting her head back, and really having my way with her mouth.

I devour her.

Claiming her mouth for however long this kiss will last.

Firecracker squeezes my neck, pulling me closer. She hikes one of her legs up, aligning our bodies.

I groan, pulling away, trailing kisses down her mouth, to her jaw, to her neck. Nipping and sucking as her body wiggles around in my lap.

Jesus Christ.

She's grinding on my dick, making him come alive. I suck harder on her neck and she cries out, a noise escaping the back of her throat.

Pulling away, I nip her nose. "Hush now. I'm working my magic." I peck her lips. Twice. "You're the one that didn't want an audience, remember?"

She bites her bottom lip, something I should be doing, and her cheeks flush. "Shut up and kiss me, Sebastian."

Not a fucking problem. Drawing her bottom lip into my mouth, I suck on it, watching her react.

She tastes like beer and mint. I slide my tongue in, coaxing her to give me more. I need more. I want more.

My hand starts to move up her thigh, getting higher and higher, when she pulls away, panting. Flushed cheeks and swollen lips. I resist the urge to pull her back to me. She holds onto my shoulders, but doesn't push away. "I have to stop."

I nod, even though my body is humming, wanting more.

It's been some time since I've had any action, but really? It fucking hasn't been long enough for my body to resort back into its horny teenage self.

She keeps talking. "If we keep going, I'm going to feel really bad when I fall asleep during it."

Words every guy likes to hear when he's with a girl.

"You saying I'm boring?" I cock a brow. I almost call her Firecracker again since I still don't know her name. *Smooth, Cleaton, it really is just like being back in high school.*

She's laughing, the sound soft and lazy. Carefree. "Oh, you're so boring. So boring that my exhaustion is catching up quicker than I'd like." She kisses my lips. "I'm Emery, by the way."

This girl is a mind reader. That's her superpower. I'm calling it right now.

Or she's recounted our night and realizes that the guy she just got hot and heavy with didn't know her name. Something about that makes me feel even worse.

I didn't pull her out here to make out with her, not that I regret doing it. Hells no.

But she should have gotten more respect before my DNA mixed with hers.

I should have at least asked for her name.

"Bash." I wink, giving her a smile with all the arrogance I've gained from being the best at what I do.

"Way to ruin a fucking nice moment. That smile is awful." She rolls her eyes. "If you make a comment about how you get girls to do this all the time, I will knee you in the balls. And if you take a look, you'll see I'm in the perfect position for it."

She's still on my lap, with one leg between both of mine. Message received.

"See, there's that violence again," I joke. "We're going to have work on that."

"Like I'll ever see you again." She doesn't sound sad, she sounds neutral. Like she doesn't have an opinion either way.

"You know—" My words get cut off by footsteps coming toward us. Emery shifts in my lap, but her grip on my shoulders tightens.

"Em, we gotta go." The guy who tried to stop our verbal sparring earlier is the intruder.

Emery just stares.

To say it's awkward that she's sitting on my lap during this, I'd have to care what the other dude thinks and I don't. He's not her boyfriend. If he were, he wouldn't have let her come out here with me.

Maybe he's her brother—no, sparing him a look longer than a glance, they don't look alike. Their features are complete opposites. From their eyes to their hair colors. Maybe cousins twice removed.

He seems kind of protective of Emery, like some type of family relationship.

At least, that's what I'm hoping. I don't feel like a fight tonight.

Emery doesn't make a move to leave as her eyes begin to droop. Fuck, she really wasn't lying about being tired. To prove the point further, she yawns in my face. My lips twitch at the small smile she gives afterward.

She doesn't apologize and I really like that.

No one should apologize for things they can't help.

And apologizing for yawning is pointless. Everyone does it. It's contagious.

My jaw stretches wide and I'm yawning back.

See.

"Yeah, okay." Her voice is small, her words slow. She tries to push off me but her body sways. Without thinking, I jump up too. My hands go to her hips, steadying her. The guy behind us watches. Doesn't comment.

His silence is probably more aggravating than if he talked. At least see if she's okay, fucker.

"I'm so tired." She yawns again, her forehead hitting my chest.

"Jesus, Emery, how much did you drink?" His voice is hard, like tires on gravel.

I'm wrong. I prefer him silent. I prefer him gone, but that doesn't seem to be happening. He seems to be her ride.

"Three beers," she says into my bare chest. Her voice is soft, brushing over my skin. She pushes away to glare at her friend. "I'm not fucking drunk, Geer, so you can stop with that fucking judgment. I got tipsy. I'm not about to blackout. I'm tired because my body needs sleep. Sue me for staying out later than I wanted to."

"Sure looks like you don't regret it," he says, folding his arms over his chest. His eyes dart to me. I give him a smug look.

Come at me, bro.

"I don't," she tells him. "Last I checked I'm a grown consenting adult who can make her own decisions. I had fun tonight. So stop being a judgmental ass and let's go find your sister, my best friend." She looks at me for the last part, like she added it for my benefit.

Ah, so that's their connection. Makes sense.

I have an older sister, but I'm still protective of her and her best friend.

Emery pulls away from me, but then stops. "Want to help us look?"

I want to say yes. I do. But I made a promise to myself yesterday that I broke today and told myself I wasn't having a repeat.

I'd get back into my routine tomorrow and that requires me getting up early. I didn't get drunk tonight for that reason. So, like Emery I should be heading home. I shake my head, but end up saying, "Sure."

Well, then. Guess that decides that. Waking up is going to be a bitch, but more people looking for a person saves time, right? Dividing and conquering and all that shit.

Plus, I'd feel worse about not helping.

Emery grabs my hand, shooting him a look. "If I see Dez's naked ass tonight, I will literally throw up."

I laugh, hoping the night doesn't end like that. I don't need to see his fucking ass, either.

Geer, unlike me, does not find it funny. As we walk by, he mumbles something about the two girls giving him gray hairs.

Yeah, being a brother is a fucking stressful job.

Emery shows me a picture on her phone of what Brit looks like. It's them outside a bar, dressed up in all green, their cheeks have shamrocks painted on them. It had to have been taken during St. Patrick's Day. There's even green beer in their hands. Emery looks fucking cute. And her friend isn't bad looking either. "Got any more recent pictures?"

I see what she looks like fine, but I want to look at more of them, *more of her.* Emery radiates happiness in person and in pictures.

She knows my game. She looks up at me, trying to pull off a serious expression, but failing. The corners of her mouth twitch. "You're trying to be cute."

"You already think I'm cute," I remind her.

She rolls her eyes, waving my words away with a flick of her wrist. "One day you'll forget I said that, but right now, let's go find Brit."

As we walk through the house with no sign of her friend, I ask, "Have you tried calling or texting her?"

"Yeah, that would be easy." She laugh-snorts. "But Brit never keeps her phone charged. I told her to charge it before we left, but did she listen to me? Noooo, she didn't, and it died on the way over here."

If I could get away with my phone not being charged, it'd be less stressful for me. As it is, my phone has been vibrating in my pocket with voicemails, missed calls, and unanswered texts since I left.

Emery's friend—Geer—disappears somewhere else, putting to use that divide and conquer method. Emery and I are sticking together. Her idea, one I'm not going to argue with.

I follow her through the house and into the open kitchen. She's walking with a purpose, her footsteps acting with no hesitation.

She has this confidence about her.

She walks right up to a guy with both sides of his head shaved, barbell in his eyebrow, and beer in hand. He's scrawny. Clothes hang off his body and his eyes are glassy. "Hey, Eddie. Hi. How's it going? Have you seen Dez?"

The guy laughs, even though there wasn't a punch line delivered. "Upstairs. Saw him with your friend."

"Let's go." She turns around, patting me on the chest before pushing me out of the kitchen. As we're walking away, I hear the guy yell, "Cockblocking, Emery?"

"Always. Gotta make sure my best friend doesn't get pregnant. Imagine the horror."

"You're awful," I say, smiling.

She looks up at me. "You enjoy it."

"I just met you," I remind her.

"And how many times do you need to hang out with a person to know if you like being around them?"

"Uh—" I don't have an answer. I've never thought in those terms before. I hang out with people I like, but when did I know the exact moment I wanted to be around them? Not sure. Don't really have a long list of people I chill with back home either, sooo. "I don't know," I answer honestly. "What about you?"

"I trust my gut," she says in way of an answer. I poke her side, making her squeal, wanting her to elaborate. "You know the feeling you get when the decision you're making is the right one? Or when you know you slayed a test? You're listening to your gut. It also does the same with people. It's a natural, instinctual way of feeling out people."

"That doesn't sound sketchy at all," I deadpan. Despite my words, I think I'm going to listen to my gut. And my gut says to have more nights like this.

*Have fun more often, Cleaton.*

My gut also says to keep this girl around. I need more people like her in my life.

"I didn't say it was a hundred percent foolproof. It's like a lie detector. There are ways people can beat it, but that doesn't mean it doesn't work—" A body backs into her, pushing her into my chest. My hands go to her waist, steadying her.

She makes a cute noise, like an attempt at a growl, but it sounds more like a cross between choking and gargling. "If I crash into your chest one more time, I will scream."

"Oooo, I'm scared." I mock shudder.

She slaps my stomach. "Asshole."

I raise a brow.

"You're not the only person to call me that," I tell her, pulling her up the stairs. Really just any excuse to touch her before this bizarre night of smiling and touching and kissing runs out.

I'm having fun for the first time in a while. I actually feel like I'm living again and don't want that feeling to end. I'm a greedy bastard that way.

"You should think about adding that to your business cards, Cleaton."

Jesus, this chick is funny and lacks a filter. She speaks without a care for what comes out, letting the first words flow. There's no calculated attack, no double meaning.

Having money changes how people act around you. Everyone wants something. The majority of people in my life back home are fake. They look at me thinking of what I can do for them. What they can take from me. It's a battle of lies, to see which ones can get me to cave, to give in. I haven't actually felt welcomed around people for some time. At least not ones that don't look at me like I am a walking sack of money.

It's obvious that Emery knows who I am. She calls me by my first and last name.

And while that should have warning signs flashing in my head, it doesn't.

She's chill.

Hasn't mentioned my career or asked what I'm doing here. She's not asking anything personal. Tonight I don't feel used. For the first time since God knows when, I don't feel mentally drained from going to a party. I feel stoked. Buzzed.

Tonight has been fun with her.

And not only because we made out.

On the second floor, Emery walks toward the first door on our left. She bangs her fist hard enough to shake the wood. When we hear no answer, she tries the doorknob. Unlocked. She pushes the door open, but the room is empty.

We try the next two and a bathroom, but all are empty.

There's only one more room left unchecked. Emery marches down the hallway toward it, not bothering to knock before she pushes the door open and walks in. Except she freezes in the doorway. I see her shoulders lock up. And she screams. Full on horror movie, voice altering screams.

She's slapping her hands over her eyes as I push her behind me. Her screams die down. Now she's murmuring, "Ohmygoshohmygoshohmygosh."

My jaw drops when I see what makes her scream, but instead of copying Emery, I push down a laugh. "Sorry guys, but Emery needs to get home and can't leave Brit here."

I close the door and I'm pretty sure I hear Brit squeak, "Did Sebastian Cleaton just say my name? And see your ass?"

I press a fist into my mouth, turning around to face Emery.

Her skin has lost some coloring, her eyes wide in revulsion, but she looks up at me. "Don't say it. Don't you dare fucking say it."

"I won't," I promise. "But do you need me to kiss you against the wall to make the night better again? Will that help you forget seeing your best friend going down on Dez?"

"You fucking said it!" she yells, her hands flying to her ears. "La-la-la, I can't hear you, la-la-la."

Gently, I grab her wrists, pulling them away from her ears. "Are you done?"

Emery shakes her head so fast her hair smacks her cheeks.

"I need bleach. Lots of it. I have to unsee and forget that ever happened."

Movement on the other side of the door starts to become louder. But Emery either doesn't hear it or doesn't care. Judging by the expression of shock that hasn't left her face, I'm going with the former. She keeps talking. "We roomed together our freshman year of college. I never saw her having sex before. We had a system! No, no, no. I refuse to believe what I just saw." She closes her eyes and exhales. Opening them again, she meets my eyes. "There. I erased it. I have no memory of what just happened. Did you find Brit?"

Shaking my head, I start to answer her, but Brit slips out the door and beelines toward Emery, her hair a mess and cheeks flushed. She definitely got some. She watches her friend in concern. "Em?"

"Oh, Brit!" Emery blinks. "We found you. Excellent. Great." Now she's smiling too wide and talking too loudly. Her friend flinches. "Did you have a nice night? I sure did."

I can't stop staring at her, trying not to pull her into my arms. She looks exhausted standing in the hallway, my shirt dwarfing her, even though she isn't a small girl. I'd guess she's around five-six or five-seven. Just watching her, I can see her energy slowly fading. Brit calls her name, but Emery only gives her friend a small, tired smile.

She's fading fast.

"C'mere, Firecracker," I murmur, picking her up in my arms.

She pats my bare chest, leaving her palm there. "I always wanted a man to carry me around. Walking can be exhausting. Can we go to the beach?"

"Nope, you've got to go home and sleep." I glance over my shoulder, tilting my head to the staircase at Emery's friend.

Brit glances at the door she came out of one last time before following us. We make it down the stairs in silence, but as soon as I'm off the last step, Emery starts wiggling in my arms. "Whoa, what's wrong?"

"I changed my mind. I want to walk the rest of the way." Her voice sounds higher, but I don't understand. She's pulling at the hem of my shirt, trying to keep it from riding up, exposing her skin. A look of panic in her eyes.

I set her down.

My mind is still a little hazy, too cloudy to think of a reason behind her reaction. I watch as she wrings her hands over the fabric. My gaze narrows at her movements and Emery stops when she catches me. Her hand goes to her thigh, her fingers drumming along the side.

Emery looks at Brit then darts her gaze away. Brit's cheeks turn pink, but before she can say anything, Geer comes stalking toward us.

"About time," he growls. I'm starting to think the dude has one octave and that's surly. "Come on. Let's go."

Brit follows without a word. Emery, however, stands on her tiptoes, pressing her lips to mine. "Thought I'd get one last kiss before I wake up from this crazy night." She winks, or tries to—but it's more like some weird blinking—before backing away from me. "Bye, Bash."

"Bye, Emery," I tell her, watching as the crowd swallows her.

It's almost two in the morning and the party still has people. Some are asleep on the couch or the ground, but the music is still blaring and people are still drinking. Digging in my pocket for my keys, Dez walks up beside me. "How was your night?" My tone is casual, but I see the shit-eating grin he's wearing.

"Fanfuckingtastic, man." His tone matches his smile. He wiggles his brows at me. "You hook up with Emery?"

"Nah, dude." I tell him. "Just made-out."

"Emery Lawson. Man, she was untouchable in high school."

I jerk my head toward him, pretty sure my face is wearing a *WTF* look. Dez, the fucking bastard, laughs. "You're not getting anything more from me, dude. I'm drunk, but not that drunk. I'm surprised you don't already know. Man, did you see Brit though? Fuck, she's hot. I mean fucking *hell*."

My mind is too busy mulling over his words about Emery to pay him any attention. What the fuck does it mean she was untouchable in high school? She's gorgeous. She's funny. She's smart. No, we didn't talk about politics or global warming, but a person's intelligence is conveyed not just with important topics but with how they carry themselves.

A slap between my shoulder blades draws me out of my thoughts. "You look like you're thinking, dude." Dez laughs. "Thinking's dangerous with these kinds of things." He glances around, taking in the atmosphere. "What time is it?" He pulls out his phone and glances at the screen, "Fuck, I have to be up in four hours. I'm gonna head out. Peace." He makes a peace sign as he walks toward the backdoor. I'm not too worried about him getting home. He lives in the house next door. I live a few streets over. I rub my eyes as I walk to the truck I'm renting; the dark green paint almost blends into the night.

As I start the ignition, I play back tonight.

Emery bumping into me. Calling me a pug. Kissing me.

Me laughing. Smiling. *Having fun.*

Yeah, this break might be exactly what I need.

# CHAPTER FIVE

## *Emery*

I HAD NIGHTMARES ABOUT DEZ'S ASS IN THE FEW HOURS I was able to sleep.

I'd blame Brit, but my poor best friend is still mortified that I saw her and Dez together.

We both spent last night at Geer's and she filled me in on what happened after I walked away. She was so high on Dez and drunk on alcohol that she doesn't even remember seeing Bash last night. Or that Bash also saw Dez's ass.

Not that I blame her for not remembering Bash. I mean, I'm sure he'd be offended if he knew, but he isn't the one that fulfilled a fantasy with their childhood crush.

I'm happy for my best friend. So happy. And a wee bit jealous. Just a smidgen though. She got lucky last night. I didn't. Bash might be a pro in the water, but he has a magical set of lips and a tongue full of spells. Imagining what he is able to do with the rest of his body had me squirming on the car ride home.

Leaving my passed out, snoring best friend in the bed we shared, I go outside, falling into my routine.

Wetsuit, board, wax, beach.

Surfing is, and always will be, a part of me. Just like breathing. I can't stop for my parents. Not even for me. No matter how much I love surfing, how much it puts my body at ease, it terrifies me. The purest passion in my life became tainted several years ago. But as much as stepping into the water spikes my anxieties, I don't let it win. Every day I face my fear and I face it alone.

Stopping would mean killing a bigger part of me than people realize.

Which is why, when I see my wave I don't hesitate to catch it. Determination owns my movements as I spin my board around, so the nose faces the beach, and begin paddling. The water under me gets shallower, my board being pulled back as my arms keep paddling.

A wave's forming.

I'm getting swept back, further into it. There's always a split second of fear that the wave will go on without me, but not this time.

Everything happens at once.

I catch the wave and push my body to pop up. My feet feel solid and I find my balance.

Water curls over me. For a moment the world slows down as I reach out my hand, touching the wave. I speed up, almost flying. A spray of water hits my face in a fine mist.

I just make it out of the barrel when a body slams into me. "Ooof!"

In a mess of limbs, we go crashing to the water, rolling under a couple of times before we break through the surface and

I find my hands on a pair of familiar muscular shoulders that belong to a very shirtless dude, who is grinning at me.

One arm is locked loosely around my waist while the other shakes some water out of his hair. I silently curse every deity I've ever learned about.

Staring back at me are those leather brown eyes of Sebastian Cleaton. "Firecracker? What a lovely surprise."

"Bite me." I push away from him, propelling backwards.

He catches my ankle, pulling me back toward him.

"Hey now, someone not a morning person?" His lips are moving and words are coming out, but all I can think of is how they moved against mine.

"I'm going to have a you-shaped bruise on my body if we keep meeting this way," I grumble. Seriously, how embarrassing and klutzy can one person be?

There are only so many blows a person can take before it starts to affect them.

Like how many times can a person keep body checking a pro surfer?

"Pretty sure if anyone is going to get a bruise, it's me." He rubs his chest. His perfectly tan, artfully sculpted chest that doesn't have a single blemish on it. No discoloration.

However, on one of his deliciously sculpted pecs is the tattoo I spied last night. It's a fancy hook-like symbol with some kind of pattern making up the inside detail. It's hot. I want to touch it. Maybe even lick it.

"You should wear protective padding next time you see me." Because apparently small town logic also applies to Bash. Can't leave the house without seeing at least one person I know. At least it's Bash and not someone that would tell my parents what I'm doing.

"Nah, I can take it." He pulls my ankle higher, dipping my

body more into the water. "It's cute that you care though."

"Cute enough that I can have my foot back?" Using my arms, I try to swim away, but Bash pulls back, tugging me closer to him.

My board is floating a little ways away from us; the leash tethered to my ankle keeps it from floating off into the ocean.

"Hmm." Bash brings his hand, the one not holding my foot, to his chin, pretending to think about it. "Nah, don't think so."

I know when to fight and when to bide my time. This time happens to be the latter. So, I willingly float on my back, letting Bash hold my ankle. I'm so tired, anyway. Which is probably why I didn't notice him in the water to begin with.

Even if that's not the reason, I'm saying it is.

Because who wouldn't be tired if they only got two hours of sleep?

I close my eyes and float, with some help from Bash.

The water rolls under my body, lapping onto my covered skin. The fact that Bash isn't in a wetsuit shouldn't surprise me. Most don't need them in Florida, even in the winter.

Hell, I don't need one.

I *want* one. It's my shield in the water, protecting me from prying eyes.

Even if I'm surfing in secret, I never think I'm alone. I'm convinced someone is always watching. I'm a paranoid person by nature, so I'm always on edge that when I walk through my front door, my parents will be waiting on me, knowing what I've been up to.

Also, in case anyone does see me, they won't have to see my scars. I don't mind them, but I know other people don't always see what I do.

My mind keeps trying to replay what happened at the

party, how I can still feel the ghosts of his hands roam over my body, but I won't let it. Shutting it down. Nope, not today. Not ever again.

As hot as it was, and it was plenty hot, I don't allow myself to think about it. Can't.

I'm not going to set myself up for disappointment. Hook ups don't mean relationships. Something I've helped Brit through a few times in college. They don't equal the same thing. Men are after one thing with hook ups, and with relationships they're after that plus more. So much more.

So, I'm not going to bring up the make out session. I'm not going to reference it. Or make any jokes involving anything relating to the events that took place at the party.

It's hard.

Very, very hard.

I like to mess with people. I like to give them a hard time. That might make me a bitch or whatever, but I don't care.

Because holding my tongue is a joke in itself. It's torture.

"Falling asleep on me?" Bash tickles my foot, making me jackknife up. Balancing on one foot that's tethered to a board is not easy, but I manage as I squeal, trying to pull away.

"I didn't fall asleep, you ass," I say between laughs. "I was relaxing."

"What's that like?" he asks playfully, but he stops caressing my foot. Thank goodness.

"Like floating in the water without having to worry about a fucker tickling my foot. You should try it sometime."

He chuckles, dropping my foot.

Finally.

The taste of freedom is enough that I pull my surfboard over and between us. A divider to keep the ankle stealing to a limit.

I heave myself onto the board, using the top to support my upper body. My feet kick under it. "How come you don't look tired?"

He had to have been up just as late or later than I was and he doesn't look tired at all. His movements aren't sluggish; his eyes aren't dull or hazy.

Bash shrugs. "I'm used to waking up early. After a few years, I guess my body has gotten used to it."

Lucky bastard. Must be nice being favored by evolution. "I don't believe you." Because I can't let him get away with that without giving him a hard time. "I think you were sitting on your couch with a coffee IV drip before coming out here. Admit it."

"I can't. I plead the fifth." He moves closer to me, the water rippling from his movements. The small set that we're reported to get is either delayed or not coming at all because the ocean is now flat. A tiny part of me is happy about this. More time to spend time with Bash and not have to worry about actual surfing.

It's a man's world, the surfing world. Even the surfers who aren't pro and do it just as a hobby don't respect women in the lineup.

They don't think that we have skills. They just like to look at us for eye candy. Sexist bastards.

Before I wasn't allowed to surf, I'd go out to the beach with actual people. The lineup always had more guys who made more catcalls than praises. There were a few princes in the convoy of frogs, but still.

I got it the worst. First for being a girl and then for having a father who was a pro.

It's one thing I don't miss about surfing during the day.

"That's a nice board." Bash gazes at my baby. I'm leaning

over it as my fingers drum on it tenderly. It *is* a nice board. It's the nicest thing I own, counting my car. Not because of the value, although it is hella expensive, but it's my prized possession.

"It is." There is no way to mistake the sighing tone in my voice. Please don't think I'm lusting for my board—I'm really lusting for you.

Wait. No.

"You love it." His voice changes a little, it has a twinge of something I don't know how to describe.

I give him a wary look. "I do. If you know what I had to go through to get it—"

"Not your board, Firecracker." His tone is still different, but I can't figure it out. "Although it is something to love. I'm talking about surfing. You love it."

"Yeah, I do. It's my first love."

Surfing has the honor of being my first love. Not a guy.

Surfing also gets the title of being my first heartbreak.

"What's that like?" he asks again, but with a more serious tone. His eyes no longer look alive, but dull. Almost lifeless.

"What's what like?" I try to keep my tone light, to brighten our conversation, but it doesn't work.

Bash's tone is as lifeless as his eyes when he answers, "Surfing."

For a moment, I'm in shock. I stare, jaw slightly unhinged, eyes a wee bit wide. I'm staring at a pro surfer, one of the most eligible bachelors, and must be suffering from a hearing problem. Because it sounds like Sebastian Cleaton just asked what it's like to love surfing.

Surely that's a mistake.

Right?

"Shouldn't you know that?" I ask, hoping he's joking like earlier.

"Nope." Deadpan. "What's it like, Emery?"

Something inside me tightens, synching around my lungs. Bash looks defeated. Like he's been fighting a losing battle and doesn't have enough strength to keep going. "Scary," I whisper, honestly. "But freeing. Like I'm facing my biggest fears and winning. I'm escaping reality, falling more in love every day. There's nothing like surfing. Nothing to compare it to. At least not for me. I think everyone takes away something different, but for me, surfing is the closest thing to magic we have."

"I used to think that." He smiles, but there is nothing happy about it. If possible, the smile looks sad and that sadness stretches to his eyes. "But I haven't felt that way in a long time." He sighs and mumbles, as if to himself, "It's been a fucking long time."

"Is that why you're here?" I ask. He sounds so sad I want to hug him. But I have the board between us and I'm not sure if Bash and I are at a hugging stage. If we're at any stage or just standing behind the curtain.

He rubs a hand over his face, shaking his head. "Listen, I—" He tries to form words but closes his mouth, swallows loud enough that I can hear, and tries again. "I—I got to go. I'm sorry, Em."

With those parting words, Bash backs away, paddling to the beach. I stay still, floating on my board, and watch as he gets out of the water, walks across the sand, and disappears down the trail.

"Bye, Bash," I say to the water. *Probably for good.*

# CHAPTER SIX

*Bash*

Y OU CAN DO BETTER, SEBASTIAN.

*Why aren't you trying harder, Sebastian?*

*You're letting yourself get distracted, Sebastian.*

Growling, I punch the steering wheel of my truck. Even when I put thousands of miles between us, the voices of my parents follow.

I can't escape them. Not even when I try running away.

Their voices from years and years of verbal lashings still follow me wherever I go. They're like my Christmas ghosts, but instead of just the holidays, they're here all fucking year and I learn nothing valuable from them. There's nothing to learn when your parents have few redeeming qualities.

At least my mom doesn't. My dad's problem is that he doesn't have a backbone. Doesn't know how to stand up for himself—or his son.

He's a spineless coward who hides behind my mother,

letting her control everything.

They have drained me dry.

If they came here, I would spiral further down that black hole.

I'm not healthy around them.

After the other day, I've been okay. Not good or even better, but I'm doing okay. Last night helped a lot. Being around people that weren't after anything from me and just wanted to let loose. It felt good to be another face, another body in a crowd and live.

Living instead of existing.

Today, I went out to try and reconnect with the ocean, to see if the feelings would come back to me after leaving months and months ago. That didn't happen.

Instead, my head is all foggy and as dull as before. I didn't feel anything in the water until Emery knocked me off my board with her body.

Crashing into the water was like a zap of energy. A recharge. The past seven years of my life were a mundane routine and today was the first day something unexpected happened.

My mood felt lifted and seeing Emery was the cause of the occurrence. She's like walking sunshine. Even with the sun not fully in the sky, the water was bright around her.

Fuck.

What the fuck was that?

Maybe I'm more tired than I thought.

I'm not a poetic person.

I don't write sonnets about the sun or make comparisons about smiles to light.

I'm exhausted. Mentally and physically. Dodging calls takes a bigger toll when actively going out of the way to do it. Maybe if I make myself busier, ignoring the parents will be easier.

Distractions.

That's what I need.

When walking onto the beach earlier, I spied a surfer in the water, but didn't know it was Emery.

I stopped walking for a moment and just observed.

Watching her was like, well, what she said. Magic. She was in control of the wave. She surfs with a power I not only saw but also felt when she crashed into me.

It seems like we've fallen into an unusual greeting, one I don't mind. I joked about her giving me a bruise, but despite her athletic, lithe body I have more weight on her and she's lighter than what I lift.

Emery has more passion for surfing than I do. The emotions are visible in her eyes, her actions. Her eyes shine in the water, a brightness that has never touched me. At least, not as purely as it does her.

Running my hands over my face, the two-day scruff scratches at my palms. My eyes are heavy, but my body feels charged.

Lulling my head back, a groan rumbles in my throat. Today's not the first day I've trained on no sleep. I've had many of those, but I know I didn't push myself as hard as I needed to. As hard as I wanted to.

I've lost my love for surfing. I'm hoping my time here, in this small coastal town, will help me find that feeling again. To find love in something I've lost.

Because if I can't, I'd have hit my prime before turning twenty-three.

I bang my head against the headrest. Again. Vibrations fill the space as my phone buzzes around in the cup holder. The name on caller I.D. has me stifling another groan. I have about ten seconds to either ignore or answer.

I hesitate too long and my mother is sent to voicemail.

With the phone still in hand, I run my free hand through my hair, messing up the semi-dried locks. The phone vibrates again, revealing that she left a message.

Of course she did.

I roll my eyes, unlocking the screen.

Instead of checking her message, something a good son would do, I open a new text message.

Dez said he wasn't going to tell me about Emery, but hopefully that doesn't apply to what I'm about to ask. I text him, asking for a certain sassy girl's number.

Calm.

Quiet.

Two words I never thought I would have back in my life.

Now that I notice it, the more aware I am of how lacking the two were before. I might not be reconnecting with surfing, but at least my life is gaining more perspective. As much solace as that provides.

It's a quick drive from the beach spot to my house. I could've walked to the beach from behind my house but that hadn't worked the first week I was here so a change was needed. A different spot, one that holds more promise.

In the short time it took me to get home, my phone went off more times than I was able to keep track of. Checking the notifications in the driveway, the screen reads twenty messages. Only one is from Dez.

The rest are from my mother.

Messages that are still waiting to be heard on my voice-mail. I think that racks the total up to thirty-five in the past two days alone. It's not even eight-thirty yet. A part of me is waiting to see how long I can push that woman until she files a missing person report or hires a P.I.

As cruel as that sounds, I don't feel bad. My mother is the reason why I needed to get away in the first place. Now that I'm here, I don't want to go back to the life I lived before.

I might be bored from this vacation but I'm not bored by the idea of a new adventure.

I want to enjoy life, soak up as much as I can.

I might not have accomplished what I wanted today, but tomorrow I get to try again and not without the company of a girl who radiates love of the sport.

Surfing is fun no matter if you go out by yourself or with your friends, but with other people, the activity becomes less lonely.

And I'm exhausted from being lonely.

Many sports are team based, taking more than one person to win in the end. With surfing, the win is between the person on the board and the wave. Every accomplishment is solitary. It gets lonesome.

At least at competitions, there are competitors around. They might be going up against me, but they also go through all the hardships I do. There's an understanding between us. A bond. It's when the competition ends, when everyone goes home to train for the next meet, that it really hits me. I'm alone on this journey.

Sure, I have my parents and coach. But they're more concerned with me winning, holding my titles of the best. It's not hard to fall into a routine, letting life pass by without noticing. Some people never wake up from it.

One day I did.

When that day hit, I left and came here.

My parents think I'm slacking off.

Even if I am slacking off here, I think I have earned that right. Some time away should be therapeutic for me, but I still feel the same. Like I'm drifting along.

While some days are better, I'm lost in what I really want.

*What if surfing isn't even for me anymore?* This is a question I don't want to know the answer to.

I grab an avocado and put bread in the toaster. As I'm chopping up some fresh fruit, I decide to play the voicemails. Some, at least.

Nobody's got time for all that.

"Sebastian, it's your mother calling." I roll my eyes. She addresses every message like this, like she doesn't know I have her number saved in the contacts. "Where are you? Honey, please call me back. We're worried you're going to fall behind." She stresses the last sentence.

I've done this for so long, she forgets that this is all second nature. Like I said, a routine.

"We're worried about *you*," she corrects, realizing her mistake. "You haven't been acting like yourself. I've also tried to access your accounts, to make sure you're not in any trouble, but I couldn't get in. The banks say you changed your information. Can you text it all to me? I need to borrow some money." End of message.

It shouldn't surprise me that my mother didn't even try to continue to lie about her concern. The only reason she pushes so hard with my surfing is because she wants the money. When I started getting big bucks as a teenager, my parents were in charge of the money.

They thought it was also their money, that they were more

entitled to it. They raised me and they were taking back all that they invested in me.

Invested. As if a child is an investment for parents that they need to collect their dues if they become successful.

Turns out, growing up I collected a lot of unknown debt.

My parents don't work anymore. They live off the money I give them.

Mom likes people under her control, like puppets to her marionette show and I'm acting off script.

The toast pops up and I shake off the message. I had planned on listening to more than one, but she confirms what I already know. The rest of the messages will be the same. All circling back to the money.

I need to find my way back to who I am without their pressuring.

Taking my avocado toast to the wrap-around porch leading out to the pool, I take a bite and send off a text.

# CHAPTER SEVEN

## *Emery*

Do you surf everyday?

An unknown number is attached to the question.

I look at the text on my phone, without unlocking it, feeling my heartbeat spike and dip, like a rollercoaster ride, beating uncontrollably in my chest.

Like it's hooked up to speakers, the sound amplifies around my room with a heavy bass.

For two years I've been so careful. To keep my secret from the world, from the people I care about. I let them think what they want about what happened. That I let my fear rule me, when I really let it drive me.

Before my panic can really send me spiraling, another text comes in from the same number.

It's Bash.

I deflate like a balloon. My heart skipping several beats as it tries to calm down.

*Fucking hell, Bash!*

I thought my secret was seconds away from going up in flames. If I ever see this man again, I'm going to kick him. In the shins.

With the identification of the number out of the way, my heart rate is slowly going back to normal. Glaring at my phone, I type out my response.

**Yeah. Same time every morning. Why?**

The little typing bubble appears on screen. Then disappears. A few seconds later it's back and stays for what feels like a while. Good Lord, is he writing a novel?

Sighing, I lock my phone and toss it on my bed. Picking up the book I'm reading, I try to find where I left off when I hear my phone vibrate. Turns out, Bash wasn't writing me a novel. Or if he did, he deleted it and settled on a five-word question instead.

**Can I surf with you?**

Can he surf with me? Can Sebastian Cleaton, the object of my youth's lust, and who reporters are saying to be the Ren Lawson of our generation, surf with me?

Do I want him to?

Surfing alone has been my thing for the longest time; there's been no one in the lineup but me for the past two years.

I don't surf to compete anymore. I surf because I have to.

Because I love it. But I can't keep up with a pro. What if he's one of those asshats that doesn't respect a woman surfer?

As ridiculous as that thought is, I'd never allow a guy to shame me for a sport that is just as much mine as his, but the more I think it over something unexplainable is assaulting my emotions. A bubbly, almost floating sensation takes over my body as I picture what it would be like to feel the presence of someone beside me, watching and waiting for a set to roll in.

It might be nice to have some company.

Maybe for a little bit.

To try it out.

I can still have time for my thoughts and my me-time, but there will be another person for when being alone gets to be too much.

Plus, if I don't like it, I can just tell him to leave. The spot is mine and I was there first.

Hopefully it won't come down to elementary school tactics, but that is my plan, just in case.

I send back my answer.

Sure.

Then another.

If you can keep up with me.

Yes, yes I did just tease a professional surfer with more wins and records than one person really needs.

This time, his response comes immediately.

What happens if I don't?

Is this flirting? Aside from the party, I haven't even kissed a guy since October of my freshman year in college, three semesters ago, so to say I'm a little out of the game is an understatement.

Flirting in person is easy. Flirting in texting, there's a fine line that can be crossed. As my fingers hover over the keyboard, I try to conjure up a response. How do I know if he's really flirting or if my brain woke up on the pervy side this morning?

Try it and see what happens.

Yep. Definitely have been out of the game for too long. *Weak response, Lawson.*

He sends back a wink, a message that is virtually impossible to carry on a conversation with, so I pick up my book again. I read a few more chapters before my phone goes off.

I sigh. I just want to read. Does he have any idea how long I've waited for this book to come out?

Can we surf tomorrow?

And another one.

What time works best for you?

One more.

I'm up for any time, just gotta get a workout in first. Where should we meet up?

I can't stop myself from laughing. Sebastian Cleaton is kind of a dork. And I kind of like him more for it.

I've spent most of the day not allowing myself to think about what happened between us last night, but I can't stop myself from touching my lips, remembering how swollen they were after. How good he felt against me. How good I felt when he his hands roamed my body.

More than good.

Amazing. Horny. Wanted.

I thought that last night would be the first and last time I ever saw Bash Cleaton. That the memory of my lips touching his would evolve into a story to tell Brit. Possibly a story to tell any future grandchildren when they asked grandma what she was like when she was their age—because I plan on being a cool grandma.

Last night was my story. Nothing more.

Then this morning happened. A little kernel to add to said story.

But now, I have a chance to see him again. And for more than the twenty minutes we had this morning.

Even if nothing happens physically between us, I have the opportunity to hang out with one of the best surfers of my generation, literally at my fingertips.

I have the chance to not be alone in the water for the first time in two years.

6:30 works for me. I always go to the same spot that you saw me at today. I'll meet you there. Just don't expect me to work out with you.

Honestly, I'd work out with him if he needed someone, but working out in the morning means cutting into my surfing time. I hit the gym and go for runs in the evening for that very reason. The time I have for surfing is already limited. I can't limit it any more.

Not for anything.

Especially not for Sebastian Cleaton.

He might be a professional surfer, but he's from California and born in Hawaii. He doesn't know these beaches. He's familiar with the Pacific Ocean, but here on the East Coast, we have the Atlantic.

Bash is in my territory now.

I can't stop yawning.

I slept even less than I did the night before. I can't even blame it on the drinking this time. No, my lack of sleep is because I'm surfing with Bash today.

Young me would be absolutely giddy at the chance for this. Present me, well, present me is tired and nervous. Tired for obvious reasons and nervous…well, nervous because this will be the first time I'm surfing with someone since my accident.

I used to be one of the best surfers in my class, on the track to following my father's footsteps, but now I don't know where I stand. I'm not competing with anyone but myself on a daily basis.

I'm a very competitive person by nature. It's been bred into me.

I get nasty when I lose.

But unless we're playing a board game or something fun with friends, I keep that unhealthy need to win stored away until I'm alone.

I'm a good sport when points, trophies, and titles are on the line, but if I mess up, I will be my biggest critic. I'm harder on myself than my dad is. I push myself harder; I challenge myself daily. Never accepting that today's surf is the best surf. *Tomorrow I have to be better.* My mantra, always.

I get in the ocean every day after almost dying from a shark attack that scared my parents enough to end my potential career right on the cusp of starting.

The accident left my body scarred. Both on the outside and the inside.

I miss competing, but my parents have done so much for me that I can't tell them I've been surfing. I won't. To see the anger, or worse, the disappointment in their eyes would hurt more than almost losing my leg.

My board is in the sand and I'm zipping up my wetsuit when I hear someone approaching.

Glancing over my shoulder, I see Bash in all his shirtless glory. Only wearing a pair of black swim trunks and a backpack strung along his back, he looks more awake than a person should be at this time. Or maybe he knows how to go to bed at a reasonable hour. My eyes eat up the sight, appreciating it more than at the party.

His stomach is sculpted in a six-pack, with the makings of an eight pack. Abs cut so deep, I imagine water running down them with my tongue chasing after the drops. His arms are big, ripped from years of paddling and popping up on the board.

What catches my eyes the most, drawing me in, is not his chest—I know, I know—but what he's carrying. He doesn't have a shortboard, but instead, secured under his arm is a longboard.

"I thought you had to work out this morning," I call out, as he gets closer. I glance down at my shortboard and wonder if I should go back up to Geer's garage and grab his longboard.

"I woke up early for it. I just got done." He sets his board in the sand. "The water colder than yesterday?" He gestures toward my wetsuit and I grimace. I don't feel like defending my outfit choice. It's none of his business. Besides, I was wearing one yesterday. I wear one every morning, keeping my scars hidden.

"I get cold really fast."

He nods, like my answer really isn't as important as I take it to be. I'm on edge. I start shaking out my limbs, yawning in the process. My eyes water and Bash yawns back.

He starts to say something, but another yawn from me cuts him off. He yawns back and pretty soon we're only communicating in yawns.

Looks like we have a yawn-off, y'all.

"I didn't sleep last night," I say around another yawn. "Or the night before. I'm just exhausted."

"Are you okay to go out there?" Concern invades his voice and something weird tickles my stomach.

"I can surf half-asleep, Bash," I tell him. "I could probably surf still asleep." And I'm not cocky when I'm saying that. It's just that ingrained into my being.

Surfing is like breathing. My oxygen.

"You're cockier than most of my friends."

"Is it cocky when you can back up the words with action?" I ask, shaking my head. "I think that's actually called confidence. Which I have a lot of."

Except in certain areas.

"Clearly." A challenge rises in his words, the competitor coming out and my body hums with what's about to happen.

I pick up my board and he shrugs out of his backpack, dropping it in the sand. "Race ya."

I don't answer until I'm almost to the water. Looking over my shoulder to shout something, I see him hot on my heels. I grin as my board and I hit the water, paddling out to sea with a pro right next to me.

If someone told fifteen-year-old me that I would be surfing with Bash Cleaton at nineteen, I wouldn't have believed them.

If they had told me I would have been surfing with a hotshot surfer from the 80s, I'd believe them in a heartbeat.

My entire life has been spent around people that used to be the talk of the surf world.

As I paddle, I sneak glances under my arm at Bash as his arms slice through the water with ease. He looks at home on the board, the ocean breeze blowing his hair across his forehead.

He really is too attractive for his own good, a surfer body with a fun personality. Making him a deadly combination.

When he was fifteen and making a name for himself, magazines called him a teenage heartthrob, but now he is something more.

Age has been kind to him. His boyish features that made him famous on preteens' walls have sharpened, matured, heightened. He's more than a heartthrob now; he's a heart-wrecker.

We don't say where we're going to stop; instead an unspoken agreement passes between us when we both halt in the same area, sitting up on our boards.

"So, come here often?" Bash asks and I laugh, shaking my head. He laughs with me before the sound fades into the breeze.

"Oh, you know." I dip my fingers into the water. "Just every morning."

"Dedicated." He tries to laugh, but it dies off in the end.

I watch him with a frown.

"When did you know you loved this?" His voice takes on a more serious tone.

"This as in…?"

"Surfing." He watches me, waiting for a reaction that never comes.

My poker face is on like a mask.

I know people can fall out of love with a sport.

It happened with Dez and baseball. He played all his life before quitting his junior year of high school when he needed shoulder surgery. But that can't be why he's asking, right?

"It's just something that has always been a constant in my life." I lay out on my board, still running my fingers over the cool water. "Growing up, surfing was as common in my house as football. A second religion where the beach was our church. I learned how to crawl, then how to surf, and then I learned how to walk. It's in my blood. I can't help but love it."

His face is pinched in thought. "Have you ever tried to break up with it?"

I nod, thinking how much I should explain. It's not like what happened to me is a secret. It was nationally televised, even internationally in some places. But there is a difference between a stranger telling my story through a screen and me telling it to someone face to face. I can't stand to see the pity in their eyes when there is nothing to pity.

I'm alive, it doesn't matter that my body has scars. What happened wasn't anyone's fault except mine for testing nature.

Nature and her inhabitants can't be controlled. They can't be tamed. Trespass on their territory to the point where they feel threatened and they will defend themselves.

"I did. I didn't even go near the water for a year." Back when I let the fear of what happened control me. Rule me.

"How'd that feel?" He doesn't ask it like my therapist did. He asks like he fears it's happening to him.

"Like I lost a piece of me," I whisper. "That year, I wasn't living. I was existing only to go through the motions."

Bash is silent as he paddles closer to me, the current bringing us out further into the ocean and away from shore. He gently splashes water onto my back. "Did you ever get it back?"

I nod, not saying anything.

"How?" His lifeless eyes tighten, a glint of light that I can't place. I don't speak eyes.

Looking out at the horizon, I see a set rolling in. "I surfed."

# CHAPTER EIGHT

*Bash*

DEZ IS SITTING ON MY COUCH, A BEER BOTTLE IN ONE hand and his cell phone in the other. He keeps glancing down at the device and I can't help but give him shit. "Waiting on a girl to text?"

Dez has quickly become the best friend I've never had in my life, something I didn't realize I was lacking until I came to this small town.

Through the years we've hung out after competitions and the times we've hung out since I got here, I like to think I know this dude pretty well and I've never seen him this borderline desperate for a chick's attention. Which is why this has become so amusing.

Since the party, he's been moody and snappy. He's hardly able to handle any jokes.

"Fuck you," he grumbles, flicking me off while his eyes are attached to the screen.

See.

I lean back in my chair, chuckling, taking a pull of my own beer. Shit's too easy. "So, who is she?"

My mind immediately goes to Brit, Emery's friend, kind of hoping it's not. I'm trying to make friends with Emery and can't have one of my friends screwing shit up with hers. That makes for an awkward friendship.

"Not a she."

My eyebrows shoot up and I fight a smirk. "Didn't know you swung that way, Daimon."

He flips me off again, repeating his insult as well. "I'm waiting on a text from my nephew."

I don't point out I didn't know he was an uncle, but I knew he had an older sister. So, rolling with it, I ask, "How old is he?"

"Seven." His voice tight, knuckles tightening around his phone.

"Didn't know they gave kids cell phones that young." Fuck, I didn't get my own phone until I was fourteen.

"I got him a prepaid one for when he goes and visits his dad. I like to be able to talk to him and I don't trust his fucking father to let him use his phone." He sounds tired, but at the same time his phone goes off. Dez gets quiet, his eyes roaming over the text, but whatever is on the screen has him sighing. "They're all good."

"They?"

"I have a niece, too," he says. "My sister and her ex-husband had Max and Ellie while their marriage was still young. They're twins, but her dickwad husband couldn't handle her job and he cheated on her. She was in the Air Force, fucking brave as hell and came home to find her husband cheating on her. On their bed, with their kids in the next room."

Fuuuuck. "What a piece of shit."

He nods, clenching his phone in his fist. "My sister's a veteran now and has full custody of the kids, but once a month she lets Dale see them. I don't know why—he doesn't give a shit about them. I keep telling her to stop sending the twins over there, but she won't."

"You're a good uncle, Dez." My parents aren't close with their siblings, so I don't have relationships with my aunt or uncles. Something I desperately wanted growing up. A big family with lots of cousins to hang out with. "They're really lucky to have you."

He rubs a hand over his face. "They're so smart and have this light in their eyes. Still so innocent and I'm always afraid it's going to go out next time they come back from their dad's."

We don't say anything after that, just sitting here, sipping our beers.

Speaking of sisters, I haven't called mine since I left Cali. She's texted me a few times and called a bunch, but I've only sent her one text. Letting her know everything is fine and I'm good—in relative terms that is.

I'm usually not such a shitty brother. I try to call Rachel once or twice a week, if I'm busy, and four times when manageable.

While my mother might not be a mom, my sister is the best. The one to always cheer the loudest at my competitions and the one making sure my ego never got bigger than my heart. She was always there to bandage my scraped knees and take me out for ice cream growing up.

"Fuck, man. I'm sorry." He takes another pull from the bottle. "Didn't mean to unload all this family shit on you."

I wave him off. "Nah, you're good. Sometimes things are easier to say to someone you haven't known for a long time."

"Ain't that the truth." He takes another pull. "So, did you get a hold of Emery?"

I take a pull of my own bottle, the condensation wrapping around my hand, as I stall for an answer. "Yep. We went surfing this morning."

He freezes, eyes wide and mouth slightly hanging open. "You and Emery went surfing? Emery Lawson? You're shitting me, right?"

I scrunch my brows together as I look at him. "I don't know you well enough for that."

"Dude, Emery doesn't surf. She hasn't since a few years ago."

My brows pinch in confusion. The memories of this morning with Emery are vivid in my head.

Clearly, we aren't talking about the same Emery. We can't be.

I don't even remember if her last name is Lawson. It could be Donaldson. The Emery I know definitely surfs, and according to her, she does it everyday.

"Maybe we're talking about different Emerys."

Dez snorts, shaking his head, and gives me a look that says he knows what I'm up to but it's not his business. "Yeah, that's it." I don't need to note the dry tone in his words, but man, can the dude lay the sarcasm on thick.

Dez drops it and we hang out for a while longer, putting on some sports channel, and knocking back a few beers.

It's fine until my phone starts going off and, without checking the caller I.D., I answer, "Hello?"

"Sebastian." Her voice makes me cringe and my skin crawl. I haven't talked to her in weeks and have successfully been able to avoid all the calls coming in from back home, but hanging out with a friend and a drinking a few beers like a normal person has lowered my guard.

*Damn it.*

"Mother." My tone doesn't even sound like me. Cold and hard.

With a realization, I startle. That's what my tone was always like. Angry and distant. Detached.

Being away has shown how empty I've been living these past seven years.

The term "finding one's self" never made sense to me. How does one not know who they are? When Rachel was in college, she did a study abroad program in Australia, taking classes that didn't correlate with her major. I brought her to the airport, hugging her tight, when I asked if she really wanted to go.

Rach laughed as she hugged me, shaking her head against my shoulder. I've always supported my sister, as she has always supported me. We're each other's number ones since day one. However supportive I was though, I didn't want her to go. It would be the first time I'd be by myself. My sister sacrificed a lot for me, to protect me from what my parents were turning into, but she told me she had to go find herself. I waited at the airport until her plane took off.

I was sixteen.

Now, six years later, I finally understand what Rachel was after.

I'm learning new things about myself that I had no idea were there. How does a person go twenty-two years without even knowing if they like IPA or lager beer?

How does one know anything unless they go out and find it?

Dez gives me a look and I get up, leaving the room and heading outside. Once on the porch, I lean against the railing.

One hand grips the phone while the other goes through my hair.

"You haven't been answering my calls or texts, Sebastian." Her tone is just as distant as mine. As if we're discussing a business arrangement.

"Correct," I state since she pauses on her end, waiting for a response.

"I've been worried, Sebastian." She keeps saying my name like it's supposed to have an effect on me.

It doesn't.

All it does is make me resent my name.

I roll my eyes even though she can't see. *You've been worried about my money. Not me, Mom.*

"I need time away."

"You have a career. You can't take time off."

"Why not?" I challenge. A knock sounds behind me.

Turning around, Dez motions that he's going to take off. I nod my chin at him. "People do it all the time. I haven't had a vacation in years. I feel like I deserve it."

What I want to say is that I've earned it, but in her eyes, I haven't earned anything until she's living in a castle made of gold and marble.

*The finer things don't come cheap, Sebastian,* was her saying to me for years.

"As your manager," she goes on, completely ignoring what I said and I bite back a groan to keep from saying, *self-appointed manager.* "It's important to run these things by me, son." *Now I'm son and not Sebastian.* "You have commitments that have been on the schedule long before you decided to pull this stunt."

She's talking to me like I'm back in high school.

The phone tightens in my grip. "I left the city, Mother, I

didn't leave the planet."

"That's wonderful to hear," she says and I wonder if she even heard me at all. "You have to be in Miami for a charity event in two days. I trust you can see to your own travel arrangements. Your father and I are taking the yacht out for a mini vacation, so I won't be able to talk to you for a few days."

*Thank God for that.*

The irony is not lost on me that my parents, who don't even have jobs, are taking a mini vacation, but my mother has been calling me nonstop to lecture me on mine.

The one who actually works for a living.

"I'll be there." I hang up, not even bothering to tell her to enjoy her time off. We both know she will.

# CHAPTER NINE

## *Emery*

"WHAT DO YOU MEAN YOU'VE BEEN SURFING WITH Sebastian Cleaton?" Brit sits on my bed, looking at me like I've sprouted two heads. Imagine all the food I could eat, though, if that was true.

"Emery!" She throws a pillow at my face while I daydream about pizza.

"What?" I hug the pillow to my chest.

"Stop avoiding and answer the question!"

"Well." I lean back against the wall. "I told you we were and you stared at me for a while before asking and now we're here."

"Smartass." She moves for another pillow and I brace for an impact that doesn't come. She puts it in her lap instead. "Now tell me."

I shrug. "There's nothing really to tell. I still surf at the same time but now I don't do it alone."

"You're keeping something from me." She narrows her eyes.

"I'm not." It's been a few days of surfing with Bash, but nothing other than surfing has occurred. Yesterday we didn't even talk past pleasantries.

"Are you sure, Emery Marie?"

Why does she have to go and middle name me! She knows I hate that. "You know me. When do I ever keep stuff from you?"

She's the only one that knows I'm not going back to school. My secrets are Brit's secrets as per the rules of best friendom.

"Because you don't get serious with guys and you've always said surfing is more intimate than sex for you—which, by the way, just means you aren't having good sex."

I'm not having *any* sex and she knows that. "He's kind of a friend, Brit. We just surf. There's nothing more."

Except that one time we made out, but neither of us have brought it up and I plan on keeping it that way. Does my time with Bash have to be something more?

Brit says I have commitment issues, both with relationships and friendships. I keep a lot of people at arm's length, only letting them ricochet off the surface. The closest people in my life are the ones that have been there since birth: Brit, Geer, and my cousin, Nori. Or the people that didn't take my brush-offs to heart and fought their way in, like my friends Xavier and Sienna.

Both lists are pretty small.

"What's going on with you and Desmond?" Not wanting the attention on me anymore, I change the subject.

"Nothing life altering." Brit shrugs, but adds, "We're going to the movies tonight."

"Is he why my calls aren't being sent to voicemail as

much?" Surprisingly, Brit's phone has been charged a lot lately. And I have a feeling our ex-friend is the reason.

She nods, biting her lip.

Dez doesn't rank really high on my list of people for Brit. Doesn't rate high on a lot of lists I have. I'm protective of people I care about and Dez has already hurt her by dropping us in high school.

I know people can change and grow, which is why he's sort of getting the benefit of the doubt from me, but this isn't a game. After one strike, he's done.

"Why aren't you happy for me?"

"If you're happy, I'm happy."

"Emery."

"Brittany." She makes a face at her full name, hating the sound. She never goes by it.

"He's not in high school anymore," she whispers, looking down, and I feel like shit for making her feel bad, but I remember the day I held her in the school bathroom as she sobbed during the first week of our freshman year. "He's not the same person."

I nod, afraid that I won't have control over what leaves my mouth. I'm not lying when I say I'm happy if she's happy. I'm on Team Brit in everything, so if this is what she wants, I'll support her. And she needs to see that. I'm not mad, I just don't trust Dez with her—with her feelings or with her heart.

I will literally destroy him if she cries over him one more time. No man is worth tears.

I push up from my spot, running toward my bed, and tackle Brit. We go down with pillows to cushion our fall. My mattress is practically made up of pillows. I'm a pillow hoarder.

I squeeze, putting my cheek to hers. "I love you, best friend!"

"I love you too, freak." She laughs, pushing me off. "Now, will you help me find something to wear?"

"Sure." I grin. "Jeans and a long sleeve bodysuit coming up. No hanky-panky will be going down in that theater."

"Hanky-panky?"

"It's a saying. For sexual relations." I shimmy my shoulders and wiggle my brows.

"Did I miss the time traveling we did to go back to the 1950s?"

"Psh, as if you'd be so lucky to go to the 50s with me."

Brit throws another pillow at my face.

My morning routine has changed. In the span of five days, I've grown used to not being alone. Maybe it's too soon to get attached, but having the reassurance of another person out in the water has calmed some of my nerves about being out there.

Having Bash around reminds me that despite pushing friends and people away with my secret, letting someone in can be worth it.

Bash has turned into a great partner to surf with.

On the days that the surf has been lacking, we float on our boards, talking about anything that isn't personal. He doesn't pry into my cagey attitude with my wetsuit and I never ask why he's in this small town.

I'm a creature of habit, so as hard as it for me to change said habits, when I start to get used to the changes, I don't like when more changes occur.

I'm sitting in the sand, my board next to me, while I stare at my phone's lock screen. The time staring back at me.

He's late.

Which isn't that big of a deal, if the person waiting on him isn't so crazy anal about her wave time.

A fact Bash knows.

The second day he met up with me, he was five minutes late and I didn't talk to him until he flipped my board over and I went plunging into the water. I forgave him for flipping me—because that was fun—but not for being late.

But today he's pushing fifteen minutes. I get things happen and people aren't as time conscious as I am, but still. I like to get places thirty minutes early when possible.

Lateness is the work of demon spawn.

The screen goes dark and I hit the lock button just as fast. Seventeen minutes late.

*Where the hell is he?*

After twenty-five minutes of sitting around, unable to wait any longer, I throw my phone on top of my bag and pick up my board.

Approaching the water, I stop before the surf can caress the tips of my toes.

The feeling of hesitation never lessens, but some days I charge the water, not allowing myself to think. Other days, like today, I need a moment.

My dad taught me a surfer's prayer he would say before a competition and I repeat it in my head, moving my feet in motion. I keep saying it until I'm on my board, paddling out.

It's a comfort as much as a distraction.

*You got this, Emery Marie.*

When I'm far enough out, my mind clicks off. Going on autopilot. I go through several sets of waves before I sit back and watch the sun fully rise—an activity I haven't been doing this past week.

A swelling in my chest rises and I ignore it. Nope. No

negative thoughts for this moment. This is the moment where the slate is officially wiped clean and a new day begins.

I stay on the beach until it's way past time for me to be back home. Geer comes out at one point, bringing me a mug of coffee and ruffling my hair. As I smack his hands away, I can't bring myself to laugh.

I wait on the beach for a lot longer than I'm proud of.

It's not until I'm in my car in the bakery's parking that I allow myself to check my phone. Nothing. No missed calls, no unopened texts. I hate the assault of feelings happening. Lonely. Forgotten.

Ignoring them, I check my phone again.

Yep. Still nothing.

As I pay the cashier at the bakery, I allow myself to acknowledge the fact that Bash. Didn't. Show.

"You sure you're okay, sweet pea?" My dad asks as we sip our drinks at our table. We're attending a fundraiser down in Miami.

"Yep." I smile. *Don't mind me, Dad, I'm just angry at myself for getting attached to a person's presence when I had no business doing so.*

It's two days later and I'm not over the event of Bash not showing that morning. Mostly because he hasn't shown up since.

As angry as I am at Bash, I'm even angrier at myself for allowing his absence to bother me so much. It's not even him I missed, but it's him that I'm mad at. Is a simple text too much to ask for? I don't fuck with people who make plans only to back out at the last second.

Tonight I'm not thinking about it. Tonight is about having fun and raising money.

"I fucking hate these things." Dad pulls at his tie. "Damn monkey suits."

Dad really hates tuxedos. He really hates pants that go past his knees and closed toed shoes. Mom grabs his hands, pulling them away before he messes up her hard work.

"Behave and I'll help you take it off later tonight," she tries to whisper. But fun fact about my mother, she is awful at talking quietly.

"EWW!" I cover my ears as my face contorts in disgust. "Children in the room! *Your* child in the room. Please refrain from saying anything that will make me want to put my head through a food processor."

"Stop being dramatic, Emery." My mom laughs, Dad joining her, and I am in desperate need of some bleach.

"Stop being disgusting, Mother."

My words go unheard as Dad kisses Mom and she laughs in the process. It is a serious wonder that I am an only child. My parents have never gotten out of that young love, must-touch-constantly phase.

It's as gross as it is sweet.

It doesn't matter that we're at an event raising money for a charity organization. My dad will never act his age. He's a child in a grownup's body.

Much like me.

Wonder who I get that from.

We've been here for two hours and I'm bored out of my skull. I leave my parents by our table to get another drink from the open bar. I get water, which I'm sipping when someone grabs my shoulders, giving me a shake. "You can come to a party but not text me back?"

I laugh at the familiar voice. Spinning around, a tall and gorgeous blonde towers over me with a smile that is full of excitement and mischief. Just the type of friend I like to have. "Things have been crazy lately, Sienna. You won't even believe me."

*Like remember that time we met at a surf competition and bonded over our adolescent crush on Sebastian Cleaton? Well, I know what his abs feel like and what his lips taste like.*

"Try me, girlie." Sienna takes my glass, drinking half of it before handing it back with a face. "That's not a vodka tonic."

"No, this is a water." I jingle the glass, making the ice rattle. "It's what people drink to stay hydrated."

"What a waste of an open bar choice." She shakes her head. "I need a real drink." Sienna grabs my hand, pulling us over to the bar where she leans over the counter, asking for a vodka tonic. The bartender makes speedy work of her order. With a smile and thanks, Sienna repeats what she did with my glass, this time coming away satisfied. "Now that's a drink."

I roll my eyes, taking a sip of water. "Excuse me for not being legal and having people here actually know that."

"Aw, look at little Emery Marie being responsible," she teases and we laugh.

"Well someone has to be. I think last time we hung out it was you, so now it's my turn."

I met Sienna when I was thirteen and she was sixteen on the surf circuit. She was standing with a group of girls, laughing, as I was walking by with my board tucked under my arm, and one of the girls in the group stretched out her leg and our ankles locked, sending me down—face first into the sand. Some girls felt like I had an unfair advantage because of my dad, that the judges went easy on my scores. It didn't happen often, but when the taunting and bullying occurred it was from jealousy.

The other girls laughed while Sienna's shadow fell over me. I still remember the metallic taste in my mouth from biting the inside of my cheek. Keeping my head pressed to the sand, I waited for the next blow that never came. She just stood over there, and while the laughter trickled off I convinced myself it was safe.

Sienna stood with her hand stretched out, waiting to help me up. We've been friends since.

Sienna has a twin, Xavier, who is very much a charmer and very much a traveling man. They're Brazilian-American and can speak at least four languages. Portuguese, English, Spanish, and French. I've never asked if they can speak more.

They've also traveled the world, from America to Fiji to Brazil, where they stayed with their family for a few years before moving back to Florida. They now live in a town not even a forty-five minute drive from my parents' house, and I've been a sucky friend who hasn't gone to see them since the start of winter break.

"So where's that charming brother of yours?"

"Did you just admit your love for me?" Arms wrap around my waist while a chin rests on my shoulder. Xavier Santos is a closer friend than even his sister is to me. "After all these years?"

He's dressed in a suit with a pinstriped tie and has a freshly shaven face. The stark white of his shirt makes the green flecks in his eyes pop. The only part of him that is unkempt, and is always unkempt, is his thick curly hair that constantly looks like he's been running his fingers through it. Twenty-two years and he still doesn't know what a hairbrush is.

"Ugh." My head lulls back onto his chest. He's a tall guy. Probably as tall, if not a few inches taller, than Bash. "Can you stop being a flirt for one point three seconds, please? Maybe I'd actually miss you then."

"You miss me anyways," he tells me and I don't deny it. I see Xavier more than his sister. He's been up to Orlando a few times to see me and Brit, and is the fifth member of our squad—the squad consisting of Brit, Nori, Geer, and me.

"Omigod," Sienna whisper-yells, grabbing my arm. "Don't look now, but Sebastian Cleaton is here and won't stop looking at you."

I've never understood why someone says *don't look* before telling you something that will obviously make you look. Like telling me Bash is here. Clearly, I am going to look.

Untangling from Xavier's arms, I look around the giant ballroom until I find the face that is starting to take up more and more time in my mind.

And he looks angry—pissed.

# CHAPTER TEN

## *Emery*

BASH IS STANDING WITH A GROUP OF PEOPLE, DRESSED IN a tux like every other man here, but his is fitted to his body perfectly. His tie hangs loosely around his neck with the knot sitting further down his chest, like he couldn't be bothered to tie it securely.

His tie is a deep violet color, the same shade as my dress. Oh, great. We're matching.

I focus on his tie. It's easier than focusing on his face. His face is compressed with so much anger toward me; I couldn't breathe when I first saw him.

*Why is he so angry with* me? I'm not the one who left him hanging the past couple of days.

Unless—I'm known for putting my foot in my mouth. The whole no filter thing really is a struggle sometimes. I've offended my share of people, not on purpose, but sensitive people just don't gel with me.

Xavier and Sienna both try to get my attention but they get ignored as I muster up the courage to look back at Bash.

Xavier snaps his fingers in my face, which I swipe away, and my gaze shifts, getting ensnared by the deep, rich brown eyes of the man I'm currently troubled by.

Putting on my best poker face, keeping the feelings closed off to use at another time, I raise my arm halfway in the air and give a little wave.

Bash doesn't return it.

I lower my arm, feeling defeated. An extended olive branch that gets stepped on.

If he wants to play games and ignore me like a child, then fine. I turn my back to him and look at my friends. What I thought Bash and I were becoming before now.

"Vodka tonic. Stat," I say and Sienna snaps into action, walking to the bar and ordering two.

"You okay?" Xavier asks, hand on the crook of my elbow, gesturing to my recent rejection.

"'Course." I shrug, putting on a smile.

His face pinches and his eyes narrow.

The thing about knowing a person as long as I've known the Santos siblings is that they know when you're lying, and Xavier is two seconds away from calling bullshit.

He doesn't get the chance. Right when Sienna is returning with the drinks, a hand lands on my waist and a voice is in my ear. "Walk with me."

I shiver, and it's not from being cold.

Bash is close, so close that I feel the heat of his body against mine. The subtle prick of his stubble against the shell of my ear. It's a sensation overload I'm not expecting.

Xavier looks like he's ready to say something and Sienna looks like she's in shock—mouth open and all.

Bash doesn't say anything to them. He's standing there, his eyes drilling holes into Xavier's hand. The one that is still on my arm.

I shake Xavier off and take my drink from Sienna. She still hasn't moved. We probably need to check for a pulse.

I'm about to take a sip from my glass but Bash takes it and places it on the table.

I don't want to have this talk, but I know Bash won't give up until we do, so it's going to be done in private, away from prying eyes and ears.

"Let's go." I push against him, trying to get him to move.

He doesn't.

I push against his chest again and this time he relents back a step before walking toward an exit.

My dad sees me walking out. He looks confused, but when he sees who I'm walking with, the confusion turns into concern as the recognition hits.

Dad might be out of the competition circuit, but he's not out of the surf game. He's a sports commentator for a lot of the competitions, both big and small. I know for a fact that he's been to more than two dozen competitions that Bash has competed in. He knows who he is. He can probably spew his stats faster than Bash can.

I smile, despite the growing feeling of dread, to let him know everything is fine. He doesn't look convinced and starts to follow until my mom sees what's going on. She says something to him, shaking her head, and pulls him back.

*Go, Mom! For the win!*

Bash leads us down the hall and into a more secluded area. I cross my arms over my dress and lean against the wall as Bash stands there. The look of anger hasn't left his face, but he says, "You look beautiful."

He doesn't sound as angry as he looks. He sounds frustrated.

"Don't," I cut him off. I'm not here for bullshit. I'm here to know what the hell crawled up his ass and has him ignoring me. "You don't get to show up here, look pissed at my presence in front of all those people, and then give me a compliment when you get me alone!"

He's never given me a compliment before and the first one that he gives me is now. When I'm pissed and he's acting weird. No. Just no.

"Emery." He takes a step closer but thinks better of it. He goes to the opposite wall in the hallway and mimics my stance. "I'm sorry about all that. I just wasn't expecting you to be here."

Standing with Xavier, is what he wants to add. I know jealousy when I see it and Bash doesn't want to admit it, but he was jealous of Xavier.

"So me being here is enough to anger you?"

"No." With a deep, heavy sigh Bash rubs at his chest, right over his heart. Where his tattoo is. "I just wasn't expecting you."

"Well, surprise," I say dryly, giving him spirit fingers that are full of sarcasm.

"Don't." He throws my words back at me. Pushing off the wall, he comes closer. "Why are you here, Em?"

My heart warms at the nickname until I make that feeling stop. He's not buttering me up. Not until I have answers. "I could ask you the same thing."

I'm looking anywhere but at him. I'm looking for an escape.

Bash grips my chin, tilting my face to look him in the eyes. "Before I went on vacation, I forgot about some of the obligations I committed to. My mother arranged this one without my knowledge, so here I am."

"I didn't know you were a momma's boy." I try to grin, but stop. His face is still hard, and I'm still mad.

I push off the wall, headed for the door, but he catches my elbow.

"Why are you so angry at me?" His voice is full of irritation.

"Because!" I poke his chest, but his body of muscle doesn't budge.

"You're the first person I've surfed with in years and it was fucking nice not being alone for once! You couldn't even send me a text saying you weren't going to show. *God,* Bash, what if I thought something happened to you?"

Did it make me a shitty person that I didn't think something serious was wrong with him?

Am I too selfish?

Answer to both: probably.

"I have a routine, Bash. I let you fuck it up by joining me and then you fuck it up again when you bail without telling me." *You hurt me, you asshole.* "I waited for you."

He curses under his breath, dropping my arm. "I'm sorry, Emery. Things came up and I wasn't thinking."

"Oh, too busy to send a quick text? Doubtful." I don't accept that answer. It's a brush off if anything. He forgot.

*He forgot me.*

The idea hurts more than I'm willing to admit. I don't like it and Bash doesn't even try to answer again. That hurts even more, in a way.

He shakes his head. "What're you doing here, Emery?"

"I was invited." I lean back against the wall.

He lifts an eyebrow at me, waiting for me to explain.

"My dad always gets invited to these things."

"And your father would be?" He doesn't say it in a condescending way, but more in a curious way.

We haven't talked about our parents. Which has been nice. I've liked having him in my life, knowing he's not there for the connections I have access too.

"Ren Lawson."

He blinks.

Blinks.

Blinks two more times.

His mouth slightly open.

It's kind of ironic that the look he's wearing is the same one Sienna was wearing earlier.

Irony at it's finest, in my opinion.

"You're his daughter?"

Biting my lip, I nod.

Growing up with surfers and having the father that I do, they always fanboyed over him. They essentially used my friendship as a way to get closer to my dad.

I really hope Bash is different.

He opens his mouth, then closes it a few times, resembling a fish out of water guzzling down air.

My heart pounds louder, like the bass in a song, and someone is turning the volume louder and louder.

*Say something.*

Silence.

*Say anything.*

More silence.

*Say something about the weather! Anything is better than this, Cleaton!*

When the silence becomes suffocating, I push off the wall with all the intent of walking away, but Bash grabs me, pulling me back. Again. "Where do you think you're going?"

"Clearly you need some alone time with your thoughts, so I'll let you be and go back with my friends."

"I don't think so, Lawson. You're not running away from me."

"You don't get a say, Bash! You've been avoiding me."

"I wasn't avoiding you, damn it! I was just going through some shit, okay?"

Throughout the exchange, the two of us draw closer to each other until our faces are close enough for our noses to touch. It hurts to suck in air. My lungs, *my body*, feels so tight. We're so close.

His breath is a soft caress over my lips as my eyes dart to his. His tongue pokes out the corner. I look back to his eyes and see the same fiery need I feel reflecting back at me.

Something in the air shifts between us; all the feelings of anger and hurt are shifting toward something else—something that gets interrupted when Xavier appears in the hallway.

"Em." Xavier sounds so casual, like I'm not in the arms of Sebastian Cleaton. He doesn't even blink at the scene.

Sienna rounds the corner next and isn't as subtle as her brother. "Oh! Sorry! Sorry!" Sienna is grinning wide. "We didn't mean to interrupt, but we're taking off and wanted to know if Em wanted to join us." Her eyes rake over Bash like he's a pair of shoes for sale. "You're more than welcome to come, too."

I roll my eyes at my friend before looking up at Bash. Since I'm still in his hold, I have to tip my head up. He looks down at me.

Our noses are so close.

I'm vaguely aware of Sienna smacking her brother's arm, saying something about her phone and needing a picture of the moment. I can't look away from Bash to say anything to her. There is something so enticing about him and the effect he has over me.

I don't like it. Makes me feel things.

"I'm going, but I won't kill you if you wanted to come too." Here I am, with another olive branch extended, showing I'm not as angry as I was. If he comes and grovels some more, perhaps on his knees, we'll be okay.

"Yeah?"

I offer a soft smile, already knowing I'm over it when I answer, "Yeah."

# CHAPTER ELEVEN

## *Emery*

THIRTY MINUTES LATER, WE FIND OURSELVES AT A PARTY that is being thrown by a guy named Stephen. A friend of a friend through Sienna. Whoever he is, he needs to get in touch with Dez.

This party is like Dez's wet dream.

Alcohol of every kind lines the kitchen counters, plastic cups already littering the floor. Loud music pours through the house, a strong bass shaking the walls.

Most of the people spill out into the backyard.

From a charity gala to a house party, this dress is not for every event. The long skirt feels constricting, the fabric starting to irritate me. I'm allergic to expensive items that only get worn once. And now I'm wearing it to the spill zone. If someone so much as drips anything on this dress, there will be a fight.

"Thanks," I say to Bash as he hands me a beer before

moving to my side.

"Want to finish talking?" He watches me as he tips back his beer.

I shake my head, sampling mine.

Beer is probably my third favorite drink—right behind Rum Runners and fruity Mojitos.

"What's your favorite drink?"

He chuckles. "Whiskey."

"Just straight whiskey?" I ask and when Bash nods, my throat burns from just thinking about it. I need some kind of chaser. I wrinkle my nose in disgust, making him laugh even harder.

"Aren't you a little young to know what that tastes like?"

I wave my beverage in his face. "Says the guy who just handed me this."

I don't add that I was also drunk the night we made out. Even though it was probably obvious. No need to drag up the awkward.

Unless he wants to.

Or I get drunk enough to lose the small filter I have on my tongue.

Whichever happens first.

He takes another swig before saying, "Touché."

We're silent for a while, just taking in the party scene around us.

"I've missed this."

"What? Beer?"

"No, you brat." He gestures around us. "This."

I must look as confused as I feel because Bash laughs at me before explaining, "Parties. Hanging out with friends." He looks down at me, and he appears a lot younger than he actually is in this moment. "I haven't just hung out in a long time."

"Aw, the life of being a pro surfer taking a toll on you? I mean, you are getting pretty up there. Age-wise, I mean."

"Ha-ha," he deadpans. "Everything in my life lately has been about work. Don't get me wrong, surfing is what I want to do. It's just sometimes the things that they want me to do out of the water aren't what I want. So I'm taking a break from everything for awhile."

"I get it," I tell him, but pause when what he said finally registers. "Wait. You're not entering any competitions?"

He shakes his head, not saying anything. Before I can get anything out of him, though, Xavier decides it's time to crash our little two-person group.

"Sup?" Xavier asks as he casually winds his arm around my neck.

I don't miss the glare Bash is giving to Zay's arm.

"Just talking about surfing," I answer.

Xavier nods, moving his hand down my body until it's around my waist. My body stiffens and Bash's eyes narrow even more.

Our reactions are for completely different reasons.

Xavier's touching one of my scars, and he knows it. I don't like it when people accidentally bump into me because I don't want them to brush against my raised skin. I hate people touching them.

I push Xavier until his arm drops away.

"Yeah, after what happened—OW!" Xavier glowers down at me as he bites back a curse.

"Oh, sorry Zay! Did I almost impale your foot?" Feigning innocence, I look up at him with big, wide eyes. I'm not even sorry I just jammed my stiletto heel into his foot—which is barefoot.

I mean, oops.

"You know, Em, you used to be graceful. I guess when you lost your board it also got rid of your balance." He chuckles, which turns into a full laugh as he sees the look on my face. "Maybe one day you'll be allowed back out in the water."

No one but Geer, Brit, and recently Bash know I still surf. After my accident and then the incident after that, my parents went ballistic. They told me I was carelessly putting myself at risk, and until I learned how to respect the sea, I was banned from surfing.

That day a big part of who I was died.

"She was in it a few days ago?" Bash looks at me with the same confusion in his voice, and I know without checking Zay is too.

Zay tries to laugh it off, but when I don't join him, he stops. With two pairs of eyes staring at me, their focus unwavering and so intent, my body starts moving like an eel. Squirming on my feet. The legs of dozens of spiders run up my back. My entire body trembles.

I hear an "Em?" the same time as "Firecracker?"

My head shakes, wanting them to go, to make them stop talking without having to vocalize it. I can't speak.

Pretty sure I'm having trouble breathing, my chest tightens and my vision begins to fade as lights dance in my line of sight.

My fingers feel the stabbing of a thousand needles and the only sound my ears pick up are waves crashing and guttural screams.

*I'm flying.*

*That is always my first thought when I catch a wave, but this time I really feel it.*

*My board is gliding effortlessly as I maneuver on the wave. I just landed a trick and I go to do another before I get caught in* the break line, but my footing feels off.

Instead of taking the time to fix it, impulse takes over and my board soars into the air, above the wave.

I give a victory cry as I come back down, but my landing quickly becomes a wipeout.

I'm flipped off from the side, getting pulled under the wave. My board comes with since it's attached to my ankle, but one of the fins slams into my head.

Pushing my way towards the surface, I only have time to gasp a lungful of air before another wave crashes on top of me, sending me under again.

I try to swim back to the surface when something sharp and powerful and painful clamps onto my leg, tugging me down.

Panic starts to fight its way inside when I look down in a blurry haze and see what's pulling me. Around my leg are the jaws of a very large shark whose black eyes are taunting me.

A scream rips through my throat, filling my body with cold saltwater.

My free limbs start flailing, struggling to get away. The shark tugs, pulling my body with it and pain rips through my leg. It becomes harder to see the shark, my blood begins to ink the water around us, making the cloudy, salty water even murkier.

I know I'm going to die.

My body is losing a lot of blood, along with energy and the surface is becoming an impossible distance to reach. But I'm a Lawson and even a Lawson getting attacked by a shark isn't keeping me from at least trying to fight back.

The jaw loosens a little, so I shove my fist into his snout the same time I stab a finger in one of the eyes.

Suddenly the weight on my thigh is gone and I see the shark look at me with a cold, calculating stare.

My lungs are starting to suffocate from the lack of oxygen

*and I feel close to passing out. After one lap around my body, my attacker swims away.*

*I don't stop to see if it is coming back. I push water out of my way, using my arms as I kick as hard as I can with one leg while my other just hangs in a bloody mess.*

*"Help!" I gasp, letting the crisp air fly into my body, to my lungs.*

*"HELP!" I scream maniacally. I've drifted a lot farther from shore. Away from the crowd, away from my parents. "SOMEONE HELP ME!"*

*My body is fading, a black shadow of sleep trying to lure me in. My vision is blurry, but I'm able to make out a small boat racing in my direction.*

*I start to scream for help again, but it turns into an ear-deafening scream as another shark, a smaller one, latches onto my torso, pulling me under the water once more.*

I crash into a hard body, arms curling around my waist. Even though the hold on me isn't tight, it feels as suffocating as the shark's teeth slicing into my flesh.

I struggle to get out of the hold, a sweat breaking out along my hairline.

"Calm down, Firecracker." The voice is like a bucket of cold water that chills my fiery skin.

I stop fighting.

*I'm not there, I'm not there, I'm on land, I'm on land.*

Blinking out the haze, the first thing I see is Sienna. The next is the moon.

It's shining proudly above us, giving off enough light to see the panic upsetting her face. Arms spin me around and Bash has the twin expression of Sienna.

I try to say something, but it's hard for the words in my brain to come out of my mouth.

Instead of talking, I begin to sob. Big, ugly, snotty sobbing and Bash is on the receiving end of it as I bury my head in his chest. His arms tighten around me again and this time I don't fight him off, instead nuzzling closer to his chest.

Bash is rubbing my back softly and if he pushes down a little harder he would feel the bumpy raised skin that covers one side of my back. If he spins me around, he would feel that it wraps around to my front as well.

My leg is just as bad.

My scars. My reminders.

Sometimes all a girl needs is a good cry fest. It's healthy. A cleanse that needs to happen to wash away the ugly and the hurt to make room for something more—something happier and good.

Unfortunately, crying into the chest of a hot surfer and thinking he won't question why his dress shirt is now one of the largest tissues he has ever seen is not that time.

As soon as my tears start to trickle down my face, Sienna grabs my hand, walks us into the house, and pulls me into the nearest bathroom.

She pushes me down onto a closed toilet seat and starts to wipe the mascara tracks off my face. While I sit, still sniffling, I watch as she searches the tiny room for a face cloth.

Once she finds one and runs it under water hot enough to cause steam to roll off the fabric, she gently places it over my face.

The steam from the towel mixes with my sticky wet face to create such an odd, yet enjoyable feeling. My pores begin to open and my eyes sting a little less. It's not a towel with healing powers or anything, but it does feel good on my face.

After it turns lukewarm, I pass it back to Sienna, who tosses it into the sink. She regards me thoughtfully with her arms crossed. "Want to share?"

I start to shake my head but stop. "I had a flashback from the day in Hawaii."

Her eyes close as the memory surfaces in her mind. Sienna was competing that day too.

"It's been two years." Her voice sounds as small as I feel in that moment.

"Three," I whisper.

After the second shark pulled me under, I don't remember anything between seeing the boat and waking up in the hospital with my parents crying by my bedside.

Seeing my dad cry is something not even sandpaper can erase from my memory.

"I never gave up surfing," I admit. The words descend around us and my heart rate starts to pick up. I bite my lip and squeeze my eyes shut, waiting for Sienna to explode with betrayal.

"I never thought you actually would," she tells me. I crack open my eyes. Well…she looks calm. "Zay did, but my brother doesn't know shit. He never competed against you."

"You're not mad?"

"Why would I be mad? I'm not your parents. Besides, they're on crack if they think they can keep you out of the water."

I snort, trying to stand up. "Right? I was born in a water birth."

For the record, my parents don't do crack.

She laughs, but pushes me back down as she shakes her head. "Not-uh. You are not leaving here until you tell me what is going on with you and Sebastian Cleaton."

"Bash," I correct without thinking and wince. "Nothing is going on. I just met him and I think we're friends. We've surfed a few times."

That sounds lame, even to my ears, but I'm not about to romanticize anything for her. Especially since there was nothing romantic going on in the first place and I'm not good when things start to be less casual.

"Yeah, friends who are in *looove*." She wiggles her eyebrows.

"What, are we twelve again?" I sputter; some spit comes out of my mouth. "Sienna, you're too into fairytales. I just met him and we've hung out a few times. If I feel anything for him it would be lust but—shit."

Sienna cackles—yes actually cackles—and punches her fists into the air. Her head is thrown back so it appears upside down in the mirror as she continues to laugh. "HA! I knew it! Spill!"

"I think it's no secret that I find him attractive. A lot of people do." Most of America—or whoever decides on those bachelor magazine picks.

"Emery Marie." Sienna looks ready to strangle me, but she's not getting anything else out of me. Nope, nope, nope.

"Sienna Santos, do you know that I love you so very much and you have the prettiest hair?" Sienna doesn't have a middle name, so she doesn't get the luxury of having one used against her.

I reach a hand out to touch her blonde locks but she slaps my hand away.

"You're so cute." She sounds anything but amused.

"Well, I know that." I stand up from the toilet seat. "Now, if you excuse me, it's time for my embarrassing exit."

More laughter follows me out of the bathroom. I hope she falls into the sink.

"Oof!" My mouth gets a good taste of shirt.

*Oh, you've got to be kidding me.*

This has to be the fourth or fifth time I've collided with the same body.

"I think you're doing this on purpose now." Hilarity colors his tone. "But I'm okay with it."

Bash's shirt is a mess. I wince taking in the sight of my mucus slathered on it.

He stands in front of me, in this empty hallway, looking like he wants to laugh. There's not a trace of disgust, despite me ruining his shirt. Good man.

The corners of his lips are twitching as he fights to keep them down.

"I'm sorry about your shirt," I tell him, not taking my eyes off my aftermath.

He glances down before his eyes return to me. "Don't worry about it."

My hands smother my face. "Don't worry about it? I sno-tafied your shirt! That's disgusting. I can't believe I actually did that."

"Hey." Bash pulls my hands away, holding them at my sides. "Don't do that. Whatever happened is done, it needed to get out and it did. I'm not going to ask about it tonight, but I think after you ruined my favorite shirt it's only fair, that later on down the road, you tell me about it. When you're ready."

"That's not your favorite shirt."

He smirks. Damn that smirk is nice. "How do you know?"

"You're too laid back for a dressy button down."

He nods, smiling a little, and I watch in rapt attention as he lets go of my hands and moves his own to the buttons of his shirt.

My heart rate kicks up into the danger zone as he slowly undoes one button, then another.

All while not taking his eyes off me.

Saliva starts to pool in my mouth, as my breathing quickens.

It's like a first class seat for all the naughty parts in my brain come to life. It is getting very hot around us, and I'm sure it's all me.

He's on his fourth button, the upper part of his tanned skin staring me right in my face. I bite my lip and I feel his gaze hone in on the movement. His eyes darken and he takes a step toward me.

I retreat back.

This is becoming too much. The intensity radiating from his eyes and the way my body is reacting, it's more than anything I've felt with any guy in the past.

I can't. I can't.

I gotta do something.

"Come surfing with me tomorrow." *Subject changer thy name is Emery.*

He blinks, and whatever seducing spell he was under is broken. My face must look as stricken as I think it does because instead of calling me on it, he only says, "Was already planning to, Firecracker."

# CHAPTER TWELVE

*Bash*

**D**AMN IT.

I see a figure further down the beach, standing with her hands on her hips as she watches the water. A surfboard sits by her feet.

I don't know how she does it, but even when I wake up earlier to get my workout in and head to the beach sooner than I usually do, she still beats me. What does Emery do, sleep on the sand?

At this point, I don't think I'd put it past her. Emery sneezes more dedication than I do. She puts me and all the other dudes I know on the circuit to shame with how much time she puts in.

I mean, Jesus Christ, the girl was upset when I didn't show up for a few days of surfing. And I feel like shit for not letting her know.

It's been a while since someone has actually cared that

much and I wasn't expecting her to take it so personally. I'm not used to people actually caring about me the person. For so long it's been about me the surfer. Those few days I didn't leave my room. I didn't do anything. I rotated between staring at my wall and mindlessly watching TV. I didn't even sleep.

I scheduled a video chat session with my therapist for later today.

Emery doesn't hear me approach, so I sneak up behind her and grab her sides. She shrieks, dropping to the sand, elbowing me in the process. I grunt, bending at the waist, and feel her eyes on me. She's glaring. I know it.

"What the hell, Bash?" Yep, she's glaring, but her lips are twitching. Like she's trying hard not to laugh. The girl likes to give me a hard time.

"Just wanting to let you know I was here." I extend my hand out to her.

She takes it and I pull her up. "A simple hello would've sufficed." She tries to wipe the sand off her wetsuit. I start to help and she shoots me a look before removing my hand from her ass. "Nice try, Cleaton."

"Only trying to lend a helping hand." I throw said hands up in surrender.

"Want to help? You can carry my board out for almost giving me a heart attack." She doesn't wait for me to agree before the board is being shoved at me. I start laughing and take it.

"Can we talk for a second?" I ask as I set her board down next to mine.

Emery's eyes get wide and she looks like she wants to bolt. If she runs, I will tackle her. Gently. Luckily, it doesn't come to that because Emery sinks to the sand again and says, "Sure."

I sit next to her, taking off my shirt in the process, in part to surf but the other part is to see Emery's reaction. We haven't talked about the night we met at all and, as much as I want to bring it up now, I know it's not something she wants to talk about—yet.

Because we will. Because I want to do it again and from the way Emery's eyes are roaming over my bare chest, I know she does too.

She's just scared.

Behind the lust and the interest I see in her eyes as she hones in on my tattoo, I see the fear. I don't know why it's there, but I don't want her to be afraid of me.

"I just wanted to say I'm sorry for last week. I should've told you I wasn't coming. There really isn't an excuse for it."

"It's okay," she says. "I kind of got used to having you with me and I don't like people who bail."

I watch as Emery mindlessly traces her fingers in the sand. Swirls and circles and zigzags. "I promise I won't bail again and if something comes up, I'll let you know."

"I want to say you don't have to, but after how I acted this weekend and how I felt, I think it's a requirement now."

"Do it."

"No."

"Emery," I sigh as she shoots me daggers. "Haven't you ever wanted to live life on the edge?"

She slaps her laminated menu down on the table, using her hands to push herself up and across the table. "You want to experiment with your breakfast, that's fine. I'm getting pancakes because this place has my favorite." She settles back into her seat. "You can't persuade me otherwise."

*I bet I can.*

I smile at her, not saying anything. Her hair is dripping little puddles on the table, still wet from earlier this morning.

After surfing, I wanted to take her out to breakfast. It took some convincing before she finally agreed. Sometimes she can be like a little deer lost in a car's headlights and as stubborn as a cat.

It's cute and frustrating.

After she finally agreed to come out with me, she suggested we go to this local place that's like a house turned restaurant.

It's super small, outdated, and packed.

Once we're finally seated, Emery doesn't even look at the menu, claiming this place happens to be her favorite breakfast spot.

I, on the other hand, need a moment. With a glance at the menu, I see something I can't help but dare her to try.

A seafood omelet.

She scrunches her face like the pug she accused me of being and I can't stop annoying her, trying to convince her to get it.

It sounds interesting.

I'm going to order it.

I just dared her because it's fun watching her get all riled up.

I want to be around her longer than just the time we spend surfing. The only people I have here are Dez and Emery and I prefer Emery's face over Dez's.

Speaking of the fucker, I've been meaning to ask if what Dez has told me is true and for her to explain, 'cause I'm hella confused. "I have a question."

"For fuck's sake, Bash, I don't want the omelet because I don't believe eggs and seafood go together!"

"Good to know." My lips twitch and I take a sip of coffee to stop an actual smile. These face muscles have been getting a good workout by being around her. "But that's not my question."

She's in the middle of raising her coffee cup to her lips and lowers it without taking a sip. "Shoot."

"Why doesn't Dez think you surf anymore?" I've waited a while to ask, not feeling it's any of my business, but now knowing that Ren Lawson is her father, I recognize her name from the surf circuit. She was good. Better than good. On her way to breaking records. Then one day, she just stopped.

Quit.

I haven't even thought about looking up the answer online. I respect Emery too much for that.

Plus, I wouldn't want her to look me up online when she can come directly to the source.

Fucking mature, I know.

"Something happened and I gave it up." She nibbles her bottom lip. My brain forgets everything as I hone in on the movement.

I want to lean over the table and nibble that bottom lip for her. I want to do more than that.

*Focus, Cleaton, you Goddamn asshole.*

"Or rather, my parents made me give it up. And I was okay with it for a little while, but not anymore." She sighs, sounding a lot more tired than she was a moment ago. "I'm not supposed to surf, Bash. Which is why I get up so early to do it. No one but Brit, Geer, and Sienna know. And, well, you." She gives me a bright smile that doesn't meet her eyes. "Welcome to the club! We have no benefits and the vote for club president is coming up, so if interested, you better start campaigning now."

"Are you always this sarcastic when you're being defensive?"

"More, usually," she says, smiling around her coffee mug.

She might think she's smart giving me a half answer, but I know what she's doing and she's not getting off the hook so easily. "What happened?"

Emery looks down at her hands, focusing on her thumbnail as she bites her lip before looking back at me. "You could look it up, you know. Ren Lawson's daughter quits surfing was a huge topic back in the day. Just type my name into a search engine."

I shake my head. "That's an invasion of privacy, Em. Even with your permission, I'm not comfortable doing that. I know what it feels like to have people know my every detail before I have a chance to tell them. I don't want that feeling to come between us."

"It's easier this way, Bash." Her voice is softer than I've ever heard it. Almost broken. "I'm a comfortable person. I will act how I act no matter where I am, with no apologizes, but talking about this with you makes me uncomfortable."

She holds up her hand before I can interject. "Let me finish. I'm uncomfortable to talk about this with you because you're the only person in this town that doesn't know what happened. I've spent the last few years being on the receiving end of pity look after pity look and if you start to give me that look I don't know what will happen." She looks down before looking back up, meeting my stare. "I like how you look at me."

"How do I look at you?" My voice matches hers, with my stare just as soft.

To me, she's always been a form of sunshine that has been bottled up, but right now it's like storm clouds are blocking the sun's rays.

"Like I'm not broken."

I don't realize how close we are to each other, both of us leaning across the table, our foreheads almost touching until the waitress comes to take our order.

We both pull away with a sigh.

Settling back into her seat, Emery orders her pancake stack and a side of home fries.

Before the waitress can ask for mine, Emery says, "He'll have the seafood omelet. Heavy on the seafood." She wears a smug smile as she reaches across the table, grabbing my open menu and passing them both back to the waitress, who walks away with a smile.

"You think you're slick." I lean back in my seat.

"Slick? I'm sorry, I didn't know I was having breakfast with one of my parent's friends."

I roll my eyes. "Really, Emery. I'm disappointed. That was one of your weaker comebacks."

"It's not my fault you're intimidated by a woman ordering for you." She shrugs.

"I'm so intimidated that when we leave I'll have to go chop some wood and drink a case of beer just to feel like a man again." I shake my head. "Order for me all you want, Firecracker. I liked it."

"Don't need to renew your man card?" She cocks her head slightly to the side.

"Don't have to." I lean across the table again. "I already did it when you called me a pug. My ego took a hit."

She snorts into her coffee, which makes me chuckle. The sound still feels strange to my ears, but less and less every time I laugh.

Emery teases me some more with her sarcastic humor while we wait for our food. Instead of going back to our conversation before the waitress came over, we talk about safer, generic topics. Like exchanging middle names and favorite colors and TV shows.

Mine: Michael, green, and documentaries on nature, especially ones focused on the ocean.

Hers: Marie, blue, and depending on her mood it's either something full of angst or a comedy.

When our food finally arrives, I cut into my omelet, forking a mouthful of delicious goodness into my mouth. Moaning as I do. Emery shoots me a look of disgust while cutting into her pancakes.

"If you want to try it all you have to do is say, 'Bash is right and I should let him pick all my meals from now on.'"

"Dream on, pretty boy." She takes a bite of pancakes and hums in delight.

I'm about to take another bite of my food when I feel my phone vibrate in my back pocket. For the third time since entering the diner.

I don't even flinch.

I'm over it.

They aren't going to ruin this for me.

The vibration of my phone wakes me up. My hand hits my nightstand, smacking the wood and searching for the device. I roll onto my back, taking my phone with me.

**What are you doing tonight?**

I blink the sleep out of my eyes as I groan, shaking my head at the text. I just saw her—glancing at the time—six hours ago.

Fuck.

Napping isn't something I do regularly, but when I do, I don't nap. I *fucking* nap. Not sleeping the best has really been doing a number on me. I've been asleep since I walked in my door and stripped off my clothes.

I don't know. I just woke up, woman.

It's been a solid week of us surfing—I haven't missed one day. The look on Emery's face when she sees me every morning tells me she's happy about that too.

She is the definition of clockwork. Showing up every morning at the same time, surfboard and wetsuit ready to go.

The first couple of times I saw her wearing a wetsuit, I was taken aback. The Atlantic Ocean is nowhere near as cold as the Pacific and Florida isn't exactly known for their cold winters, but to each their own.

Well, chug an energy drink. I need your full attention.

Intrigue and concern flood me at the same time. What if something happened? What if she needs my help? What if she doesn't want to hang out anymore? Just waking up makes me paranoid, evidently.

Using my elbow, I push myself up against the headboard.

She has my full attention now.

What's up?

The little bubble with the three dots pops up and I clench my jaw, not allowing my brain to jump to any ideas. I'm trying really fucking hard to be rational and wait for her response, but with Emery, she can say anything right now and that makes me nervous.

Tuesday nights are taco and trivia night down by the water at this bar. My friends and I always do it when we're in town. Want to join?

I feel like a fucking moron for overreacting. My entire body deflates. Jesus, what is up with me?

Emery is what's up.

I can't stop thinking about her and it's driving me insane not knowing if she can't stop thinking about me.

**Are you saying I'm your friend, Emery Marie Lawson?**

Friends who made out one time. Friends who want to make out again. At least this friend does.

Badly.

I want to explore her body, to see if her skin tastes as sweet as her mouth did.

Last week at the event when I saw her with that guy, it made me want to rip his arms off her and throw him across the room. In total caveman fury.

I haven't so much as hugged her since that night. I'm a patient man in the water, waiting for the right wave, but I can only see Emery for so long without wanting to touch her. If she wants me.

**If that's what the kids are calling it these days ;)**

I smile, typing out my response to her, telling her to tell me the name of the place and a time. As it sends, I make a decision.

Whether we win this trivia shit or not, my night is ending the same.

With Emery's lips on mine.

# CHAPTER THIRTEEN

## *Emery*

TRIVIA NIGHT HAS BEEN A TRADITION SINCE LAST YEAR. It's hosted by a bar on the beach every Tuesday night. Trivia Taco Tuesday is my favorite day of the entire week. Mostly because I can get my favorite tacos for half the price, and who doesn't love tacos?

Brit and I already have a table by the window, looking out toward the ocean while we wait for the rest of our party. A plate of half-eaten fries sits between us.

Usually, she and I get to the bar a half hour early to have a little best friend bonding time.

I spin the straw around my cup, stirring my soda, as I watch Brit pick nervously at the napkin-wrapped silverware. Her camera sits to her side.

Pushing my drink away, I wave my hand in her face. "If you don't stop that, there's going to be hamster bedding on the table."

Brit blinks before looking down at her shredded mess. "Oops."

"Yeah, oops." I smirk. "Want to tell me what's going on with you?"

"I invited Dez."

"Ah." A sound, not even a word, is all I can think to say for a moment.

As far as I know, they hooked up at the party and then went to the movies. She never told me if anything happened after.

Her phone vibrates on the table and she grabs it, clutching it in her hand. "We've hooked up a few times since the party and he wanted to hang out tonight so I invited him."

"You've hooked up more than at the party?" I repeat her words as they swim around my head. When she nods, I make a noise, earning me a few looks from other patrons. Their looks go ignored as I lean across the table. "How come you didn't tell me?" My body is so far over the table that my butt isn't in my chair anymore. Using my foot, I try to hook around the leg of the chair and end up losing my balance, falling on my ass. "This is what happens when you keep things from your best friend," I grumble. "They get hurt."

"You're crazy," she tells me, laughing and flicking a fry my way once I'm back in my chair. "But he texted me two days after the movies to come over and I did and, well, things happened…"

I blink, giving her a bland look as my excitement instantly melts from my face. "Seriously? *That's* all you're going to tell me? I feel cheated."

"Yeah?" Brit leans back in her chair, arms crossed. "Now you know how I feel about finding out you've been hanging out with Sebastian."

"There's a big difference between platonically hanging out with a hot guy and getting serviced by his dick."

Brit spews out the soda she's drinking, a mist of liquid spraying in front of her, layering the table and my shirt in a mixture of cola and saliva. She doubles over, clutching her stomach as she howls with laughter.

After the shock of getting an unwanted shower, I join in and we're both laughing until our stomachs tighten and tears paint our faces.

"I can't believe you just said that." She pauses. "No, wait. It's you that I'm talking to. Of course you would say something like that."

I grin, throwing a soggy, gross fry at her. "Now I'm covered in your spit and drink. Fuck you, Brit." I stand up but give her a sharp look. "When I get back, I need details. All the details."

"Where are you going?" she asks before I can walk away.

"To change." My trunk is always full of clothes. Somewhere along the way, my car turned into a portable closet. Which is really handy for scenarios involving your best friend spitting on you.

Popping the trunk, I shuffle through the mound of clothes, looking for a shirt.

Maybe it's more like a moving closet floor. Articles of clothing are unfolded and thrown about.

Finding a shirt, I back away, slamming the hatchback closed, and am walking back to the bar when I hear my name being called.

I spy a familiar looking green truck and feel myself smiling at the figure approaching. His hair is shaggy and damp, looking relaxed in khaki cargo shorts and a dark green shirt. A pair of sunglasses hang around his neck. He looks good.

He looks really good.

But Bash always looks good.

For a moment, he distracts me enough to forget my shirt is sticking to my chest and that the white fabric is stained and sheer.

Bash draws close enough to hear me squeak in alarm.

"Stop!" And he does. Freezes mid-step, raising an eyebrow. "Sorry, but my shirt is wet and you can totally see through it."

The grin that stretches across his face can only be described as shit-eating. The fucker. He steps closer, engulfing me in his scent of natural man, detergent, and shower gel. "More reason to come closer."

"Bash," I warn, holding my dry shirt between us. He might see my scars.

"Emery." He steps into my personal bubble. I want to retreat but my legs have stopped working. He dips his head down, angling our faces close together. "Hi."

"Hi," I whisper. "You came."

"Did you think I wouldn't?"

Honestly, a part of me didn't think he would. The small, pessimistic side of my brain wouldn't let me.

I've been bailed on by guys before. A lot, actually.

So, my wariness in guys wanting to hang out with me is just a natural reaction. And yeah, Bash has hung out with me before. Every morning, in fact, but this feels different. This *is* different.

Like our friendship is developing and evolving into something more.

I squeak out an, "I don't know." Then quickly add, "I'mgladyoudidthough!" My words come out so fast, they blur together.

Bash levels a look my way, sees my internal panic, and

turns me around so I'm facing the bar. He's giving me my means to escape.

Before I can walk away, he leans in close. Warm breath tickles the spot behind my ear. "I'll see you inside."

Bash has Brit laughing at something as I walk toward them wearing the clean shirt. The dirty one is tucked into my bag.

Sliding back into my seat, the seat right beside Bash, he turns his body toward mine. "Where have you been hiding her?"

I groan, not even wanting to know what these two were talking about. "I haven't. Dez's dick has been entertaining her."

"Emery!" Brit says, her cheeks going red, but she's laughing. "My friend has no filter. What she means to say is that I've been busy."

I laugh, biting my cheek to refrain from adding on. *See! I do have a filter! I just choose to ignore it.*

The waitress comes over, asking Bash for his order. After ordering a beer, she lingers, flirting with him across my head.

A strange feeling rises in my stomach. One I try to ignore until her blatant flirting becomes too much. Glaring up at her, I snap, "I'll have a rum runner."

"Aren't you a little young, hon?" Her eyes don't leave Bash's as she talks to me. Almost as if she is trying to get him to join her in her attempts to make me feel inferior.

Too bad for her, I'm not easily scared.

Smiling with more venom than honey, I hand her my fake I.D.

The I.D. is as legit as it gets. Florida license, my birthday just three years before, same address as my house, and a picture of me. The only difference is the back. Which the waitress doesn't even look at before she passes it back with a huff.

I take it with a swell of triumph.

With one last look of longing at Bash, who isn't even trying to fight a smile, the waitress walks away, her steps are a little too forceful as she goes.

She's barely out of earshot before Brit starts cackling. "I really hope you're not going to drink that."

"She's probably going to spit in it or something," I say as I look over my shoulder towards the bar. "I did really want a drink though."

Chuckling, Bash throws his arm around the back of my seat. I shift, feeling the heat of his arm. "She's going to hate our table now."

"No, she's going to hate me now." When I look up at him, his brown eyes crinkle at the corners. "She's still going to love you."

"She doesn't love me."

"Don't be dense." I poke his chest. "Girls here keep glancing at you with heart eyes. It's like some love at first sight cliché."

He lowers his head, coming closer to my ear. I shiver as his breath hits my neck, as his words roll across his tongue. "I think the word you're looking for is lust. They want to fuck me, Em."

I try to pull away from him as something uncomfortable settles into my stomach. But Bash doesn't let me. His arm tightens around my chair as he pulls it to him. He won't let me escape. "But I don't want to fuck *them*. I wouldn't be here if I did."

I stare at the condensation ring my soda has left on the table, eyes dazed, and at a loss for words. Nothing runs through my brain except *uuuhhh* and *mmmhmmm*. Really, I don't know what to say to that. There is nothing coming to me.

Not even a sarcastic, deflecting comment.

I have nothing.

For the second time tonight, I am speechless. This never happens.

Brit clears her throat, looking up from her phone. "If you two are done, I'd like to get back to not feeling like a third wheel."

"You're not a third wheel. We're a tricycle," I tease.

"No," Brit disagrees, shaking her head. "The three of us aren't a tricycle. No offense." She looks at Bash and he shrugs, waving her off. "You, me, and Nori are the tricycle."

My phone vibrates on the table. Checking the screen, I laugh. "Say her name, and she hears."

Nori's texting to say that she's on her way, but doesn't know if she's going to stay until ten, when trivia ends. She just got back from a diving competition earlier today and she's going back to the pool tomorrow at six in the morning.

*No rest for the determined* is what she always says when someone tells her to take a day off.

Nori has plans, plans that involve the Olympics and gold medals. She's had her eyes set on that podium since she was a little girl.

The Lawson girls are pretty dedicated to their sports.

I'm in the middle of sending my reply when our waitress comes back, placing our drinks on the table. I give her a smile, much nicer than the last one. She doesn't return it. Nor does she look at Bash before walking away.

As I'm reaching for the glass, hands knock mine away.

"What the hell?" I say to Bash, who's ignoring my glare and reaching across me, picking up my glass instead of his beer.

I grow even more confused as he stands up, walking back toward the bar. I turn to Brit. "What the hell was that?"

"I don't know." Brit shrugs. "Maybe he's offended by pink."

I give her a look, seriously doubting that the color of my drink offends him.

She shrugs again. "I don't know, Emery. I've lived with men my entire life and I still don't understand how their minds work."

"The same can be said for women as well," a deep, gravelly voice says as he sits on the other side of Brit.

I grin as she shoots her brother a look. Oh, this is going to be good.

I don't say anything, just sitting back to enjoy the bickering that is about to happen.

"And who asked you to chime in? Not me."

"It's not like you're talking in a soundproof box between you and Emery. Therefore, I can join."

"Excuse me? Did you just say *therefore?* Since when do you know words that have more than six letters?"

He flips her off, not bothering to give her a response.

Brit can verbally spar with her brother for hours, but Geer usually stops it after a few volleys.

Bash comes back, placing my drink in front of me again.

I scrunch my eyebrows at it. "Was this a weird game of bar tag? Was I supposed to chase you to be able to drink it?"

"No." Bash bends down and kisses the top of my head before sitting down. "Saw the waitress spit in it so I got you a new one."

"That stuff actually happens? Spitting in drinks?" Brit asks.

My mind is too busy reeling from his lips touching my head to focus on their conversation. Warm lava settles in my stomach from the action. Where did that come from? When can it happen again? Do I trust myself not to run away before it does?

Pushing these thoughts into the avoidance cave for now, I pick up my drink, taking a sip that is spit-free. "Thank you," I mouth to him before my world goes black.

"Guess who?" a voice asks, in a faux, high-pitched volume.

Long, calloused fingers cover my eyes, blindfolding me in darkness. Reaching a hand up, I pull on their arm hair.

With a yelp, the hands drop away and I can see again. Cursing sounds from behind me and I don't even have to turn around to see who it is. Throwing my arm back, I elbow him in his side. "Fucking asshole, what is this? Second grade?"

Xavier snickers as he sits next to Geer. Geer, who is fisting his phone, checking the screen every fifteen seconds and mouthing something to himself.

"Nothing wrong with getting in touch with your youth," Xavier says. He dude-nods to Geer and Bash. Geer responds right away, but Bash takes a few extra seconds. I stiffen, worrying tension will ruin the night.

I don't relax until Bash nods, taking a pull of his beer after.

"Xavier!" Brit jumps out her chair to give him a hug. They've been friends almost as long as he and I have. "Where's your sister?" Brit asks when she pulls away.

"With her boy," he says with a mocking tone. He can't stand the guy Sienna is dating and makes his feelings clear about him with every chance he gets. "Where's Anora?"

"*Nori* is right here," the girl in question replies as she slides into the empty seat next to Bash. Which also happens to be across from Xavier. She juts her thumb at me. "I don't even let my cousin call me by my full name so stop calling me that. Please?"

Nori's as sweet as overly sugared sweet tea. She hates drama and conflict, would rather be submissive in friendships, not loud or talkative. Except when she's with us.

But even then, she tries to stop arguments before they happen. I asked her why she acts the way she does with her other friends and she reminds me that she's still in high school. A senior, but she doesn't want to spend it as a loner.

*Better to be alone in a group of people than by yourself.*

Her words still break my heart and I want to get up and wrap my arms around her. She's the closest thing I have to a sister and I will protect her at all costs.

We all watch as Xavier concedes to her request, at least for tonight, with a nod. He reaches across the table and taps her nose. "And what has you looking like you're two seconds away from passing out?"

Peering closer at my cousin, I notice she *does* look like she's about to flop down on the table. Her skin looks pale and she has deep, dark circles under her eyes.

As Xavier and I study her, she covers her mouth as she lets out a long yawn and rubs her eyes. "Insomnia and my diving schedule aren't getting along."

"You told me you were sleeping better."

Words I think, words I want to say, but can't because Xavier beats me to it. I scrunch my face as I look between my cousin and friend. Mouthing to Brit, *they talk?*

She shrugs, mouthing back, *I don't know.*

Oblivious to anything else going on, Nori looks at Xavier. Shyness clouds her face. "I was, but I've been traveling and when I travel I can't take my stand of Himalayan Salt Crystals."

I groan.

Xavier looks confused.

And Bash is staring at Nori like he's found a kindred spirit.

"What?" Nori gives me a look. "They work."

"What the hell are himmabablyn crystals?" Xavier asks, growing more confused. His features pinch and a frown lines his face.

Laughs chorus around the table, making Xavier even more lost. Nori giggles one more time before explaining, "They're these rocks that essentially act as an air purifier and help with a bunch of sleeping issues like insomnia, sleep apnea, and snoring. They're magical and I love them."

Xavier doesn't look convinced, but neither was I when Nori first told me that. Another thing about my cousin is that she really loves her crystals. "I'm calling bullshit."

"Nah, man," Bash says. "It's true. I have really bad insomnia but a year ago, I got them and it helps. I left them when I came down here and have really noticed the difference."

"No, Bash," I groan as I dramatically drop my head on his shoulder before pulling away just as quickly. "Not you too."

He chuckles as Nori explains, "She thinks I'm crazy over my crystals since I tell everyone about them. Now she probably thinks you're going to do the same."

"They're amazing, I get it," I deadpan. "I just don't need to constantly hear about it."

At some point during the crystal debate, I look over and notice Brit's chair is empty. When did she get up?

I'm a crappy best friend for only noticing when she comes back with two pads of paper and a pen in her hand. Uncapping the pen, she asks, "What's our team name?"

"Save a tree, eat a beaver." Xavier holds out his fist to bump with Bash. Who declines.

Smart man.

"No, funny boy. Nice try though." Nori pulls out her phone. "Hold on." Typing away on it, she looks up and asks, "How about The Trivia Troupe?"

"You can do better than that." Brit reaches for Nori's phone, but my cousin leans away.

"Les Quizerables?"

"No," Geer contributes before glaring at his phone.

Nori looks offended. "It's a fantastic musical. You should be honored to carry the trivia equivalent name."

"It's also a book I had to suffer though in high school." He growls. The normal tone of Geer. "So, no."

"So surly tonight," Nori tries to tease, but the corners of her mouth dip a little. I frown.

Something else is going on that she's not sharing.

Xavier catches my eye, looking as worried as I do. I'll stress about him later.

"Hey, Nor?" I call, leaning a little toward Bash in the process.

My call goes ignored by her, but not Bash. He turns more of his body to me, brushing the hair out of my face in the process. A small smile forms as I whisper, "Hey."

"Hey, Firecracker." He gives a small smile back.

"I'm really glad you came."

Surfing might be the secret I keep from half the people present at the table, but I don't want to keep Bash a secret. I want to share him with my friends, introduce him to the weirdos that are us, and maybe help him not feel so lonely. Because even if he doesn't say it, I know he feels it.

"You said that already." Gah, can his smile be any hotter?

"Some of these are seriously disturbing." Nori's voice pulls us out of our soundproof bubble, something I didn't realize happened until the steady hum of conversations around us fills the room again. "Like this one." She reads it aloud and we all cringe.

"Fucking sickos," Xavier spits.

"Ew." Brit looks sick.

"Just no." I am horrified.

"Just pick a name, damn it," Geer snaps, glaring at Nori. She shrinks back from Geer.

*What is going on?*

Geer can be an asshole, but he's never been so snappy and rude like this. Especially to Nori.

"Lay off, Jackson," Xavier warns. "She suggested one that you shot down. So don't fucking get snippy unless you want to pick the damn name."

Nori leans a little more into the table at his words, but her phone screen is black and sitting on the table.

Brit's glaring at her brother, shoving the pads of paper in front of him. "Congrats. You get the honor, asshole. Better pick a good one."

He takes the pen from her, mumbling something under his breath—curse words I'm sure—as he scribbles something on the trivia sheets. "There."

Taking the paper back, Brit smiles. "Periodic Table Dancers."

We all laugh.

"My mom would be so proud."

"So, Bash." Brit's suddenly serious. Her fingers make a bridge for her chin to rest on as her elbows are propped on the table. "What were your best subjects in school?"

I'm about to interrupt, telling her that he didn't go to school after he was on the track to go pro. But I stop myself.

1.) Because it's really creepy I know that—damn the

teenage gossip magazines I read when I was younger.

2.) Bash puts his hand on my knee as he leans back in his chair.

"History and science," he says.

"Hmm." Brit taps her ring clad pointer finger on her chin. "I think we can use you."

"Glad I've been deemed worthy."

"You're only worthy if you contribute," Nori explains before pointing with her index and middle finger to Xavier. "If you don't, then you're like this one. A pretty face but nothing else."

"I always knew you were attracted to me, Anora." Well, not calling her by her full name lasted about twenty minutes. We should have placed bets. He leans over the table. "But you know if you really want me, you just have to ask."

"Hey!" I get out of my seat, leaning over Bash before I realize what's happening. Snapping my fingers in Xavier's face, he blinks up at me. "Stop fucking being weird with my cousin. She's seventeen. In case you weren't aware of the law, that's considered a minor. And since you're twenty-two, that means it's illegal."

With his hands around my waist, Bash directs me back to my chair. I sit down stiffly.

Watching Xavier.

"Actually, Em. I'm well aware of the law here since I have dual citizenship and in the state of Florida it's legal to be with a minor up to a seven year age difference."

"How the hell do you know that?" Geer snaps, not looking up from his phone.

Okay, *seriously*. People think I'm dependent on my cell phone. I don't have anything on Geer. I haven't even touched mine since Nori sat down.

Despite Geer's rude behavior, I have to agree. We all look at him, waiting for an answer, but he shrugs. "I like to be informed on all the laws."

"That's creepy." Brit scrunches her face.

"He's lying," Nori tells us, rolling her eyes. "I told him."

"I don't even want to know why," I mumble and Bash chuckles.

# CHAPTER FOURTEEN

*Bash*

N OT A LOT OF SOUNDS COMPARE TO EMERY'S LAUGH. From the octave that vibrates her throat, the smile brightening her face, to the happiness that shines in her eyes.

My gaze is fixed on her as she laughs again at something Brit says.

It's weird being around so many people who have known each other for years, people who have inside jokes, their own lingo and looks. But I still feel comfortable. Like I fit in with them. Like I belong.

Back home I have two close friends. One of my buddies was my neighbor growing up and the other is a guy I met when I started surfing. But the three of us never hang out together.

Not like Emery and her friends. They're a unit. And for tonight, I feel like I'm a part of it.

At some point between the waitress coming to take our

order and Emery ordering three tacos with a side of chocolate lava cake for dinner, our chairs move closer together. I can feel the heat of her body mixing with mine and as she laughs, her body pressing into my side, I don't want the pressure to subside.

Moving faster than she can pull away, I wrap my arm around her shoulder. Keeping her near.

She looks up at me, eyes sparking, and gives me a knowing look.

I smirk back, pretending not to know what she's seeing. Or thinking.

These mornings of surfing with her have been some of the best practice sets I've done in almost a year. She doesn't know it but our mornings together are my favorite part of the day.

Even sometimes when there aren't any waves and it's just the two of us out on our boards, bullshitting around, it's the most fun I've had in years.

For so long my career has been the only thing that's mattered in my life. It's been all I've focused on. I had been living with tunnel vision, only seeing surfing.

But being around Emery and her friends has made me realize just how much I've been missing.

A hand squeezes my wrist and I meet Emery's eyes. "You okay?"

"Yeah, just—" I lean in closer. "Thanks for inviting me tonight. I'm having fun."

"You're hardly talking!" she points out.

I have been quiet tonight.

Quieter than I usually am, but I don't know if Emery realizes what a strong bond she and her friends have. There's a dynamic between them I'm unfamiliar with, but I've been having fun sitting back and trying to figure it out.

"But you're welcome. Any time, Bash." She gives my hand another squeeze. "Any time."

"Careful, Firecracker." I tighten my arm around her shoulder. "I might just take you up on that."

"I'm counting on it, Surfer Boy." She tries to wink. It looks more like a squirrel having trouble mid-sneeze and now it's my turn to burst out laughing.

Her cousin, Nori, and Xavier, who were talking (er, more like arguing) about something I haven't cared to follow, are now looking at us, seeing Emery's "wink."

Geer is on his phone, the same activity he's been doing all night, and his sister has adopted his method of distraction as well.

"Oh gosh," Nori giggles and Xavier gives her a look so soft I almost wait for him to produce a blanket and wrap her up in it. "Emery, you can't wink! Why do you keep trying?"

I'm laughing again, harder this time, as Emery gives her cousin a dark look. "If I don't practice, how can I get better?"

"There are some things you can't get better at."

"Oh please." Emery waves away the words. "You're an athlete, you should know that practice makes perfect."

"What? Now that you don't surf, you're a competitive winker?" Xavier teases, and it's then that I remember that no one here knows she surfs.

No one besides me, Brit, and Geer that is.

Next to me, Emery sits a little stiffer, smiling a bland smile. "Just because I stopped competing in one sport, doesn't mean I stopped being competitive. I had to find *something* to fill the void."

Suddenly, Brit throws her phone down on the table and looks over her shoulder. She gives someone a quick wave before turning back around.

"Hot date, Brit?" Xavier quirks an eyebrow.

"No, but hopefully a hot hookup afterwards." She waggles her brows and Xavier laughs, holding out his fist to bump when Dez appears at the head of the table.

"Sup?" He looks around the table, nodding at me, before sliding into the only seat left. Brit passes the lone menu on the table to him. He takes it with a nod and a smile.

"Desmond," Emery says.

"Emerson," Dez quips back.

I raise a brow at Emery. "Is that your real name?"

"No," she tells me, rolling her eyes. "He used to call me that because he said it sounded like a better retort for when I used his full name. It'd work even better if it wasn't a lie."

"Emery," Brit warns. Her tone pleading. Emery glances at her best friend and I catch Brit mouth the words *you promised.*

Dez gives me a look. My mind goes back to our conversation the other night, about me surfing with Emery, and she doesn't know I mentioned it to him.

I take out my phone and shoot him a text.

Don't mention anything about the surfing.

He reads the text, nodding. His fingers fly over the screen before he locks it, sliding the device into his pocket.

My phone goes off with his reply saying:

Wasn't planning on it. Not my business dude.

I don't bother replying.

Brit pulls Dez into a conversation about a movie they saw recently or something.

The waitress comes by, not saying a word to Emery or me, dropping off our food and takes Dez's order. The trivia announcer comes on with the first four categories.

"Trivia is about to begin, but I'd like to remind everyone

to turn their cellphones off. Cellphones are not to be used during the game. There are four rounds with four different categories. After each round, all tables will be put in a pitcher and whoever gets drawn will win a free pitcher of beer." Cheers ring out, including everyone at our table. "The first four categories are state capitols, politics, pop culture, and lakes."

Groans ring out throughout the bar.

"Lakes?" Nori asks. "Has that always been a category?"

"Yeah, Nor. It has been," Xavier says. "A category I'm hoping you're an endless pit of knowledge on, since we always get that one wrong."

"It's a wide variety," I tell the table as the announcer comes back on with the first question. The one for state capitols.

"What is the state capitol of Missouri?"

Everyone falls silent. Nori rubs her eyes. Geer locks his phone but doesn't contribute to the brainstorming. Xavier is thinking out loud, mumbling words. Brit is asking Dez, but he appears as confused as she is. Me? Missouri is a state I always forget about.

Emery is the only one who doesn't look lost. She has a look of concentration as she moves her head in a silent beat of her own, until she leans across the table so fast she blurs. "Jefferson City!"

Brit hesitates before she writes it down. "Are you sure?"

"Yes." She rolls her eyes. "But only bet six and let's save the eight for pop culture."

The way this trivia game is set up is that the game is divided into four rounds and each round teams can bet a two, four, six, or eight on their answer but they can only bet each number once.

Brit writes the answer down and passes the paper to Geer, who gets up to deliver it to the host. Brit writes the answer down again on another sheet of paper to record the results.

We have to wait a few more minutes for the answer to be revealed, but when Jefferson City is announced, cheers ring out—our table being one of the loudest.

"How'd you know that, Em?" Nori asks before she yawns. The poor girl doesn't even wait for her cousin to answer before she folds her arms over the table, resting her head on them.

For the first time since I've been hanging out with Emery, she looks sheepish. And she blushes. I've never seen that reaction from her, but I want to know what else makes that pink color brush her cheeks. "I might have listened to this one song about the state capitols for the past week to prepare."

"You studied during break?" Geer gives her a look.

"Yeah? So what?" she challenges. "Learning isn't something confined to a classroom."

"Is that why you dropped out of college?" Brit asks, but she's not looking at Emery. She's watching Dez at the bar, flirting with our waitress. The table quiets and Brit looks at Emery with her mouth slightly open, eyes wide.

Emery sits next to me, glaring at her best friend. "You are no longer privy to secrets."

Nori denied coffee earlier, but hearing her cousin dropped out of college is like the espresso shot that she needs. Her head pops up. "You dropped out?"

"Says the girl who already has a diving scholarship. You have your wants and I have mine." She's deflecting. She does *that* enough around me that I'm familiar with it.

"Are Brit and I the only two that stuck with higher

education?" Xavier asks.

Not many people know I went to college, but I am going to shock the hell out of him. "I have a Master's degree in International Business."

Eyes rotate from Emery to me, and I feel, more than see, her deflate in relief.

Dez comes back to our table soon after I tell them about my Master's. "What'd I miss?"

"Nothing as important as getting that girl's number," Emery snaps and even though she might be mad at Brit, she's still sticking up for her best friend.

He gives her a look, sitting down. "What'd I miss?" he repeats to Brit, who doesn't look at him when she answers.

"Emery's not going to college in the spring and Bash has a Master's degree in International Business."

"Dude, you do?" When I nod, he leans across the table for a knuckle touch. "Badass."

I shrug, shifting in my seat.

The only reaction I've gotten from people when I tell them I have a Master's is, why? Why do you have one when you already have a career? Isn't it splitting your focus? Do you really need it?

My parents didn't even know I was enrolled in online classes until I invited them to my graduation. Finishing high school early thanks to being homeschooled had me able to enroll in classes at an early age, which led to early admissions, finishing my BA at twenty and graduating in August with my Master's.

No one talks more about Emery leaving school and as the

second round of trivia begins, I drop my hand on her knee. She looks up at me, mouthing *thank you*.

I give her knee a squeeze.

"Why haven't we won our free beer yet?" Xavier asks, fists on the table.

I'm starting to like him a lot better than I did. I'm not a jealous person. I'm a competitive person, but last weekend I didn't like seeing him all over Emery. At all.

Maybe it's because we've been living in a bubble where it's just her and me. And in that bubble I forget we have friends here outside of the two of us. At least she does anyway.

I just have Dez.

So, yeah. Reality set in a little but I'm adjusting.

"Maybe when we stop listening to you, we just might," Emery says, smiling. "The one time you've decided to help and we're losing."

Xavier feigns hurt. His hands clutch over his heart, frowning. "I am a well of knowledge."

"Of Xavier knowledge. Not facts," Nori adds, her head resting on her folded arms on the table.

"*Et tu*, Anora?" He turns puppy dog eyes on her.

My feelings toward Xavier are also getting better because it's obvious he's not into Emery. But her cousin is another story.

At least, she's the one he's been heavily flirting with all night. I wonder if Emery has noticed.

Emery makes a sound at the back of her throat, eyes on the pair. I think I have my answer.

Dez and Brit are oblivious. For different reasons.

Dez was busy flirting with the waitress that wasted no time following him over and Brit is glaring at the back of his head. Looks like her night isn't going as planned.

We make it to the third round of trivia before Nori starts to really crash. "I gotta get home." She throws an arm over her closed eyes, mumbling noises.

Xavier stands up, walking around to help her out of her seat. "You can't drive, Nor."

She falls against his chest, fisting his shirt. "I can't drive. But I gotta get home. I'm so sleepy."

Emery stands up, my hand falling away. "You follow us in her car and bring me back here to get mine," she tells Xavier and he nods.

Disappointment.

I feel like a dick for feeling like I do since I don't want Nori driving home either. She can't. She looks like she's about to keel over. And if she falls asleep at the wheel, no telling what would happen to her.

One thing though—it wouldn't be good.

"I'll bring her to the car." Xavier gathers Nori's things, pulling a set of keys out of her bag. He says goodbye to the table before gathering Nori close and walking out.

Emery gives hugs to everyone but Dez, although he doesn't seem bothered by it. He's wearing a smile and waves bye before turning his attention to the waitress. Brit's shoulders slump. Emery goes in to hug me, but I tell her, "I'll walk you out."

She smiles, sliding her purse onto her shoulder.

It's a quick walk to the parking lot and too soon, we're there. "That's her car."

I spy her cousin's car before eyeing Emery. "You good to drive?"

"Yeah," she says. "I promise. I only had that one drink earlier and didn't even finish all of it. It's been a few hours now, I'm good."

"Okay." I pull her into a hug now, but I don't want to let her go. In my arms, it feels right. "I'll see you tomorrow?" The question's more rhetorical.

I see her every morning.

"Actually, I was wondering." She smiles at me, her arms still around my neck. "Can I come over once I get my car? I don't want tonight to be over yet."

I don't want tonight to be over yet, either.

# CHAPTER FIFTEEN

## *Emery*

**I** DON'T WANT TONIGHT TO BE OVER YET.
My words replay as I drive over to Nori's. I shake my head for the hundredth time over those words.

Tonight has to end because I have to be up early tomorrow. I never stay out late. Neither does Nori, my poor cousin.

What a trooper she is. It was only nine-thirty when we drove off, but when she says she doesn't sleep, she doesn't. Even with her rock crystals. Insomnia and her have a very intimate relationship. One that dates back to eighth grade. She's a semester away from being a high school graduate.

She's used to be a very light sleeper. Any shifting or movement would stir her awake.

Her mom says it's because when she was a baby she refused to fall asleep in fear that she'd miss out on something. It doesn't help that when a Lawson baby is born it's a family affair. People fly in from out of town, grandparents camp out in the guest bedroom. It's basically a party for weeks.

Especially when Nori was born. My aunt Hilary got pregnant by her boyfriend—a guy everyone thought was great, until he found out he was going to be a dad. Then he took off, leaving my aunt pregnant and alone.

I don't remember much, since I was a toddler, but when the family tells stories, they share so many from when they all came into town for Nori's birth. I still tell her to not let the popularity go to her head—I'm still the favorite grandchild.

She might've been a light sleeper when she was younger, but over the years that changed. Once she took up diving, exhaustion become a frequent visitor. Tonight has been no different.

A minute after Xavier put her in the car, she was out.

Sleeping and making these weird little noises.

She doesn't even wake up when I pull in her driveway, putting her car in park. I barely have the keys out when the passenger door opens and Zay is scooping my cousin up, carrying her to the front door.

He doesn't put her down once.

Not as I am unlocking the door.

Not when I am guiding us to her room.

He only puts her down when we get to her bed.

Nori doesn't stir as he gently places a blanket over her, passed out cold. Something I've never seen from my cousin.

Something else I've never seen is the look on Xavier's face. It's so foreign on him, I don't even know how to describe it.

Soft.

Sweet.

Caring.

I bite my tongue from saying anything as we leave her house and get in his car.

Neither of us say anything on the ride back to the bar.

Not until I'm about to get out of the car.

I give him a look. "What's going on with you and my cousin?"

He doesn't answer for a beat. The low music cooing from the radio fills the silence until he says, "I'm worried about her."

"Me too," I admit, turning in my seat toward him.

"She's lost weight." He sounds helpless. "When I was helping her out of the bar, I felt how thin she's gotten."

My stomach clenches. Weight has been a hard topic for my cousin. She eats, just not enough. As an athlete, as a diver, food is really important. But Nori is spending so much time chasing her dream, she forgets to stock up on calories.

"We have to help her," he continues.

Nori also pushes herself hard. Harder than she probably should. She's told me she does it to distract from her problems, and from what Zay says next, it's clear she's told him too.

"She needs a therapist. Someone who can help her with all the shit in her head. She won't talk about it with me." The last part he practically growls.

"Believe me. Unless she wants to address the problem, it won't do any good. Her mom doesn't have the money anyway." Nori wouldn't want to see anyone at the hospital where her mom works, either. I remember what it was like being forced to see a therapist after my accident. I didn't want help. I didn't want to talk.

And I didn't. Not for several sessions.

My therapist didn't force me to open up. To talk about anything. She didn't pressure or push. She waited.

Waited until I was ready.

"She's going to pass out from hunger one day while she's on the board and get seriously hurt."

"As much as I love your concern, why are you stressing yourself out over this? I didn't think you and Nori were that close." Please don't be that close. I can't have them be that close. I love Xavier. I really do. He's a great friend, but he travels everywhere, going on adventures—chasing waves and not taking names.

If he makes my cousin fall in love with him, he'll break her heart.

And then I'll have to break him.

"Fucking hell, Emery. Your cousin is slowly killing herself! You should be more concerned if I didn't care."

True, true, true.

I don't think she's killing herself. She's forgetting to eat and has an extremely fast metabolism. Tomorrow, I'll just go over there and hang out with her, taking her to lunch and dinner. Xavier doesn't need to worry. Nori will be fine.

I hope.

"I think Xavier has a thing for my cousin," I say in lieu of a greeting as Bash opens the door, stepping aside to let me in.

"Hello to you, too." He chuckles.

"Hi." I turn around, hands on my hips. "What do you think?"

"About Xavier and Nori?"

I nod.

"Aren't they a couple?" His joke is not appreciated.

I growl, spinning around to walk into his living room. Bash lives in such a dude's place. Minimal decorations, a three-seater couch, two recliners, and a TV. Aside from a coffee table, the only other place to eat is the island bar in his kitchen.

He needs a lot of help with decorating.

But not right now.

There are more important things happening.

Plus all the stores are closed.

"No! They aren't. As far as I knew, they only talked when we hung out. That's what she does with Geer. She says she doesn't even want to date. Says she doesn't have time. He's going to distract her."

"Is that what he's going to do?"

"And break her heart. And make her hate men. And—"

"And?"

"Take her virginity."

"Em," he says, but I don't want to hear how ridiculous I'm being. I don't need to be told. I'm well aware of it. Doesn't mean I'll stop my tangent. And it's not just Nori I'm worried about. I don't want Xavier to get hurt either. I love Xavier, he's one of my ride or dies, and Nori has just as much power to hurt him as he does her.

It's just Nori's like my little sister. I've been protective of her since she was little.

I nibble on my bottom lip. "And he's older than her. Why does he want to get with a high schooler? Can't he get girls his own age? Nori already deals with dipshits in high school. She doesn't need one in the form of a twenty-two-year-old."

I remember this one guy she told me about in her chemistry class last year. He'd tried calling her all the time while he was jerking off. It was gross. But she refused to give me a name.

Which was safer for the dipshit.

"Am I a dipshit?" he asks and I look at him.

"Whaa?"

"I'm a twenty-two-year-old guy who likes a girl younger than him. So, am I a dipshit?"

Pause. A moment to acknowledge that Bash just admitted he likes me.

At least, it better be me. Or else I will smack some sense upside his head.

Okay, moment over but not forgotten.

"No, but would you still like me if I was seventeen and in high school?"

"Depends." He moves closer to me, gripping my arm and pulling us toward the couch. I tuck my legs under me and he spreads his legs apart. "If you acted like a girl who's seventeen, then no. But if you were mature for your age, probably. Nori doesn't seem like a kid; she's three years younger than you, right?"

I hold up two fingers. She's two years younger than me.

"Well, no offense, Firecracker, but you act more immature than she does."

"How do you know? She was practically napping the entire night." I give him a look, then a smile. "I do act like a child. But what's wrong with not growing up when you can be young forever?"

"Never said there was. You just asked if I would date a seventeen-year-old and I'm telling you my answer."

I pout. "It would have been better if you just said no."

"What's the harm if he does like Nori?" Bash pulls me closer, my shoulder pressing into his side. Just like tonight at trivia. "You said it yourself, she doesn't date because she's too busy."

I concede with a nod. Too tired to talk about this anymore. Plus, there are other things that we can talk about, instead.

"So, you like me?"

The look he gives me sends a shiver down my spine.

# CHAPTER SIXTEEN

*Bash*

S HE THINKS SHE'S CUTE, ASKING ME IF I LIKE HER WITH
that smile on her face. If she's fishing for an answer, she
isn't going to get it.

No, I already said that I liked her. Now it's time to show
her.

Shifting around so my chest is facing her, I lean over.
Closing the distance between us. Bringing our mouths closer
and closer together.

Before my lips touch hers, I hear her sharp intake of
breath and I can't stop the smile that forms as I capture her
lips, demonstrating to her just how much I like her.

Moving my mouth slowly over hers, I feel her body fall
onto mine. Melting against my chest. Hooking an arm around
her waist, I haul her up onto my lap so her thighs are on either
side of mine.

Straddling me.

Hands move up her jean-clad thighs, I slide my fingers into her belt loops, keeping her close.

The tentative kiss I began quickly turns into a frenzy. Lips crash, tongues tangle, and bodies collide.

Her hands lace behind my neck and she rocks her lower body into mine. We both groan. She rocks again and I have to move my hands to her waist, holding her still.

She makes a strangled noise, pulling her mouth away from mine. She doesn't go far.

Her hot, swollen mouth moves to my scruffy jaw, down my throat, kissing my bobbing Adam's apple as I inhale a sharp breath. Her mouth moves further down, closer to my collarbone where she begins to suck on my skin. Hard.

My breathing is labored, but I'm able to find my voice enough to get out a breathy laugh and ask, "Trying to give me a hickey?"

"Maybe." Her voice is a caress on my skin.

Taking her chin between my thumb and forefinger, I tilt her face up. Her eyes are hazy and heated; lust boils within the depths of her green eyes. "If I get one, so do you."

My hands slide under her shirt and she stiffens, jerking off my lap so fast she trips and falls to the ground. I glare, confusion and concern conflicting with each other as I bend down to help her up. She scrambles away, holding her hands up. "Above the clothes action only." Her tan skin washes out several colors as her eyes plead with me. Her voice is desperate and shaky when she says, "Please."

It's the please that worries me the most. I'd never force myself on her, on any woman. Whatever man does isn't a man but a sick, twisted fuck who deserves to be castrated, among many more uncivilized punishments.

I force myself to soften my expression, pushing the

confusion aside and focusing on the concern for her.

Emery is brave, so brave she surfs before the sun breaks the horizon. She says what's on her mind, does what she wants, and doesn't care what others think.

She's her own person, so sure in her footing, but right now, she looks small.

Like a child afraid to fall asleep because of a monster hiding in the closet.

Scooting closer to the edge of the couch, I lean closer to Emery. She's shaking. A horrible realization washes over me.

What if something happened to her? What if someone put their hands, or other parts, on her—unwelcomed?

Rage, fire-burning rage unlike anything I've ever felt tries to rise to the surface. I barely have it contained but try to keep my voice calm when I tell her, "Okay, Em, okay." I fall to my knees in front of her, my tone soft. "You set the pace."

I remember the party, how she stopped my hands from going under her clothes. And this past weekend when she had her panic attack. A lump forms in my throat. "Whatever you want to do or don't do, that's what we'll do. I promise I won't rush you or make you feel like you have to do something you're not comfortable with. Just tell me what's too much or if I cross the line with you."

"Okay." She nods, voice small. She won't meet my eyes. Her gaze is focused on her hands that are splayed out on the carpet on either side of her.

Slowly, *so slowly,* so I don't spook her, I scoot closer. I wrap my hands around her ankles, connecting us. I need to have part of her tethered to me so she feels my touch, knowing I won't change or think of her in any other way, when I ask her, "Have you—have you been attacked, Emery?"

Forcing the words out feels like swallowing chunks of glass.

She freezes and my heart breaks.

Breaks into uncountable pieces for the girl in front of me, who's brighter than any light I've ever seen, but now, this conversation, has dimmed her shine. I want it back. I release her ankles. "I promise I'll never hurt you, Emery. I promise."

"I know, Bash." Her eyes grow wide and she sits up higher, pulling her legs to her chest. She reaches her hand out and touches my arm. "Bash," she repeats and I cover her hand with mine, giving it a squeeze. "I wasn't raped."

My chest collapses and a wave of crashing relief comes down on me.

"But I was attacked." *So much for that relief.* The fire is slowly building again, but I don't ask questions, seeing her struggle for words. Emery wants to talk about this. I see the need to in her eyes.

She has to get this out at her own pace. I won't force her. For her, I have all the patience, even if I want to trash every piece of furniture in this room and then go find the fucker who hurt her.

Both of her hands rub her face and she makes a sound between a sob and a laugh. "I don't know why it's so hard to tell you. It's not like it's a secret. If you just searched my name you would already know. But you don't look at me like I'll break or I can't handle something because the memories are too much." She's talking in circles, not making sense, but I sit beside her, squeezing her knee again. My thumb is moving across her skin in rhythmic strokes.

"Anyway," she goes on, "I got attacked by two sharks during a competition. It was pretty bad and my parents made me stop surfing. I was reckless when I was younger, still am. But my body has scars, a lot of scars, and I am really weird about people seeing them. I've accepted my body for what it is, but I just don't like showing them to other people. The stares, the whispers, the questions are just something I don't feel like dealing with day-to-day."

"And if you don't like people seeing them, you don't like people touching them," I fill in.

Her reaction makes more sense now and I like the reasoning behind it a lot more than my initial thoughts. But I wished to God she'd never had to go through a shark attack.

As uncommon as they are, they still happen. Even I forget how dangerous sharks can be since I see so many when I surf.

Fuck, I've seen them in the actual waves I'm riding before and have even fallen on one or two in my time.

"How old were you when it happened?"

"Sixteen, but I didn't get back into the water until I was seventeen."

"Two years? You've been surfing alone for two years?"

Again, she nods. "After a few months of being lonely, I fell into a routine and hardly noticed. Until you came along and missed that day. That was when I realized just how lonely I had been. It's been nice having you around."

Lonely. In a sport full of other people, we've both been so alone.

Isolated.

"The first time I surfed in months was the day you crashed into me."

She blinks. "The morning after the party?"

I nod. "I came here because I needed a break from everything. You missed surfing so much you came back, but I was starting to hate it so that's why I left."

"Going pro isn't all that fun, is it?" She scoots over, pressing her body to me. I wrap my arm around her shoulders. "Dad always said that surfing was the only part of the job he liked."

"The endorsement money isn't bad either," I tease, then soberly add, "For about two and a half years I've hated surfing. I was bored with my dream job. It's what I lived for. But somewhere along the way I stopped living and just existed. I went through the motions because I had to and it's been hard to get back ever since."

"But you always look like you're having fun when we're out there."

"It's hard not to when you're there."

She inhales, looking into my eyes. I refuse to look away.

We stay like that until a phone, *my phone*, rings and breaks the silence around us.

But even then, I hold her eyes as I reach for my phone and answer.

That's the move that proves I made a mistake. For the second time, to be exact. If I checked the caller I.D., I would have seen who was calling and could have avoided answering. I made the same mistake at Dez's. I paid for it then and I'm paying for it now.

Whatever good mood I was in is now gone with my mother's voice in my ear.

I give Emery's knee one last squeeze as I stand up. I mouth *I'll be right back* and am moving out of the living room and onto the porch. Fast.

"Sebastian, you need to come home." Her icy voice contrasts the humidity of the Florida weather. "Now."

Groaning, I roll over and roughly turn off the alarm on my phone.

My body aches.

My neck pinches.

And my bed feels uncomfortable as hell. Like a plank of wood.

"Uuung." With eyes shut, I roll onto my side despite the stiffness of my body, an arm stretched out looking for my pillow. Instead of a pillow, I'm met with a softness of another kind.

The softness of a woman.

Opening an eye, I see the soft waves of Emery's brownish-blonde hair as they tumble down the back of my T-shirt. The one I gave her last night when she got too cold in hers. The long sleeves were rolled up to the crook of the elbow.

Her arms are folded and tucked under her head, breathing steady. My hand touches her side, making her shiver, skin freckling with goose bumps.

With a curse, I sit up, going for the blankets that must have gotten kicked to the foot of the bed sometime during the night.

Except.

Except, we're not in my room. The reason for my body aching this morning becomes a lot clearer.

As I slowly start to wake up, the surroundings come into focus.

We're in my living room, on the floor, where the fan is on full fucking blast.

With another curse, I get to my feet. Making an executive decision, one that will no doubt piss off Em, I gather her in my arms and walk us into my bedroom.

Emery will kick my ass for not going surfing, but right now I don't give a single damn.

She can take one day off—especially after last night and opening up with what happened to her.

Once the phone call with my mom was done, I came back in and Emery must've seen the mood written on my face because she asked if I wanted to watch a movie. I think we both needed time in our thoughts after that, so I put on the first movie I saw on TV and Emery cuddled into my side. I think we watched two movies, completely forgetting about the morning.

My body was too keyed up to relax. I wanted to touch her, to feel her skin against mine, but she set the pace.

After seeing how she reacted, I relinquished whatever power I had and gave it to her. She controlled everything from there. I wouldn't push her for anything she wasn't willing to give.

After a while, my body deflated and I was lulled to sleep by her steady breathing.

Now, I tuck Emery into my bed, making sure she won't get cold. I walk into the bathroom to piss before climbing in beside her.

I doubt I'll be able to sleep for long, if at all. But somehow I'm able to fall asleep for maybe forty-five minutes before something wakes me up.

Correction, *someone* wakes me up.

Opening my eyes, I see a sight that makes my morning wood very happy.

Emery is straddling my waist, sitting right below the waistband of my shorts. Her face is flushed, with slightly pink cheeks, either from sleep or from anger. Green eyes that shine like grass after a rainstorm narrow down at me.

Holy fuck she looks hot.

"You better not fucking pinch me." My voice is harsh from sleep. "This is the kind of dream I like."

She glares harder and my dick twitches. Sometimes he's a kinky bastard.

"I'm not going to pinch you. I'm going to strangle you."

"Kinky." I raise an eyebrow and grin. "To what do I owe the pleasure?"

I'm not into choking or being choked; it does nothing to get me off, and I know she's not talking about it in a sexual way, but it's way too good to pass up. Especially since Emery's too cute when she's mad.

And hot as fuck as she straddles my body, right above my dick.

Fuck, Cleaton, think of something else besides that.

Emery's fist collides with my chest. It barely even tickles. "What the hell, Cleaton?"

I know I probably shouldn't, but I really like her saying my last name in her pissed off voice. My amusement must show on my face because Emery slams her palms on my chest as she leans closer to my face. I try to fight a grin. "Why did I wake up in your bed? And more importantly, why aren't we surfing right now?"

"We're in my bed because we fell asleep on the floor last night and I like to think this mattress is better than hardwood floors, but that's just me. As to why we aren't surfing, I was sore and tired from being on said floor and I liked seeing you in my shirt." I lean up on elbows, bringing our mouths closer together. "So I made the executive decision to sleep in today."

It wouldn't take much to close the distance. All I'd need to do is sit up a little bit further.

Jesus, I'm horny this morning.

Emery's hand is over my mouth before I'm able to put my plan into motion. It's probably written all over my face. "Don't even think about it, Bash." At least I'm back on a first name basis with her. "Not only am I pissed right now but we also have morning breath."

The way she says morning breath makes me believe she's really repulsed by the idea of kissing with MB.

I don't care either way. I want her lips on mine.

With her hand still pressed to my mouth, I dart my tongue out. Licking her palm. Running it from the base all the way up to the joint in her middle finger, I watch her. My gaze never wavers from hers as she shivers above me and some of the anger turns to a different kind of heat.

"Stop being cute." She retracts her palm, pushing away and off of me.

I roll over to face her, my grin still in place. "Am I being like a pug?"

She groans, crossing her legs, and looking down at me. "Will you let that go?"

"Nope." I make the "p" pop as I reach over, grabbing her waist. Rolling us over so she's on her back and I'm above her, I brush some hair away from her face.

"I'm still mad at you."

"I can handle that," I tell her.

"I have a rule to never miss a day when I'm in town. You don't know how hard it was to be landlocked at college and have the closest beach like an hour away."

"That sounds like torture for you." For me too. The beach has always been in my backyard and I need to smell salt in the air. "Can I ask you something about that?"

"Sure." She runs her fingers through my hair.

"How come your parents don't want you to surf?

"After my accident when I got released from the hospital, I snuck out and went to the beach with my board. You know that whole cliché saying about falling off a horse and getting back on? Well I did that. And had a panic attack because I saw a shadow that looked like a shark. It was a turtle. I fell off my board, got caught in a rip current, and panicked even more. It was a mess and I scared my parents shitless."

Jesus H. Christ.

"And technically I'm an adult and can do what I want but I live with them, you know? I don't want to disappoint them, so I don't tell anyone. Because word of mouth is a real thing in this town." I rub my hands up and down the back of her calves. The fabric of my gray sweatpants she put on last night move with me. "Plus I'm scared. I'm scared if I stop for a day, I won't go back out there. I want to be a pro surfer, for fuck's sake, but I can't even tell my parents I've been surfing again. And have been doing it for years."

"Emery, following your dreams takes a lot of courage. It's the uncertainty that scares you but that's where the adventure begins. I wish I could tell you that you can hide behind your alarm clock forever, but the second you go back on the circuit, people are going to be all over you because of your name. You have to be ready for not just your parents but for everything that comes along with this life."

Silence.

My words are greeted by silence.

Emery stares at me, eyes a little glazed over, and I wait.

And wait some more for her to say something. Anything.

I didn't mean to lecture her. I didn't mean to actually say any of that yet. She deserves every chance to go pro, but she can't do it in secret.

It's not just the fear of disappointing her parents, but it's also the fear of failure.

"Can we go get pancakes?" Emery asks, her voice not quite off but not normal either. She's deflecting and for right now, I'll concede.

So, we get pancakes.

# CHAPTER SEVENTEEN

## *Emery*

"**H**EY MOM," I ANSWER MY PHONE, TURNING DOWN the radio. "What's up?"

"Hi, baby." I haven't seen my mom all day—she's been running around with my grandma. "I'm stopping by the mall on my way home, is there anything you wanted me to pick up?"

It's four days before Christmas and the malls are hell on Earth. Brit's at the mall, working, and has already texted me no less than a dozen times telling me the horrors of the day.

It's ten past one.

"Nah, I went down to Jensen and picked up a few things." Drove over an hour to another mall because the mall in my town is dying, with barely any shops while the one down South has ten times as many. The drive is a bitch, but my trunk is full of gifts to be wrapped and stuck under the tree. "Now I'm going to stop at Beans and Cream before I head home."

"Is Brit coming over tonight?" Usually Brit and I do a weekly movie night on Sunday, but because of the holiday rush we had to push it to today, since she isn't closing tonight.

"Yep." I turn my blinker on, a driving skill people here are seriously lacking, and pull into the turn lane, waiting for the green arrow. "She's coming around six."

"That's good. You two haven't been seeing a lot of each other lately." Mom's not saying it to make me feel bad, but that doesn't stop the guilt from happening anyway. It's true I haven't seen Brit as much as I'm used to. I've been a shitty best friend.

Usually during winter break, Brit and I are attached at the hip.

But this break, I've hardly seen her.

I have, however, seen a lot of Bash. Not just in the mornings for our early surf sesh, one neither of us have missed since the morning I woke up in his bed, but we sometimes meet for lunch too, or he cooks us food at his place. Homeboy is a really good cook. And yes, most of the time there is kissing and groping going on. Okay, all the time that happens now.

He's been different since I stayed at his place.

When we surf, he's pushing me. Challenging me. Making me go more at his level than for fun. Which, until he started pushing, I realized is what I had been doing for the past few years. I had been dedicated, yes, but I haven't accessed the potential inside.

Now, because of his lessons, I've been more tired. More sore. But happier.

And not just from the surfing.

I still see Brit at Trivia Night, with the gang, and we meet up for dinner or lunch at the mall once a week depending on her shift. We just haven't gotten to hang out for a longer period of time. We both blame the holiday season. Whatever free time she has gets sucked into more hours for work. Sometimes her boss even works her past her weekly max.

And I know for a fact she's seen Dez a lot this break.

I'm not the only one hanging out with a man-friend.

"Yeah, but we have movie night tonight and Trivia Night tomorrow," I remind her as I pull into the first parking spot I see. As I hang up, I can't help but wonder what exactly Dez's plan is with my best friend. All I know is if she gets hurt because of him, he's going to get more than a sarcastic comment. He's going to get my claws.

"Sup, stranger?" Brit says as she leans in my doorway, wearing an ugly Christmas sweater that features a sad and deformed reindeer. She's holding a bag of tacos. "I brought the goods."

"You can stay then," I smile, shifting the laptop off my lap and onto my bed. "I got the movies."

I point to the stack of movies on my desk. Yes, I still buy movies. If I love it enough, I buy it to add it to my physical collection. I even still have a box full of my childhood movies on VHS and a VHS player that still works.

I'm a child of the 90s. What can I say.

"Superheroes then space battles?" Brit asks, holding up two of the movie cases.

"Sounds good." I make grabby hands for the taco goods, which she hands over on her way to put the disc in the DVD player. "I see you didn't kill anyone today."

"Ha-ha," she deadpans before flopping on the mattress next to me. "I just don't see how people can be so dense. I mean, you're really going to leave your leaking drink on a pair of white jeans or try to return something that has clearly been worn and washed multiple times?"

"Both of those happened today?"

"Just a fraction of what went down. My manger went back in the stock room like three times within five minutes just because she had to scream. She said it was very therapeutic."

She presses play and sprawls out next to me. I pass her the bag of food.

We munch on tacos while my screen gets double-teamed by hunky heroes. There's not a more attractive sight.

Unless, of course, they're shirtless. On the beach.

Then I'd really be a goner.

"Imagine if men actually looked like that," Brit says, some lettuce flying on my duvet from her taco.

"Brit, you are aware that they are real people, correct?"

"Correct." She takes a bite of the taco. "But you know what I mean. Men in real life. Like where are the everyday hot men? The ones you meet at the grocery store and flirt with only to find out you two are actually neighbors."

She's describing a romance novel. Probably one she just read.

I'll have to get the title from her later.

"What's up?" I lift an eyebrow.

"Nothing." She shrugs. "Everything's fine. Why wouldn't it be?"

"Yeah, okay. What'd Dez do?"

She glares. "What makes you think he did anything?"

I stare at her, letting her words process for the both of us before answering. "You just got really defensive when I brought up his name. Proof. Now spill."

She doesn't. Instead she counters with, "Tell me about Bash."

"Why? You already know everything that's happened." I call or text her when we are up to bat and get on a base. Although, I've never had a clear idea on what base means what.

Except a home run.

Pretty sure that means sex.

Which hasn't happened yet.

"I doubt I know everything." She rolls her eyes.

"Pretty sure you do." I laugh. "Unless you know something I don't. But, anyway, spill. Tell me about Dez and what he did now."

"Nothing." She sighs. "And that's the point. He hasn't done anything. We've barely texted or seen each other since the last trivia night he showed up for, where he spent the entire night flirting with that waitress and ignoring me. So why am I so upset over this?"

"Because you like him, dork," I tell her. "And he treats you like a secret he keeps from the world. Which is fucked up."

She cringes. "I really don't want to. I want to go back in time and shake high school me for ever finding him attractive. I want to tell younger me that his cock might be impressive but his attitude isn't."

"Here, here." I raise my half-eaten taco in support.

But Brit isn't done. She's on a roll now.

"And why did I even think this time would be different? Because he noticed me at a party? Really? Am I wanting a boyfriend so bad that I'll put up with all this less than stellar crap for what? An hour or two of play every two weeks?"

She takes a deep breath, filling her lungs with energy to continue her rant. "It's like I'm wanting to live out a high school dream of mine, like I'm making high school me proud. I shouldn't care if I make her proud. I should be making the me today proud."

"And are you proud?" I ask, but I already know the answer.

She shakes her head. "I shouldn't have to put all this work into whatever the hell this actually is. Head games aren't my thing. Either you tell me you like me or tell me you don't. I shouldn't be freaking out that I've done something wrong for him to ignore me."

"You haven't done anything wrong," I reassure her. Dez has always been a player. I think he had one serious girlfriend in high school. And that relationship lasted *maybe* three weeks.

If he comes to the next trivia night and flirts with that damn waitress again, I'm fork stabbing him. It'll be more painful than those dull knives. Brit doesn't deserve the shit that is running through her head over this.

"Don't let him get to you. You're only here for a few more weeks before you go back to Orlando for school. Winter break is a time to de-stress from finals and just have fun before the spring semester starts."

She nods, a small smile on her lips. "I like having fun. Sometimes I think I want to have a relationship. But then I start talking to a guy, like Dez, and just assume that it'll lead to dating. When in actuality it doesn't."

"What's this relationship you speak of?"

"Oh, I forgot. I'm talking to the girl that runs from commitment."

"I don't run. I avoid," I clarify.

I "dated" a few guys back in high school but never have had a serious boyfriend. And this time, I don't even know what I'm doing with Bash. Am I dating him? I have no idea, but I'm trying to take it day by day with him. Not overthinking and keeping the freak outs to a minimum. So far, it's been working. "So what are you going to do?"

"Would you judge me if I said I wanted to try and keep having fun with Dez?" Brit tilts her head down, looking at her hands in her lap.

"Of course not. But just because you want to have fun with him doesn't mean you shouldn't make him work for it."

"Oh, you know I will." She finally smiles. "And I'm going to tell him things have to be exclusive if he wants the all access pass to my fun town. No other hook ups while we're doing our thing."

"And if he doesn't go for it?" I will always support my best friend. With anything. It's me and her against the world.

"Then he doesn't get a pass to my fun town." She shrugs, still smiling, but her tone isn't light-hearted to match.

I pinch my brows trying to figure out what's off when my phone vibrates against my leg. Brit spares me another quick glance before she turns back to the movie as I read the message on my screen.

I bite my lip as my eyes move across the screen. My leg starts to bounce, shaking the mattress and Brit.

"What?" She puts a hand on my leg, halting the movements.

I ignore the slight annoyance in her tone and debate asking. Wondering if she'd be down. Wondering if I can do it.

"How do you feel about cutting movie night short, since we've already finished all the food, and doing something different?"

"Well, we already are having it on a different day than our usual Sunday so I think we can cut it short. Depending on the offer. Is it better?"

"I think it is. But if you don't want to go then we don't have to."

"Does it involve water?" My best friend knows me so well.

I would never leave my bed at nine o'clock at night if it

didn't have to do with water or water activities. Or alcohol. "Yep."

I shove past the cotton balls pressing against my throat as I answer. My love of the water has never wavered, but talking about something and actually doing it are two different things. I have to pump myself up. I've gone paddleboarding a few times after my accident, but never at night.

Going out surfing in the morning as the sun tries to rise provides some light. The moon shares less.

I'm tired of letting fear run my life. I'm going to do this. Hopefully.

"Are you going to tell me what it is?"

"Paddleboarding with glow sticks." I try to keep my voice calm as a mix of apprehension and excitement builds, but hardly succeed. Brit whoops, jumping to her feet on the bed.

I laugh and join her. Her excitement is making mine grow, making it outweigh the fear. I won't miss out on memories because I'm nervous. I can't. I can't let the past win.

We've had this activity on our bucket lists since high school. But after my accident happened we kind of let it fall to the back burner.

Until now.

"I have one of your bathing suits in my closet," I tell her, jumping off my bed, grabbing my essentials. With my bikini in hand, I start changing as Brit dashes into the closet for her own. After I put it on, I shimmy into a long sleeve t-shirt and cropped leggings.

It might be December, but it's not even below seventy tonight.

Brit comes out wearing a similar outfit, but instead of leggings she wears shorts and a t-shirt, the strings of her bikini top peeking out of the shirt's collar.

I pack an extra wetsuit from my closet in a canvas bag, throwing my wallet in there as well.

"The paddleboards and the LED lights are still in Geer's garage, right?" I ask as we walk toward the front door and to my car.

She nods. "I already asked him to put the lights on our boards for us."

A while ago we bought these colorful lights for our paddleboards. You put them around the edges of the board and the colors light up the water under you. They looked too freaking cool to pass up.

Now I'm glad they're not going to waste.

After we drive to Geer's, and secure the paddleboards to the top of my hood, Brit finally asks where we're going and who invited us.

It's about time. I was beginning to wonder when she'd grow curious.

"Bash invited us." Which is why I felt so weird asking her if she wanted to do something else tonight. I didn't want it to seem I was bailing on her for my guy.

Is he my guy?

Do I want him to be my guy?

Gah, I feel the hives forming.

But Brit doesn't seem bothered by who invited us at all. She just smiles and nods. "Whose house are we going to?"

I show her the address he texted me that is programed into my GPS.

She reads the address and curses.

"What?"

"That's Dez's parents' house." She mumbles something about them moving two months ago.

*I forgot.* "Shit."

# CHAPTER EIGHTEEN

*Bash*

"I'M BORED," DEZ SIGHS AS HE PLOPS DOWN ON THE chair next to me. The TV is on, playing a rerun of some game show. Not sure how it got on, but neither of us have gotten up to change it.

It's strangely entertaining.

I tip back my beer. "Well, if you're asking for me to entertain you, I'm not that kind of guy. You gotta buy me dinner first, at least."

"Fuck you, Cleaton," he growls. "I'm not house sitting for my parents all weekend and not doing anything fun."

Dez's parents went out of town for a few days but will be back tomorrow night. Apparently Dez has an aunt who spends Christmas with them every year but hates driving, flying, and doesn't really like to leave her house.

His parents drove up to Charleston, South Carolina on Friday to get her.

And since it's the holiday season, they didn't want to leave their house empty. In fear of break-ins or something. So, Dez has been here since and apparently is going a little stir crazy.

Dez quiets for a while before clapping his hands together. "Let's have a party."

I chuckle, putting the beer on the coffee table. "Did you not trash this place enough in high school?"

This house is a high school kid's dream for a party. Open floor plan, insane square footage. Given the person Dez is, and the few parties I'd been to at his actual place, I have no doubt that he went balls to the wall in high school.

"Ha, I wish! My parents just moved here." Dez pushes up off the couch, pacing around the living room. "We can't have a party, though. Not enough booze. We can do something. Have to do something or I'm going through the wall. Can't go to a bar, they're too packed with everyone in town. What to do, what to do?"

He wanders to the giant windows looking out toward the river and snaps his fingers. "I got it! Paddleboards."

"Paddleboards?"

"Yeah, we'll invite some people over and get them to come party on the river with us. Get some glow sticks and shit. Who should we invite?"

I stare at him. "I only know a few people. All of them know you." Not to mention I don't have a paddleboard here. When I left home, I only packed two of my surfboards.

"You can borrow my sister's board," Dez says, as if he can read my mind. "I'll text a few people. Not a lot. Do you think Emery and Brit will want to come?"

"Don't know." I shrug, fisting my phone. I don't bother mentioning that they already have plans. Dez stopped listening as soon as he asked the question, his phone in hand as his fingers type furiously across the screen.

"How are things going with the surfer princess?" he asks, looking up.

That's the name the media gave her when she competed and Emery told me the other day that she hates it.

"She'd kick your ass for calling her that," I say, laughing. "Things are fine. We're good."

"Bang her yet?" He locks his phone, wiggling his eyebrows.

I flip him off. "If I have, I'm not telling you shit. Because she'd kick *my* ass."

Emery has made it clear that she can't stand Dez.

He chuckles. "She doesn't really hate me that much does she?"

I guess he isn't as oblivious as he pretends to be. I shrug. "Sorry, dude. When we're together we don't talk about you. Much to your ego's dismay."

"Next time you're with her, ask her why she hates me."

"Two guesses as to why." He looks at me, not understanding. "Two words. Best. Friend."

"She doesn't like me because of Brit?" Now he sounds even more confused. How many beers did he drink tonight, again? "Brit and I are cool."

"How do you possibly get laid as much as you do and not know shit about women?"

"Hey!" he starts, looking slightly offended. "I know women. I have an older sister, you know. She made sure I was well versed on all things women."

"Then how are you still so bad at it?" He has to know that girls stick together. One for all and all for one or some shit like that. Chicks before dicks.

"I don't have time for a relationship right now. Not with the shit that is going on in my life. I need fun and simple. Not committed and complicated."

Dez doesn't talk about his personal life a lot. Hardly ever. Something he and I have in common. But from what I gather he helps his parents a lot by taking care of his sister's kids while she's away for work. After getting out of the military, she took a job that has her traveling at least twice a month. He hasn't mentioned their dad after that one night at my house, but he hardly mentions his sister either.

Family is a sore subject for Dez.

Something I get a hundred percent.

With Dez, though, I feel his cagey attitude comes from a place of protection. That he wants to keep his fam close and safe.

"Have you even talked to Brit lately?" I ask, already knowing the answer. I might have lied when I said Emery and I don't talk about Dez. We talked about him once after trivia night when Emery came over for a little bit. And then one time this weekend. Both times, it was basically the same. She doesn't like Dez for messing with Brit and her emotions.

"Dude, this is the first weekend I've had free since school got out for break and that's only because my parents, niece and nephew are out of town. I can breathe for once and take the day a little slower."

"You might know women, but I do too," I tell him. "If you haven't told her you've been busy, she's going to be hurt that you've been ignoring her. Especially after last time I saw you two."

"What are you talking about?"

"Are you really this fucking dense, Dez? You spent the entire night ignoring her, putting your attention on another girl and now you haven't talked to her. Jesus Christ dude, the first time I met Brit she was sucking your dick." He glares. I ignore him. "And I know you two had sex after that because you wouldn't shut up about it. You're being a fucking idiot."

"Should I invite her tonight?" He looks lost standing in front of me, holding his phone limply.

I shake my head. "She probably won't come if you ask. She's with Emery right now. I can just text her and see if they want to come." I don't mention that they probably won't, as much as I want to see her. I know how important her friends are and how much she values her "best friend bonding time" as she likes to call it.

My fingers hover over the keyboard, trying to figure out how I'm going to get her to agree to come.

I send a message, wondering if Emery will or won't show. If her smile will light up the night sky like it does the mornings.

I'm at my truck when a car honks. Pulling up beside me, Emery rolls down her window, smiling. "Fancy seeing you here."

I smile back. "Hi yourself."

"Do I not get a kiss for showing up?" she teases. This morning when she opened her car door, I leaned into her car, kissing her just "because she showed up." She clucks her tongue, tilting her head to the side. "Or do you not kiss me in front of other people?" Her words are drawn out, dramatic. "Am I your secret affair for spank bank material to use in years to come?"

I chuckle, not really following where she's going with her last question. I do, however, lean into her window, sucking her bottom lip into my mouth. Kissing her hard and slow. Right as I'm about to greet her tongue with mine, a gagging noise sounds from the passenger seat.

I pull back, nodding to Brit. Not apologizing for mauling her best friend. Kissing Emery is something I'll never apologize for. "Sup, Brit?"

"Just lost my appetite." She gags again.

"Don't listen to her, she just ate tacos," Emery says. "Quick, kiss me again."

Laughing, I do.

"You two are gross." But Brit's smiling, her words light. "Break her heart and I'll break your face."

"If he breaks my heart, *I'll* break his face," Emery says, and the look these two share has me fearing for my life.

Mental note: don't break Emery's heart.

I've noticed that Emery has no problem with PDA or acting more affectionate when we're together, but when we're texting or the few times that I've called her, she's different. More distant.

I know she's got issues with commitment. I don't even know if she's aware of it, but it's clear that she doesn't want to get too attached.

I'm trying to show her that she has to take risks and put herself out there if she wants to get what she wants.

And I want her to want me.

Brit looks out the windshield and her eyes narrow.

I don't have to turn around to know she sees Dez standing on the porch. He's been out there waiting since I told him the girls were on their way.

He says he wants to try and explain, but I think he's going to fuck it up more.

"I'm going to go say hi to Tucker and Carly," Brit mumbles as soon as she's out of the car and Dez steps off the porch, heading toward her.

He tries to stop her, but she spins away from his reach and

walks away. Not looking back.

Mental fist bump to Brit.

Dez looks at her retreating backside until she reaches two people standing on the other side of the yard, near most of the paddleboards, before he walks over to us.

Emery mumbles something under her breath I don't catch as she gets out of her car.

"Be nice," I warn.

She looks up at me, eyes wide with faux innocence. "I am always nice, Sebastian. I don't know what you're talking about."

I chuckle, pulling her close to my side. Partly because I want her close and partly to hold her back so she doesn't go off on my closest friend. I've been trying to be a third party up until this point. Now it looks like I have to get involved on both sides.

Mediating and shit.

Fucking joy.

"Emery Lawson, you look radiant." Dez smiles, a little wobbly from all the beers.

"And you look like a drunk idiot." Em smiles back but it lacks warmth, her words sugary sweet and fake. Dez seems to know it, too. He looks down at her.

"I don't know what I did to you, Lawson. We've barely talked since high school."

"We barely talked *in* high school," she tells him. "My problem with you has to do with a girl you are treating like dirt. Just stop playing your fucking games, Dez. Brit's too nice of a person for you to be doing this with. She wants something you'll never give her. Stop now and let her be happy, and enjoy the rest of her break."

Dez is still looking down at her. His expression shifting around. "What if I want to try?"

"Try what?" Emery stiffens. I squeeze her waist until she relaxes into me.

"Try to give her what she wants. Do you think she'll let me?"

Emery nibbles her bottom lip, thinking. "I think she will," she starts, slowly. "But only if you're serious and not going to bail after two weeks. Your attention span is shocking."

"Have you always been this snarky?"

"Only when my protective side comes out." She smiles, the smile of a feral cat.

I try to contain it, but a cough slips out with the word, "*bullshit.*"

Emery elbows my side.

I laugh, kissing her head.

Dez watches both of us before nodding and walking away.

"Leave her alone tonight," Emery calls and Dez turns back long enough to nod one more time.

She turns in my arms, kissing my neck. "Why am I here again? I could be at home, in my PJs, watching hot men on my screen."

"Should I be jealous?" I rumble, wrapping my arms around her waist, pulling her up on her toes.

"Only if you have their number in your phone. I'd hit them up instead," she teases, her arms going around my neck. "So, unless you want me to reunite with them back home, you should get on with reminding me why I came."

I smile as I lean in to kiss her. It feels good having her here, having her in my arms. I try to keep the kiss innocent and light. Just a quick slip of the tongue. But I haven't been able to be just sweet with Emery, so why would now be any different?

The sweet kiss turns into something packed with a lot

more heat. Emery's nails dig into my neck as I devour her mouth, teasing, tasting, nipping.

Kissing Emery is something I never want to stop, but someone's hooting and whistling breaks through my lust-filled haze and I pull away, pressing a kiss to her forehead as I do.

"Need a hand?" I ask as I start working the cables on her roof, undoing them to take the paddleboards down.

Emery goes to the other side, doing the same motions as I am. "You know I can do this by myself." She glares at me. "I don't need your help."

Have I mentioned what a turn-on her independence is?

Because holy fuck it is.

I grin as if she isn't wanting to chop off my balls. "I know you can do it by yourself, Em. But I'm trying to earn my keep with you."

She snorts as her glare fades. I know the glare isn't a real one. "Catch!" She has the cables done on her side before I do and she throws them at me. I catch them, jumping to the side so the hooks don't smack me in the face.

"Dude." It's my turn to glare.

"I didn't mean to throw them at your face." She nibbles her bottom lip. "I have really shitty aim."

I shake my head, throwing the cords on the driver's seat. "How about from now on you don't throw things that could potentially blind me?" I grab one of the boards, heaving it off with a shallow grunt as Emery does the same, not making a peep.

Again, her independence turns me on.

She walks around to me, holding the board to her side, looking every bit at ease. Even though paddleboards are heavier than surfboards. By a lot.

"Deal." There's an evil quality to the way she's smiling at

me now. "And since I'm a lady, I've decided that you can carry both the boards to the river. You know, since you want to earn your keep."

I tilt my head back and laugh. Wordlessly agreeing. She's just doing this because she's sassy and wants to mess with me, to see how far I'll go with what she throws down. No matter what she tries, I'll be willing to catch or hit.

I played little league for five years.

I can keep up.

Motioning for her to hand the board over, I ask. "Ready to head over?"

"I was promised glow sticks, Cleaton. You better deliver." She reaches into the backseat, clutching a bag to her chest. Protectively.

I frown. "You okay?"

"Yep!" Cheer, too much of it, is forced through her tone. "Just point me in the direction of where they are stashed and I shall get all colorful."

"Emery."

"Bash, do you not want me all colorful? Because, again, I can find them without your help."

I sigh. She's deflecting. "Come on, I'll show you."

As I lead her into the house, I rub my hand over my chest tattoo.

"You do that when you're aggravated, you know?" Emery's voice is smaller beside me as she watches my face.

"Yeah?" My grandma always used to say it was the little things that mattered. Not just in relationships, but in life too. A shot of emotion swells in my chest at her words.

She's paying attention to me as much as I am to her.

"Bash, you know I have issues from my accident I'm still trying to deal with."

I do know that. I just wish she wouldn't hide herself from me.

We're walking through the front door and I grab her hand, leading her away from the kitchen where the glow sticks are and down an empty hallway, pushing through the first door we come to.

Walking us straight into a bathroom.

"I know you do." I put my hands on her shoulders, giving them a squeeze before running them down her arms. "And I'm not pushing you to tell me anything you don't want to. But I want you to know that you don't have to hide from me."

"Don't I?" She looks up at me. "This doesn't even feel real, whatever we've been doing. I feel like we're in a bubble and you're going to leave soon and the bubble is going to pop, taking everything I've told you with it."

She's talking like we have an expiration date, an expiration date for something that hasn't really begun. I don't like it.

But she's right, isn't she?

As much as I've been trying to avoid it, I'm going to have to leave one day.

Soon, if my mother has her way.

"Even if I leave, Em, it doesn't mean we have to end." I don't want whatever we have to end. I want it to grow. I want to define us. I want to be invested in her, in us. The time frame has been short, but spending every day together has brought us closer in this short time than some people I've known for half of my life. We've formed a friendship that is starting to develop into something more. "It's not like I'm never going to come back. Or that I'll even leave."

This vacation has turned into so much more than I'd hoped. More than I had originally planned.

"Bash—"

I kiss her, capturing her words with my tongue, swallowing them down. Unheard and unsaid.

"I'm not leaving anytime soon," I promise her. "We don't have to rush anything. You set the pace, I'm good with whatever you want. As long as I get to see you." My hands travel to down her sides, to her hips, sliding over her ass. Giving her cheeks a squeeze. "And, hopefully, touch you."

She laughs, pressing her face to my body and the sound vibrates my chest, traveling everywhere. She digs her fingers into my arms, not lifting her head as she says, "I have scars."

The words are mumbled into my shirt, making them not as coherent.

"We all do, babe." I kiss her forehead. Something I've been doing a lot of tonight. But each time I do, she relaxes. It calms her and it calms me.

"Mine are pretty bad." She still won't look at me.

"Ask me about mine sometime, Em. Mine aren't pretty either."

"I'm not talking about emotional scars, Bash. Although I have a lot of those, too." She pushes away from me. Not far. Just enough so her face isn't pressed into my chest anymore. "I'm talking about physical scars."

Oh.

Right.

She told me how bad it looked, but I've seen her in bikinis and haven't noticed any—

Wait.

No, I haven't seen her in a bikini.

Ever.

She's always in a wetsuit when we're in the water and wearing jeans or long dresses and skirts. I've never seen her actual legs.

Her actual body.

My mind goes back to all the times I've touched her body. Felt the raised flesh on some places, never fully registering or questioning them.

"Do you want to show me?" My voice soft, like cashmere.

She shakes her head but pulls away. Grabbing the hem of her t-shirt, in a way similar to the night I first met her. My own hands shoot out, capturing her wrists. Holding them steady. "You don't have to do this."

I see the fear in her eyes.

I don't know if it's fear of me seeing her scars, specifically, or if it's fear of her showing them to someone else in general.

Whatever the reason is, I don't like it. I don't want her to do this out of fear. I don't want to see them if she isn't ready to actually show them.

"Bash, I want to." She tries to pry her arms away, but I hold on. Loosely. "Let go."

The sternness in her voice causes me to listen.

I let go.

I step back.

I wait.

With a deep breath, Emery pulls the shirt over her head, holding it at her side. Her eyes are closed and my eyes are on her stomach.

*Fucking hell.*

# CHAPTER NINETEEN

## *Emery*

CLOSE MY EYES BEFORE THE SHIRT IS OVER MY HEAD. IF Bash were just a little closer, he'd see that my body has a slight tremble. A vibration struck from within, born of nerves and apprehension. Aside from family, no one has seen my scars after the doctors didn't need to look at them anymore.

It has taken me years to love my body again. It might not be smooth and soft in places anymore, but the scars are a sign that I survived.

And I love the way I look—now that I'm used to it.

Doesn't mean other people will see the same thing. I can't handle the pity, the questions, the glances, and the speculation.

It's easier to hide the scars behind clothes than feel the eyes of strangers when I go somewhere.

Hiding them forever isn't an option. I mean, I live in Florida where seasons don't really exist and it's miserable wearing jeans in the summer, when the humidity is at a kill level. Death by denim is how I'll go if I keep wearing them.

I'm just scared and find it easier to hide behind clothing than hear the whispers of nosy people.

Yet, there was something in Bash's words that gave me the small courage to show him. Something unexpected that caused a rush of strength in my veins.

So now, I'm standing in only the cropped pants and my bikini top with nothing covering my stomach. Cold air brushes against my belly in a tentative caress.

My eyes are tightly shut. Body shaking. Adrenaline steadily flowing.

My shield has been lowered and I can't look at Bash. Refuse to.

He doesn't say anything.

I hear no intake of breath.

I hear nothing and the soundless air hanging between us has me almost opening my eyes to see if he silently slipped out the door.

Almost.

My eyes remain closed. I remind myself to breath.

Still no words are spoken.

I'm about to yell *fuck this* and put my shirt back on when large, calloused hands run slowly up my stomach.

I shiver for a completely different reason now.

He doesn't falter at my scars. Tracing them, learning them, as if committing them to memory.

His hands move at a snail's pace, fingers working over every inch of skin, smooth and raised.

I keep my eyes closed. Lids squeezed tighter as I lose control of my breathing.

His fingers are the first to touch this part of my body in

years and I don't want to see what is reflecting in his eyes.

I don't want to know.

Soon, too soon, his fingers are pulling away. My eyes flicker, about to open, when hot breath and soft lips touch the very place his fingers just were.

His tongue flicks over once, twice, and for a moment, I have no beating heart. No working lungs.

My fingers dive into his hair, pulling him closer.

The nerves on the scars are extra sensitive. Sometimes I don't feel sensations as intense on that side, sometimes I feel too much.

Right now, I feel *everything.*

With my eyes shut and Bash's mouth moving methodically over my flesh, my nipples tighten. Fireballs race down my body as my core tightens, heavy with a need so strong I feel tears prick my eyes.

Soon, Bash's mouth is working its way up and over my scars, moving higher up my stomach. His pace never wavering as the skin transitions from raised to smooth. He grazes my nipple through the fabric with his teeth.

"Bash!" I cry out, my fingers tightening around the locks of his hair. He sucks one last time. Hard. So hard that I feel my breath start to become labored, heavy lungs and sharp gasps. "*Fuck.*"

"Open your eyes, Emery," his growls in my ear.

His voice. His voice is so strong, so thick, like rich whiskey and cigar smoke. So different from his usual carefree attitude.

I shiver again, my body responding to his command.

My eyes snap open and the heat in his eyes is so intense, I'm sucking in a breath the same time his lips crash into mine. He might have slowly explored my body, but exploring my mouth is a different story.

His lips are hungry, rough over mine.

Hands graze my stomach and then cup my breasts in a flurry of stolen touches as his wandering fingers journey north.

His hands go to either side of my neck, tipping my head back, creating a whole new angle for him to invade.

As his mouth destroys mine, moans escape from my throat only for him to steal the noises, locking them away.

"You're beautiful," he growls into my lips, his hands on the move again. Caressing my scars.

His rough mouth is at war with his soft touches.

He's destroying and cherishing me.

"C'mere." His teeth and stubble nip my chin. He lifts me up, setting me on the sink countertop and spreading my legs apart. Stepping between them, he lifts my thighs high around either side of his waist, pulling me close, angling our bodies so I can feel how hard he is.

With only the light fabric of his swim trunks and my leggings, I feel *everything*. Every hard inch of him as he rubs our bodies together. Hard. Fast. Rough.

Losing myself to the sensation, I break away from Bash, my head hitting the mirror.

The cool glass does nothing to quench my scorching skin.

"Fuck, Emery." Bash grunts. "You're so fucking beautiful, you don't even know, Firecracker." His voice is so deep with need. "You don't even know what you do to me. How many times I've thought of your sexy as hell body." He sucks my neck and I groan at the feeling. "But no matter how many times I've fantasized about you, the real thing is so much better." His stubble scratches my jawline as he moves toward my ear.

He doesn't push for more. He doesn't ask for more, taking the limits I've set and running within them. Each touch has power, but tentative. It's like we're back in high school, two teenagers daring for exploration.

I reach out to trace the curve of his swollen bottom lip.

He buries his face in my neck where he takes a nip of skin before placing a kiss, when loud banging on the door douses us like ice water.

We stiffen.

"Fuck off," Bash yells. It comes out muffled with his face still cradled in the crook of my neck.

"Dude," Dez yells back and I groan. *Of course, it would be him.* "We're heading out."

"Give me a minute."

I bite his ear to keep from laughing. He's going to need more than a minute.

His fingers dig into my thighs.

"No can do, broski." Dez sounds causal. Way too casual. Casual like when a situation is anything but casual. "Can't have you and Emery fucking in my parents' house. There are children who stay here."

We both stiffen.

Dez knows.

And if Dez knows, how many other people?

Gah, how good are these bathroom acoustics?

"We both still need a minute," Bash growls, turning around to face the door in case Dez decides to barge in. Pretty sure neither of us thought to lock it when we came in here.

We hear Dez's laughter, not as muffled as his voice, and I notice the door is slowly moving.

I smack Bash's shoulder, frantically pointing at it.

"Fucking hell, Dez!" I scream. "Close the damn door, what is wrong with you?"

"Calm down, Surfer Princess."

That name. That fucking name. Red swarms the edges of

my vision. I am going to strangle that fucker.

"Don't get your bottoms in a twist—if you're wearing any that is. I'm just bringing my boy these. Figured he might need them."

Another pair of swim trunks come flying from the other side of the cracked door and, by some twist of fate, hits me in the face. "You better run, Desmond. Or I'm going to throw my shoe at your head so hard your ears will be ringing until Christmas."

"Sheesh, Emery. Not even a thank you? I'm wounded." He sounds anything but.

"Go the fuck away now, Daimon." Bash's tone leaves no more room for jokes. He's serious. And this voice is kind of really sexy.

We're rewarded with the sweet sound of Dez's laugh, retreating down the hallway.

"Come on, Em," Bash calls through the door. "I got the glow sticks."

I'm standing in the bathroom, alone this time.

I told Bash to give me a few minutes and I'd join him. Not sure how long ago that was.

I'm not hiding, per se, but I'm not rushing to get out.

After Dez interrupted, my high crashed hard and the full gravity of what Bash saw sunk in.

I still can't believe I did it. I've been hiding behind my shield of fabrics and showing Bash has left me emotionally bare. Raw. I feel lighter, more exposed, and free.

I want the high back, sipping the intoxicating adrenaline.

I want to show someone else. I want to show Bash the

rest of them. All of them and all of me.

But not yet, not while I'm feeling impulsive and lightweight.

I need to wait for this night to end, when my rational, sane thoughts return.

Well, as sane as my thoughts can be.

Inhaling a deep breath, I look at myself one last time in the mirror.

I tried to tame my hair as best I could, but this is as good as it's going to get. A mess of controlled tangles and waves. Less sexy-times-messy and more of a I-tried-to-make-this-messy-on-purpose-and-failed.

Whatever.

It's fine.

It's dark outside.

I wiggle my eyebrows at Bash as I open the door and he smirks, holding up the goods.

"Hand them over, Surfer Boy." I hold out my palm and he places the sticks in it.

He's already wearing a necklace, one bracelet on each wrist and the same goes for his ankles. Bare essentials.

I, on the other hand, make quick work with the multitude he gives me.

I slip a small stack of bracelets on each wrist, three necklaces around my neck and two on each of my ankles. I'm a glowing mass of color and I love it.

"How do I look?" I ask, twirling around slowly.

"Like one of those lights that flashes different colors."

"Perfect! Let's go."

We don't say anything as we walk outside to grab our boards, but when I see what his looks like I can't stop laughing. "Nice pink hearts and—*is that* a princess crown?"

Laughing.

So much laughing my abs clench from the workout they're getting and I wipe tears from my eyes.

"Yes, it is," Bash deadpans.

*So serious,* I think as my laugh keeps rolling.

"It's Dez's sister's, funny girl."

I can barely hear him.

Laughing.

"Did you find laughing gas in the bathroom while I was gone?"

"Nonono." I gasp for breath, trying to calm myself down. "I'm just really happy and apparently when I reach this level of happy, I can't stop laughing."

I flick on the lights around my board, making it come to life. Colors fade and bleed into one another as we walk toward the bank.

"What kind of happy? 'Cause, I might just keep you in a constant state of this."

"Ugh." I bump his shoulder with mine and he laughs. "You're trying to be cute-funny, but you can't be me, Bash. This relationship will never work if there are two Emerys. Plus, I love myself, but not enough to date me. Although that would make holiday parties a lot more bearable—Bash?"

He looks a little dazed, a little crazed, but I can't tell if it's on the good or bad side.

He grabs me, pulling me as close as our boards will allow. "Relationship?"

Oh.

Right.

"What? Relationship? Are you trying to tell me you're in a relationship, Bash?" I wave my hand, as if that will somehow carry our words into the breeze. Taking the memories of this conversation with them.

As it turns out, my superpower is not erasing memories. It's creating awkward tension.

"I'm trying to fucking be."

*Oh.*

Well. Then.

"Emery." He's trying not to be amused, the corners of his mouth are fighting to turn up, rebelling against his serious tone.

"Sebastian."

"Do you want to be in a relationship with me?"

"Do you want to be in a relationship with me?" Is it childish to parrot his words back to him? He doesn't get a chance to answer. "You don't want to get in a relationship with me, Bash. I'm going to fuck it up. I'm not an easy person to deal with. Commitment scares me and when I get scared I run—"

"Emery."

"What's our expiration date?"

He blinks, his grip tightening around me. Like he's not sure if he wants to pull me closer or push me away. "Do we have to have one?"

"I mean, yeah. We live on opposite coasts," I remind him. "Even if you don't want to admit it, you have to go back home one day, Bash. You have a career. Responsibilities."

"Last time I checked, you have oceans here. I don't have any ties really holding me in California. I had planned on staying for a vacation, but then I met you—get that scared look off your face, Emery." Is my face scared? If it is, I can't help it. Did he just hint that he'd move here? For me? "I'm not talking about moving here for you. But I can come see you and have it not affect my surfing. You can train with me when

I'm here. It'll help you get back on a routine at a pro's level."

"We haven't even gone on a date."

"So let's go on a date."

"Do people still go on dates? Dates that don't come from a dating app?"

"I don't give a fuck if people don't go on dates anymore. They should. We should. Go out with me. Tomorrow night. For our first date."

"You don't want to date me, Bash." I shake my head. I continue my sentence from earlier as I retreat a few steps. Bash moves with me. "Seriously, I'll drive you up the fucking wall and I run when I get scared and being in a relationship will send me running. I'm already terrified."

"You, the most fearless girl I know, are too afraid to go on a date with someone you see every day, anyway?" Well, when he puts it like that...yes, very much so. "It's a date, Em. The start of many—"

"Aren't you getting a little ahead of yourself?" I can't stop myself. When things get serious, a joke is almost guaranteed to slip out, which is how I hear myself asking, "Who says I'll want to go on more than one?"

Bash ignores my question. "Say yes, Emery."

"Yes, Emery." Despite the uncertainty and the queasy feeling in the pit of my stomach, I want this. I want him.

Bash tweaks my nose and I laugh as he says, "I'm taking that as a firm yes."

I don't disagree.

He's supposed to. As much as I'm a pain in the ass, I really want this. I'm tired of being afraid of living my life, of doing what I really want. I have a voice and I need to use it. For more than just sarcastic quips.

We don't say anything as he puts his board in the water.

I stand off to the side, watching him step on it, finding his balance before he uses his paddle to push himself out further into the river.

I haven't mentioned this to anyone, but I'm more afraid of going in the river than I am the ocean.

With the ocean, it's almost guaranteed you'll see a shark. When I don't see one, I make a wish. It's that rare while surfing. But with a river, where it's home to a lot of bull sharks, who are very territorial, it's that much more dangerous, especially since they breed in the river.

With the ocean, I'm okay because it holds no secrets of danger, the hazards are present in the back of my mind the entire time. With the river, it masquerades as serene, peaceful, but underneath that calm there are threats unseen.

But I can't back out. I've wanted to do something like this for years. And as if the party people, who are already paddling out on the river, can feel my hesitation, they let out loud whoops, cries, and cheers.

Laughter ringing into the night.

Fun.

That is what this night is supposed to be about.

That's what the night has been so far.

Bash isn't too far out; he stopped when he noticed I hadn't joined him. He's out there floating, waiting for me. His arms are open as if to say, *well, aren't you coming?*

I get on my board. I get on because I want to. Because I can. Because I have to.

I can't let this fear rule me forever.

The light from my board illuminates the water in my path. That creates more comfort, knowing I can see under me.

I paddle harder toward Bash, who is still waiting for me to catch up. He shouldn't have stopped. As I get closer to him,

I decide that Bash and I are going to race to the rest of the group.

Ready, set, go starts now.

I'm passing Bash before he realizes he's in a race and he's losing. I laugh, picking up as much speed as I can.

The thing with paddleboarding is that it's not easy. At all. It takes a lot of strength. Both physical and core strength. Even after years of surfing, I find it challenging.

Once you find the balance and a rhythm, there isn't much that can stop you.

My muscles pull and stretch with every stroke.

Power. That's what it feels like to be on a paddleboard.

Exhilarating.

"Slow down, Firecracker." Bash pulls up beside me.

"Why?" I taunt. "Afraid you'll lose?"

"Ha! I don't lose." Maybe in surfing he doesn't, but he hasn't competed against me in a paddleboarding race. "I don't want to join the rest of them just yet."

"You're not sick of me?" Warmth floods my belly.

"Not yet," he teases and I splash him with my paddle.

We slow down and sit on our boards, under the full moon and the shining stars, facing each other.

There are no street lights to drown out the beauty in the night sky, so for a while we lay back on our boards, hands linked together, tethering us so our boards don't drift with the current, and see who can find the most constellations.

It's Bash, with all of them.

I can't even find the North Star. Every time I think I've found it, it moves quickly through the sky.

If we were counting airplanes, I'd kick Bash's ass.

The wind starts to pick up around us, bringing a bite of cold breeze.

I shiver.

"Are you cold?"

"No, I just felt the urge to shake my body in a spasm-like way."

"Smartass." He shakes his head.

It's the perfect night.

# CHAPTER TWENTY

## Emery

**M**Y COUSIN IS A LOT OF THINGS—DRIVEN, SELFLESS, kind-hearted. One thing she is not is punctual. Unless she has a date with a springboard and a pool, she will not show up on time.

Which is why I'm sitting in this booth at a restaurant alone.

The waiter has come by twice to take my order and both times I've had to send him away.

After twenty minutes of scrolling through my social media accounts, my cousin settles into the opposite side of the booth with a flourish. Nori tosses her bag onto the table that causes a loud *bang* to ring out. She's breathing hard—her cheeks flush. "I'm so sorry I'm late!"

I wave her apology away. No matter how hard she tries, she will always show up late. I've accepted it. She's the only one that tends to get a late pass from me. "Traffic?"

"No, I fell asleep after practice and slept through the alarm I set." She yawns.

Oh, Nori.

The waiter swoops in when he sees Nori is sitting at the table, but Nori still needs a few minutes. She's never eaten at this place before.

Once he's out of earshot, I give my cousin my full attention. "How's practice?"

"I've decided that I'm going to up my training to more hours." She shrugs like it's no big deal. She practices early in the morning before school and then for a few hours after. How long is she planning on staying? Until it's midnight?

I don't say anything against it. She wants this and there is no stopping Nori from going after her dream.

"How's your mom?"

Nori shrugs as she plays with the glass of water I ordered for her. The condensation has created a thick ring of water on the table. "I haven't seen her. She's not home when I'm there."

*Wait, whaa?*

"You mean at night?" I sit up straighter and lean across the table. "How long does the hospital keep her?"

"She's not there every day, Em." Nori won't meet my eyes, which is probably a good thing as I process this.

My aunt isn't a bad mom. She was a single parent at twenty and has worked her ass off to support her small family. Still, for the past few years, she's been distant from us. Going long periods without coming over or answering our calls. The only time we get to see her is when we go to her house—and that's only if she's there.

"Is she dating again?"

"I think so."

"Have you seen the guy?" Her mom has dated a lot over

the years, but I've only met one guy. I was seven and he gave me a chocolate chip cookie before dinner. I wanted them to get married right then and there.

Nori shakes her head. "She hasn't been there at all. I've talked to her a few times, but it's like having a roommate when all I want is my mom."

"How long has it been since she's been home?" If it's been more than a few days, I have to tell my dad. See if he knows what's up with his sister.

"Two weeks and a day." She sounds so broken. "And when she calls she doesn't stay on the phone for long. Just to check in and see if I'm okay or that I've been eating."

I don't want to bring it up, but I once heard my parents talking about how Nori's mom used to disappear with her dad, only for him to take off again, leaving my aunt alone and hurting. The likelihood of these two connecting is doubtful but one can't help but wonder.

"Do you think your parents will mind if I stay over for a few nights?" Nori asks. "I just don't want to be alone anymore."

I look at her for a good while. Just looking. Not saying anything. "Seriously? Of course they'll think you're the biggest inconvenience to ever walk through their door."

Nori blinks. Then smiles. She knows I'm being sarcastic as fuck right now. "Pretty sure that's Brit."

"True that." I grin. A grin that slides off my face. "I won't be home for a lot of tonight."

"That's fine. I can just hang with the coolest aunt and uncle in town. I'll probably crash super early, anyway. I need to talk to my coach before practice tomorrow. Where are you going to be?"

I take a sip of my water. Stalling. "I have a date."

Now it's my cousin's turn to stare. "Excuse me? You don't

date." She's not lying. Haven't really gone out with a guy since before my accident. The guy I kissed in my freshman year of college was the first guy to touch me since I was sixteen. "With who?"

"Who do you think?" I mean really, what other guy have I been spending all my time with? "Take a wild guess."

"Bash?"

"Ding-ding-ding we have a winner!" I take the straw out of my drink and point it at her. "You get a prize."

She rolls her eyes. "You were supposed to stay single with me. Team Forever Single!"

Now I roll my eyes. "You're not going to be forever single."

"I will be for the unforeseeable future. Last time I tried it ended poorly, remember?"

Last year, she tried to go out with a guy and ended up sleeping through their date. The dude called her a few times and knocked on her door for a solid ten minutes. The next day at school, homeboy ignored her completely.

"So, you're not seeing anyone?" I ask casually, not only to change the subject away from me, but to find out what is going on with her and a certain Brazilian friend of mine—ours.

Nori scrunches her face up. Like a pug. "No. You know my stance on dating now."

Right. After the one guy wasn't understanding about the date, Nori said that a guy would only distract her and she had other, more important things to worry about than who was taking her to the prom. Something she plans to skip anyway. Nori doesn't want a man until she gets a gold medal around her neck.

Smart girl. Now if she was only smart enough to stay away from someone in particular.

"About Xavier," I start and she groans, her head hitting the wood behind the booth.

"He's my friend." She glares at me. Uh-oh. Her glares are as scary as an angry kitten.

"But what kind of friend? A friend you see on social occasions, a friend you converse with on the regular, or a friend you lie to your other friends about being just friends with? Hmmm?"

"Did you smoke or something before coming here?"

"You know I haven't smoked weed in like two years. Nice try, though," I tell her right when the waiter walks up. Nice.

After we order, my burger and a lettuce wrap for Nori, I try to get her to spill. "Seriously, Nori. You do realize he's older than you, right?"

"You mean he's not an eighteen-year-old high schooler?" She tilts her head to the side. Man, when Nori takes naps she is some kind of sassy. "No, Emery. I didn't know that. Tell me, what is his birth year? Zodiac sign?"

Under the sarcasm, there's hurt in her words. She's seventeen, but has been on her own for a lot longer. She's more independent than I was in high school and Bash was right when he said that Nori is more mature than other people her age. More mature than I was at her age.

"I'm sorry, Nori. I didn't mean that." Never wanting to hurt my cousin, I wish I could swallow those words. Choke on them. "I'm just concerned."

"About what? You know Zay. He's your friend too."

He was my friend first, but now is not the time to be petty and territorial. "Exactly. I know the kind of guy he is. He's a shameless flirt that will be here one day and gone the next. He doesn't stay in one place for long and I don't want to see you get hurt."

"He stayed in college to get his degree." Point Nori. "He's

been in Florida longer than he'd been in South Carolina." Another point. Xavier moved to South Carolina for about forty-nine days. "He has a good job here, an actual adult job that has him working five days a week."

*He does?* As long as I've known Xavier he's always worked jobs that allow for a flexible schedule. Ones that allows him to pick up and leave whenever he gets sick of whatever town or state he was in at the time.

"Since when?"

"The past three weeks or so." Nori shrugs like it's no big deal, but it is. It *is* a big deal. The biggest, actually. Xavier has had a nine-to-five job for over three weeks and he isn't itching to leave.

My face must express my shock since Nori says, "He's my friend too, Emery. It's not a big deal that he tells me things."

I know it's not, but I want to protect her from getting hurt and me being angry with my friend in the process. "Nothing has happened, right? *Sex-ually.*" I drag the word out.

"What?" Nori's face pinches and she's gone a little pale. "Of course not. Nononono."

She's flustered and I watch as she stammers to find composure.

"Breathe, Nor," I coax. "I believe you. It's fine. I get you two are friends, I just don't want you thinking it will turn into something more."

"I don't think that. He's just a really good friend," she whispers. "You don't find those a lot, right?"

Right. Nori's friends in school aren't the best and while she's close with the people she dives with, she doesn't usually hang out with them outside of the pool. My friends are her friends but her friends aren't mine. If Xavier wants to be her friend like Brit is for me, the best friend that puts shame to other best friends, then I'll try to let go of my worry.

Until I see cause for it to come back.

Our food arrives and we eat in silence for a while. I'm stuffing my face with the juicy, beefy goodness while Nori is hardly picking at her wraps. Maybe I've upset her more than I realize and that is a knife plunged deep into my heart.

After wiping my hands and mouth with the napkin I placed in my lap, I reach across the table, giving her hands a squeeze. "I'm sorry and I love you."

"I love you too." She squeezes my hand back while giving me a smile.

It's not until I'm paying the check, ignoring my cousin trying to give me cash for her half, and we're walking out of the restaurant that she asks, "So where's your date tonight?"

# CHAPTER TWENTY-ONE

*Bash*

T HIS IS EASY, SEBASTIAN. ALL YOU HAVE TO DO IS KNOCK.
*Hand to wood.*
*Knuckles to wood. You got this.*
*You know how to knock.*
I've forgotten how to knock.

My palms are fucking sweaty as I go to wipe them on the denim, but stop before flesh meets fabric.

I've already wiped them on my jeans enough times that I worry my handprints are visible streaks on the fabric. Maybe the slight cool wind, what the air feels like without humidity here, will dry them off before the door has a chance to open.

You know, when I remember how to fucking knock.

Since I woke up this morning, my stomach has been tied up in knots. Food hasn't had any appeal and time has moved too fast. Tonight is supposed to be important.

It's my first date with Emery, one that doesn't involve

surfboards—since the times I've taken her out to breakfast don't count and I can't even bring myself to knock on the door.

About a dozen times while driving over here, I thought about texting her when I pulled in the driveway so she could meet me outside and I wouldn't have to get out.

But my grandma always taught me to pick a girl up at her door. She also taught me to hold the door open and pull out a lady's chair. A twenty-first century gentlemen is what she tried to raise me to be.

I think of my grandma's smile and how proud she'd be of me as I raise my knuckles, that totally *aren't* shaking, to knock on the door.

Three quick raps and I'm taking a step back.

I hear footsteps. They sound too heavy to belong to my girl, who walks like she's always on sand, but that doesn't stop me from chanting:

*Please be Emery*

*Please be Emery*

*Please be Emery*

*Please be Em—*

The door opens and I feel my lungs seize.

*Holy motherfucker.*

It's not Emery.

It's her father.

Ren Lawson.

One of the best surfers of all time.

My idol.

I stare at him, mouth slightly unhinged from my jaw, unable to form thoughts, much less words. He looks the same as he did in his pre-retirement days. He looks like the same Ren Lawson I worshipped as a kid. Just older.

*Fucking duh, Bash. You fucking idiot.*

"Hi, sir. I'm here to pick up Emery. I'm Bash—" I stick out my hand for him to shake. Wait, or do I introduce myself as Sebastian? "I mean, Sebastian, but you can call me Bash." Pause. "Sir."

I hate myself. Is this how people feel when meeting me? Tongue tied and nervous?

Ren doesn't say anything, just stares at my hand that is between us until he grips it in his own. He gives a firm shake and an even firmer squeeze. "Ren."

I flex my hand behind my back when he lets go.

"She didn't tell me she had a date." He eyes me, assessing me.

Fucking hell, I want to pull the collar away from my neck. I'm sweating everywhere. I wasn't this nervous in the past, right? When meeting girls' parents?

"Oh," is what I say in response.

"Does she know you're here?" he asks and I shake my head. I should've fucking texted her when I got here.

I'm vaguely aware of him pressing a button on a little white box on the wall, telling Emery she has a visitor. It's hard to hear, but I think Emery says she'll be right down.

"You can come inside and wait for her. She's upstairs with Nori." He opens the door wider, stepping aside. "You know Nori, right?"

I think I nod, but I can't really process anything at this point. *Ren Fucking Lawson* invites me inside and I barely even hear the words as a steady pounding fills my ears. I'm too awe-struck. Is this even real life?

Somehow my feet still know how to move, carrying me inside.

Then it's just Ren and me in silence.

As cool as this might be, standing in my idol's home, I

can't help the urge that surfaces, to run out the door and into the truck.

"You look familiar," Ren says as he stares at me shifting in the entryway. "What did you say your name was again?"

Emery never told me if her parents cared if she was with a surfer or not. Her friends surf so it shouldn't be a big deal, but I don't know if I should answer or not.

A part of me wants to talk to him about my surfing. See if he has any pointers or advice.

Where the hell is Emery?

She has about three seconds before any control I have leaves and I make a fool of myself in front of her father.

I'm about to answer, no idea on what will come out, when I get saved.

"Ren, come here for a second?" a voice calls from somewhere in the house.

Ren looks over his shoulder in the direction of the voice before looking at me.

"She'll be down any second," he tells me. "Have a seat if you want."

I'm finally able to breathe as my idol walks away, disappearing into the house.

I'm about to plant my ass on one of the chairs when Emery comes running down the staircase. Nori's behind her whisper-shouting, "Go, go, go!"

She's wearing a long dress with a floral pattern and tan sandals that smack the hardwood staircase with each step. Her body is crouched, hunched over, as she rushes down the stairs.

*What the hell?* She looks like a frog with her knees kicking up to her chest.

The smile quickly changes to a frown as her foot gets caught under her dress and she goes down. I move my feet, lunging toward Emery, but not fast enough to catch her before her elbows crash down on the hardwood floor.

"Ooooow!" She curses as her eyes get watery, but she's also fighting a smile.

Nori is standing above Emery, gawking. "Seriously, Emery? I thought we planned on a quick exit, not making an entrance."

"Remind me next time I want to wear something floor length that I'm a klutz so that might be a bad idea," she tells us, hugging her elbows.

"But I like seeing you throw yourself at me." I reach down to help her up. "I will say, though, I prefer when you run into my chest instead of the floor."

I take one of her arms in my hand, extending it out to get a better look at her elbow. There's a little red mark with some skin shaved off that I kiss before doing the same to her other. "You swoon every time you see me."

"I do *not* swoon." She definitely swoons. "You're like an unlucky rabbit's foot."

I laugh as her dad clears his throat. He must have come back in when Emery fell. She wasn't quiet about it.

Standing next to him is a beautiful woman with dark hair. Despite differences in hair color, she shares the same delicate features as Emery. Emery's mom. I remember seeing her when she was younger in some of the pictures with Ren.

"Hi Mom, hi Dad," Emery waves, smiling. Her cheeks are a little red. "I'm going on a date."

I clear my throat to keep from laughing again. I'm less nervous around Ren when Emery's here. My palms aren't as sweaty, my heart isn't threatening to beat out of my chest, and my breathing has regulated. Everything is fine. Or it is until Emery grabs my hand, pulling me toward her parents.

"Bash, meet my parents. Ren and Ruby Lawson. Parents, meet my date, Sebastian Cleaton." I don't know what I'm expecting, but Ren's face flashes with recognition and there goes any calm I was feeling a moment ago.

How do you breathe again?

"The surfer, Bash Cleaton?" he asks, sharing a worried look with his wife. "That's why you looked familiar."

"Yea—" My throat catches, making Emery laugh, and I have to clear it before saying, "Yes, sir." Then, because I'm having an out of body experience, I add, "Um… it's, uh, great to meet you too, sir. Truly, it's an honor. I've looked up to you so much growing up and I still do. You really are an inspiration to me."

I hear giggling to the side of me. Nori leans close to Emery, failing at whispering when she says, "Please tell me I'm not the only one finding this funny."

"Oh, it's hilarious." Emery laughs and I want to pinch her side.

"You have the world speculating about what happened to you," Ren says, and by world, I know he means the surfing world, and I hear his unspoken question. *How the hell did I end up here?*

I shift my feet and wring my hands together. "I took a much needed vacation, sir." I have never said sir so many times in my life. Now I can't stop. "I just needed to clear my head and get away from everything for a while."

I don't say that I fell out of love with my sport, my job, and my life, but I don't need to. Ren seems to understand what I'm saying without me having to actually say it.

Did we just share a moment?

"Well!" Emery slips her hand into mine, pulling me toward the door. I follow with a grunt. "As much fun as this has been, we actually have places to be and food to eat, so byeeee!"

"Emery Marie, you act like I embarrass you," her dad says, his tone light.

"Oh trust me, Daddy." Emery opens the door, pushing me out first before calling over her shoulder. "It's not you I'm embarrassed of this time."

# CHAPTER TWENTY-TWO

## Emery

"I'm sorry," Bash mumbles into his beer.

We're sitting in his kitchen with me on the island counter and him leaning against it. One of his hands resting on my upper thigh. My feet swing leisurely as I half-heartedly nurse a beer of my own. "Don't be."

"You shouldn't have to deal with that." He throws back the rest of his beer, placing the empty bottle behind me.

"It's not your fault," I reassure him. "You didn't know she'd say that."

"I should've known better than to have you answer my phone." He pushes himself off the counter and steps between my legs. Without looking away from my face, he takes my mostly full beer out of my hands and takes a sip. "She was a bitch."

I nod my agreement as my hands go under his shirt.

"She had no right to say those things about you, Firecracker."

Again, I nod.

"It just pisses me off," he all but growls. "But you, babe, you were amazing. You took what she said and brushed it off, no problem. I don't think you realize how strong of a person you really are."

This, right now, is my kind of date. Just hanging out. I only wish Bash would stop being hard on himself.

We ate at a cute place by the river, where I spent most of the meal messing with Bash about his fanboying. We were having fun until we were on our way home. Bash's mom called and since he was driving, he told me to answer it. Thinking it was Dez.

But the feminine voice made of ice and steel on the other end was definitely *not* Dez. As soon as she heard my voice, she tore into me, calling me names and throwing accusations. Then I went off on her, saying that if she was just going to throw out insults, she can shove her words up her tight ass. In a polite way. Or as polite as I could be with someone calling me a gold digging bitch. Among other things.

Bash looked at me in alarm as he asked what was wrong before taking the phone from me. I've never seen Bash as mad as he was when he was on the phone with his mom. He wasn't even on for long. He said some words, telling her to back off and he'd talk to her later, before hanging up.

He's been brooding in silence since he ended the call.

"I'm not strong, just resilient."

"Pretty much the same thing." He sits the bottle down next to my leg before cupping the back of my neck. His lips graze my cheek before he pulls back. "You were kind of hot when you were defending yourself. Kind of turned me on."

I smile up at him as my hand moves down his chest to grab his growing erection through his jeans. "Kind of?"

He groans and heat shoots down my body, through my stomach, settling between my legs. Feeling a little bolder, I tighten my grip around him, stroking up, but he pulls away.

Bash's face is unreadable as he backs up until he presses against the opposite counter. The only sounds to fill the room are our labored breaths and pounding pulses.

The silence in the kitchen is too much. My heart starts to beat faster and louder the more I sit here.

Bash has said I'm resilient, that I'm a fighter, but when it comes to him I feel off balance.

Like there are a million butterflies in the pit of my stomach every time I'm around him. The urge to throw up is also present. I'm a mess around him. It scares me.

The only thing I've ever taken seriously is surfing, but even surfing doesn't feel as dangerous as this. What if he doesn't feel the same way?

I need a minute. Sixty seconds to pull myself together.

I begin to move away, toward the hallway, when he grabs my arm. "Where are you going?"

"Uh, I was going to—"

"No."

"No?" I parrot.

"No," he confirms as he reels me closer to him. "Come swimming with me."

"What?"

"There's a pool in the backyard. I want to go swimming and want you to come with me."

*What?* I silently repeated in my head. "What—"

Before I finish talking, I'm upside down, staring at Bash's very nice *ass*ets as the room moves in a blur. "Hey! Put me down!"

He doesn't.

Instead, he chuckles and smacks my ass. The resounding noise of his palm against my butt echoes down the hallway. I try to push away, to push against his lower back, but he's hardly affected by my movements. "Sebastian Michael Cleaton, put me the fuck down!"

"Nope." Another ass slap.

I retaliate by pounding my fists on his muscled back.

He laughs. "That's cute, babe. Thanks for the massage."

I huff. "Massage, my ass, Caveman!"

"Well, if you insist." He squeezes a butt cheek before kneading into it.

"UUUGHH!"

"You asked for it."

"I so did not ask for it!" I pound on his back again. My fists thumping against muscle in a musical drum beat. "Put me down, Cleaton!"

"Okay." He grabs my waist and throws me off. A scream escapes my lips as I fly through the air and bounce against his soft mattress. Propping myself up with my elbows, I glare at him. "I hate you."

He laughs as he prowls onto the bed toward me, caging me in with his knees. "No you don't."

"I kind of do."

"Okay." His tone is riddled with thinly veiled amusement. It's clear he doesn't believe me.

"I thought we were going swimming."

"We are." He makes no move to get off of me.

"Well," I look around the room, "This is your bedroom and as far as I can see, there's not a pool in here. And another flaw to your plan, Surfer Boy, is I don't have a bathing suit. I'm not going nude," I add when I see him perk up with an idea.

"This is where I keep the suits." He smirks that arrogant

smirk I like so much on him. I want to lick it. Wipe it away so he stops being so smug.

"I'm not wearing a pair of your swim trunks," I warn.

"Or you could just wear the one you left here."

*Huh?*

He gets off me, pulling his shirt off as he goes.

*Really? Is that really necessary?*

Hard and sculpted is how I would describe his body, along with sexy and lickable. Pulling out a pair of swim trunks, he flicks the button of his jeans and slowly unzips his fly. His eyes not leaving mine, a challenge as he waits to see what I'll do next.

I sit further up on my elbows. Daring him.

His expression turns darker, a hunger consuming him, as he pushes the denim down his thighs, taking his boxer briefs with them. His hands move up, slowly grazing his thighs as he grabs his semi-hard dick, giving it a lazy tug.

My focus hones in on his dick, my breath catching at his hand working over it.

I'm fixated on his movements when something smacks me in the face before landing on the bed.

I blink. Bash gives me a look as his hand moves up and down his length, his dick fully hard now. I lift my eyebrow in question at seeing what hit me in the face. I pick up my missing swimsuit. "I've been looking for this, you know?"

He laughs darkly before the sound turns to a groan. Forgetting the lost swimsuit, I crawl off the bed and move toward him. He eyes me, his hand still moving at a lazy pace.

I kiss him hard and before he can slip his tongue into the tango, I pull back. I give him a smile as I bite my lip. He watches me with rapt interest as his speed takes on a new vigor.

I drop to my knees, smacking his hand away and replacing

his grip with mine. Stroking from base to tip, I watch my hand move over his length with heat pooling in my core. After a few more pumps, I replace my hand with my mouth.

Bash groans, his fingers entangling in my hair as I run my tongue from the base and around the tip before taking him in as far as my mouth allows without gagging.

Bobbing my head, Bash's hips thrust in tune until he goes too far and I pull back retching.

Really, it's as sexy as it sounds.

"Sorry," Bash rumbles, his voice full of lust and need. But even through the haze, his hand goes to the side of my neck, tilting my jaw up. "Are you okay, Firecracker?"

My eyes are watering from the sting as I say, "What a fun way to test your gag reflex."

Bash's thumb caresses my jaw. "Em—"

His concern is sweet, but right now I don't want sweet Bash. I want hungry Bash.

Reassuring him, I slowly run my hand down his stomach until I wrap my hand around the base and wrap my lips around him before going down until my mouth touches my fist.

"Fuck." Bash pulls at my hair and my free hand grips the back of his thigh as I work him over.

I tease, I taste, I control as I make Bash mumble incoherencies.

My knees dig into his carpet.

I give the underside of his dick one long and thorough lick before tightening my hand around the base.

The movement is enough for Bash, and without warning, he grips my hair so tight he removes my mouth from him before bending down and scooping me up.

"Not a fan?" My voice is like sandpaper. It's distracting

from my pounding heart. The nerves of what's to come.

Yet those thoughts stop as Bash tosses me back on his bed. My back bounces against his mattress, once, twice, before he climbs over me, spreading my thighs with his knees so I can feel his heat against my aching core.

I shift around and that does *nothing* to help.

Heat courses throughout my body, igniting fire in my veins as Bash grabs my hands, raising them above my head. My knees bend, hiking up the fabric of the dress, bringing it dangerously close to the starting line of my scars along my thigh.

But Bash doesn't glance down; he keeps his eyes on mine. Brown eyes so dark with lust they look black. "I need to know my limits." His voice sounds as scratchy as mine did.

He needs to know if he can see the worst of my scars. If I'm ready to bare all. My throat tightens and it's a struggle to swallow. It's been such a long time since anyone has seen me. All of me. Yet, I know what I want to do. Even if the consequences cost me this tomorrow.

"There are no limits."

Bash nods, bending down to kiss me hard and fast before he drags his teeth along my cheek to nip at my chin, before trailing kisses down my neck and sucking hard at the base where neck and shoulder meet. His tongue swirls around the skin before he applies more pressure and I arch against him.

Jesus, he's giving me a fucking hickey. It's like high school all over again, but better. His lips are torture in the purest pleasure. Once he has me thoroughly branded, because Bash is feeling like a caveman tonight, his teeth skim along my shoulder, capturing one of the straps to my dress between his teeth, dragging it down my arm as his hands cup and squeeze my breasts.

My breathing is labored and I truly believe he's going to kill me tonight.

My nipples are puckered, straining against the cups of my bra.

Bash repeats his movements to my other dress strap, until they're both hanging around my elbows.

"You're beautiful, you know?" he says as he kisses the valley between my breasts.

"Well," I pant, all sweaty and squirmy, "I do try."

Bash peers up at me, his chin resting on the spot he kissed. "I wasn't talking to you. I was talking to our friends." He squeezes each breast like they need reassurance.

Pulling down the cups, he pinches and twists one nipple, while his mouth closes around the other peak, lapping with his tongue and pulling with his teeth.

"Oh *fuc—*" I flex my arms, bucking up, as he sucks a nipple so hard his cheeks hollow. My breath is reduced to pants.

Bash pins me down. Digging my wrists into the mattress. His hips press against mine.

His straining hard-on pulses between us.

"If you don't let me move," I threaten, not sounding intimidating at all as I'm struggling to process words. "I will—"

My words turn into a gasp as he pulls more of my dress down, exposing my stomach. His tongue and hand tracing and following along to the patterns of my scars.

He kisses down my stomach until he reaches the fabric of the dress, which is now pooling around my waist. He doesn't pull it down any further and kisses the dress, the barrier to my skin, instead. The action is so small, but holds so much weight.

My throat catches and I strain against his hand still keeping me captured. He lets go, somehow knowing I have to touch him for this. My hands go around his neck and his back.

Nails press into the skin as tears well in my eyes at his action, at not pushing. He takes all that I give and doesn't try for any more.

He kisses down until he can feel the thin strap of my thong. I feel him smile as he grabs it with his teeth, pulls it, and lets it go so it snaps back against my skin.

I jolt.

"Bash." I dig my nails into the nape of his neck to get his attention. "I'm ready whenever you are."

My heart drums to the words. A symphony of emotions come over me and now I'm shaking for what is about to happen.

It's not from being scared, but that doesn't mean nerves aren't involved. I'd be concerned if they weren't. But I'm ready. As fast as my heart is racing, it's the engine that's carrying me to a destination that I never fully thought I'd reach.

My man wastes no time getting off me and pulling us both to our feet.

"Strip."

His words are erotic, but they fill me with power. Power I've had this entire time. He's let me set the pace, controlling, guiding. Bash might take charge, but he's giving me all the influence. Knowing I need to do this at my pace. Not anyone else's.

"Can a girl get some music first?" I ask to distract. To take one final breath, knowing that no matter how bad I think others will judge me, Bash won't see me any differently.

*The darkness within you is where beauty shines the brightest.*

Bash doesn't give in to my music joke. He's standing before me naked.

My arms reach behind me, unclasping my bra and letting

it fall to my feet. Bash's stare feels like I'm standing too close to a bonfire.

As slow as I can, I wiggle my hips as my hands push the dress the rest of the way down. My body bending, following the movements until the dress and myself are crouched over the floor.

Bash's nostrils flare out as I uncurl my body back up, kicking the dress away, leaving me in nothing but my thong. Before I can register that I'm baring all the scars, Bash pounces. Grasping my waist, he spins me around until I'm facing the full-length mirror. I shiver despite the heat rolling off our naked bodies.

"You." His nose runs up my neck, tugging at my ear as his hands run over the raised flesh on my thigh. I watch him through the reflection. "These?" He runs a finger over the longer and more raised scars. "Should never be hidden."

"They're not," I whisper as I follow his tracing through the mirror. "Not from you."

# CHAPTER TWENTY-THREE

## Emery

Bash leads me back to the bed. I drape my body over his, before he rolls me onto my back. He slides down my body and I sit up on my elbows as I watch him studying my thigh.

He drags a finger up one thigh, over a scar, and chases it with his mouth. He moves to another one, repeating the pattern over and over. Moving up and down. His mouth chases his finger and he starts to get higher and higher until he reaches my thong.

Eyeing it like a cat eyes a mouse, he rips it away.

Cool air hits my core before Bash's head disappears between my thighs. His tongue plays with my clit and his finger slides into my folds. Every few pumps, his finger hooks—hitting just the right spot. I gasp, with little noises escaping behind it, as stars, such pretty stars, dance across my eyes.

My body feels like an instrument that has already been

thoroughly tuned so when his fingers start to play the actual strings I can't hang and am coming hard and fast.

My nails dig hard into his shoulders, holding him close as I come down.

Through the fog, I hear the sounds of a foil packet opening.

He kisses me as our bodies line up and I feel my arms shake as they wrap around his neck. Bash stops, feeling my limbs tremble around him, but I shake my head with a glare. The nastiest one I can muster, which probably isn't intimidating as my eyes are hazy with lust, to let him know he better get back to moving.

Bash is looking down at me with amusement while his dark brown eyes are molten, blazing with the same want inside me.

I cry out as Bash slides into my body. Filling, filling, *filling* me until I swear his tip touches my spine. I can't breathe, I can't move, all I can feel is myself clenching around his pulsing dick.

"*Fuck*," Bash breathes as he runs a hand down my body, around to my ass. Giving the cheek a squeeze as he tilts my hips up.

Bash begins to move and my mouth opens but no sound comes out. His hips flex and roll and my body responds instinctually, but Bash grabs my hips. Halting my movements. Holding me still as he pulls out and slams back in. Hard and fast.

As he moves, I find my voice. Shouting his name, praises, and all together incoherencies.

"*Aah, Bash!*" My body bucks as he flicks my clit.

His smile is full of sin and desire.

Bash is playing my body, pulling up to a climax he won't

let me touch. It's right *there* when he stops moving and I growl in protest when he pulls out. "Bash—"

He silences me with a kiss. "I want to take my time with you. I'm not going to rush this."

"So you're going to torture me instead?"

"What an excellent idea, Firecracker."

With those words hanging between us, Bash flips me around so I'm on my stomach and he slides back in. His sweaty chest presses against my back. He raises my arms over my head and holds them together in one hand at the wrists. Bash's other hand skims down my back, gliding over the curve of my—

*Smack!*

I make a noise at the back of my throat as my body bends upward. Looking over my shoulder, I see Bash looking at the reddening spot on my ass. His handprint on full display as his hips roll slowly in shallow thrusts.

My eyes close and I give myself over to the feeling that is building inside of me, chasing after it.

"You don't know what you do to me." Bash's scruff rubs against my neck as he growls in my ear.

"Show me," I say, or I think I do. The words might not travel outside my head.

Bash's answer is a growl and his pace picks up, sinking even further in with each thrust. "*Fuck,*" he rumbles, the word vibrating against my back as I cry out at the blinding sensations that overtake my body.

He moves the hair off the nape of my neck, the cold air kissing the skin before his lips do.

I shiver and he squeezes my bound wrists in one hand. His other wandering hand snakes to the front of my body. His palm brushes and glides over my breasts and down my body until it slides between my folds and flicks my clit.

"*Ahhh.*" My body trembles as my back arches. His fingers start to play and pluck as his hips pound into me from behind. Feeling him in me, on top of me, and hearing his moans of approval and desire are becoming too much.

My arms shake and my legs tingle. The feeling that has been building steadily is about to erupt—

I come with Bash's name on my lips and he's not that far behind me. He tightens his grip as he stiffens, my name rolling off his tongue in the next breath.

We both ride out our waves and Bash kisses up my spine and over my shoulder before he pulls out and walks into the bathroom to discard the condom.

I go in next to cool down my burning face and pee.

After splashing water on my cheeks and forehead, I get a good look in the mirror of what being freshly fucked looks like. My hair is a tangled, sweaty mess. My lips swollen and red, and my skin is peppered with bite marks. My eyes are tired, cloudy, and happy while my limbs and body feel spent.

With a half-assed attempt to smooth down the tangled bird's nest masquerading as my hair, I smile, thinking I could get behind this look.

My body is curled into Bash's side, his hand lazily stroking my shoulder. The sun is rising through his window and for once I don't make myself get up to go in the water. I'm too tired. Too comfy. Too sore.

The floor around the bed is littered with torn foil wrappers. Sleep clocking in at a max of two and a half hours.

"You've made me lazy," I tell Bash.

"I'm on vacation," he reminds me. "I'm allowed to be lazy. You're a college dropout. You should be the one working extra hard."

I twist his nipple and he twists mine in retaliation before biting my shoulder.

"Why aren't you sleeping?" he asks, as he nuzzles his face into the crook of my neck. "Didn't I tire you out? My mind is too lax for your sass right now. I need you to sleep so I can recharge the sass meter."

"I'll go to sleep when you can thoroughly exhaust me." That would have had more of the zing that I wanted it to if I hadn't yawned at the end of the sentence.

"Go back to sleep, Em."

He sounds as tired as I am.

So I do. I sleep with my body pressed against his and his arm around my waist.

Sleeping for a few more hours leaves me sore and starving. Yet I'm too comfy to move from Bash's bed to do anything about it. But after convincing Bash to carry me down the stairs, an easy task to do when naked, we find ourselves in the kitchen trying to cook breakfast.

My stomach is weeping for nourishments.

Bash is wearing nothing but gray sweatpants as he stands over the stovetop scrambling some eggs.

"About your mom—"

I come up behind him, wrapping my arms around his waist, but he pulls away from me, frowning. I frown back.

We didn't talk much about her last night, too busy doing other stuff—sexy stuff—but I know they have a rocky relationship. He's mentioned it before, but I had no idea she was as cold as that phone call.

She makes the ice queen look like the queen of summer.

"Don't, Em." His protest does nothing to stop me. Really, he should know better.

"She sounds like a pleasant woman." My sarcasm is thick, but Bash doesn't smile. His lips don't even twitch.

I want him to smile—he doesn't do it enough. He's out of practice and it looks like broken jagged glass that someone has tried to repair. Except, his cracks can disappear. He can fully heal. The damage isn't permanent.

"She isn't, but that doesn't mean she's not a compassionate person. She has that inside of her somewhere."

A snort fights to come out, but I refuse to let it. I don't like the woman, but she's still his mother. He knows a side that I will never see. A side that loves her child unconditionally.

At least for Bash's sake I hope she has that side. Somewhere within her being.

He tries to end the conversation by whisking the eggs with a fork. His arm is moving vigorously and the sound of the metal hitting the ceramic bowl fills the kitchen.

*Clinkclinkclinkclink.*

"Are you going to tell them where you are?" I ask when he stops and spills the yellowy mess into the hot frying pan. No egg whites for him today. The yolk is the best part. A thought pops into my head. "Why haven't they tracked your phone?"

"My parents aren't tech-savvy and won't spend the money on someone to find me. They just keep hoping if they badger me enough, I'll come home." He sounds tired and not from lack of sleep.

Bash doesn't add more, so I let the conversation drop for now and help him get breakfast ready.

He finishes making the eggs and takes the bacon out of the oven. I butter some toast and stack the slices on a plate. We make our plates in silence, but on Bash's way to the fridge he gives my ass, which is hidden under one of his shirts, a firm pat.

Right over the bite mark he left.

So sweet, my man.

I follow him out onto the porch, the humid air attacking us as we step away from the sweet sanctuary of air conditioning. The humidity clings to my skin in a sticky sheen as I sit down.

"Bash, are you not even going home for Christmas?" I ask after a few minutes of eating in silence. Really, there is only so much silence this girl can take.

We've been steering clear of the Christmas conversation because:

1) We just started dating.
2) He doesn't like to talk about his parents.

Being close to my family, I could never imagine not spending holidays with them. I could never imagine going on vacation and not telling my parents where I am.

Then again, I have been lying to them about surfing for years. So maybe I get it more than I'm willing to admit.

"My plan is to stay here, order Chinese food, and watch movies all day." He tries to hide it, but fails to mask the bleakness. My heart clenches as the eggs in my mouth turn to ash.

An idea that will probably backfire for loads of reasons pops into my head. I shimmy my chair closer to his, sitting next to him. My legs cross as I fold my body into the chair, palms stretched out in front of me. Warning him, silently, to not freak out.

I'm also warning myself not to freak out with what I'm

about to suggest.

He looks calm, curious as he watches me. Meanwhile, my heart is hammering away as if it were in a construction zone. I feel my forehead prickle with beads of sweat. "You know how I'm crazy, right?"

"In a total lack of the actual definition of a crazy person, yes."

"You say the sweetest things to me, babe." Is this me deflecting? Yes, yes it is. Can he hear the radical beat of my heart like I can? 'Cause it feels like it's going to beat out of my chest.

"Emery."

"Right." I take a deep breath, filling my lungs with air. To stall for time, I take another deep breath. "Well, no one should spend Christmas alone. Because it's Christmas and it's about spending time with family, being thankful, and in the case of my family, seeing who can out-drink each other before the ham is served."

The only response I get is a raised eyebrow.

"See where I'm going with this?"

"Maybe." Does he sound cautious? Scared? Why is he so good at hiding his feelings? Or maybe I'm bad at reading people. "But how about you spell it out for me. 'Cause I don't want to be wrong."

"Do you want to be right?" My heart jumps and crashes. He doesn't answer. Just waits. Damn him. "Do you want to spend Christmas with my crazy-ass family?"

He shrugs, giving me a crooked smile—one less broken and a little more full. "Sure."

I look for a sign to see if he's lying. "You're totally fine meeting my parents? My cousin? My relatives?"

"Em, I've already met your parents." Neither of us mention his fanboying over my father. "I see your cousin once a week, at least. I think I can handle meeting your grandparents and whoever else is there."

"You sure it's not too soon? I feel like there is a dating rule about when it comes time to meet the relatives. A timeline of sorts."

"Says the girl that didn't want to go on an actual date," he deadpans.

"Well, you did!"

"We had sex on the first date, too," he points out as he pushes himself up, leaning his elbows on the arm of my chair. "So if we're going by traditional social norms, we're doing shit wrong. Do we have to follow the timeline in someone else's book? Why can't we just do what we want?"

I shrug, not finding the words to answer.

"Yesterday over dinner you told me you wanted to put a lavender stripe in your hair," he says, reminding me how non-traditional I can be.

"Well do you blame me?" I think I'll look really good with a lavender streak in my hair.

"You have the attention span of a squirrel." He laughs. "We'll be fine."

# CHAPTER TWENTY-FOUR

*Bash*

A SENSE OF DÉJÀ VU WASHES OVER ME AS I STARE AT Emery's front door. This time I'm a whole new level of nervous and my sweaty palms are holding a bottle of wine and a case of beer.

What does the last minute guest bring to a Christmas dinner? Booze to make them forget you're the last minute, pity guest.

Everything on the walk up to the house is the same as last time, aside from the slew of cars already around the driveway. The door has a huge dark green wreath with a red plaid bow hanging in the center.

I told Emery that it'd be fine meeting her family and while that's true, there's still a lot of pressure. I really like this girl and I want her family to really like me.

I want them to see something that my parents never did. For them to see more than just a surfer.

Before I can knock, a small, lithe body slips in front of me, blocking the door. She's holding two big bags of presents that seem to outweigh the body holding them. "Hi, Bash!"

Nori is decked the hell out in Christmas attire. Oversized sweater with a crocheted Santa face on it and leggings decorated with reindeer. They look like sweater material—*how is she not dying?* It's a decent eighty-six degrees out right now with a side of hella humid.

Around her neck is a long necklace of flashing Christmas bulbs that are blinking to a silent Christmas tune. To round out her outfit she's wearing gray fuzzy boots.

Has no one told the girl she lives in Florida?

Her smile is blinding and I return it with ease.

"Hey, Nori." I motion toward her bags. "Let me take that for you."

"Thanks." She hands one of them over and I grab it, wrapping the strings around my fingers while I try not to drop the bottle of wine. *Jesus*, the thing is heavier than it looks. "Why aren't you inside?" she asks, looking from the door to me.

Coal. I've come to the conclusion she's gifting everyone coal for Christmas and that is why my fingers are bending backwards in pain.

"I was about to knock when—"

"Bash, if you want to be a part of this family—" I really hope she doesn't say that in front of Emery. Even joking, my girl is likely to spook. "—there's a little rule you should know. We don't knock. Yep, it's true. Emery and I don't know how. We lack manners. Raised by wolves, as our grandparents say." She puts her hand on the doorknob, but doesn't open it. "So as long as you're with us, you don't have to knock either. Rules don't apply from here on out, okay?" She doesn't wait for me to nod before she's pushing the door open. "Come on."

She's a lot more talkative today, I note as I follow her in. Usually, the Nori I've come to know is more subdued, a little sassy like her cousin, but not as talkative. At least not to me.

I figured she was shy, but maybe she's warmed up to me. Or maybe she's not as tired in the middle of the day as she is at night.

"Does anyone know why I found a famous surfer outside digging through your trash?" Nori says by way of announcement as we walk into the kitchen. Her words go unheard as attention is divided elsewhere.

Emery's mom is standing over the stove while Ren hovers by the food placed on the bar. He tries to grab a hotdog wrapped in a puff pastry, but his wife smacks him on the head, shooting him a look. He holds up his hands while leaning in to kiss her. Grinning as he does it.

"Was Ren looking for a snack again?" a tall man asks. "We all know he doesn't have enough food in his actual house."

The new guy has intense features, a smiling face and dark eyes. He has a receding hairline, but the hair he still has is dark, almost black. There's something about him that looks familiar, but I can't put my finger on it.

Ren Lawson—I still can't believe we're in the same room, but I'm trying to contain the fanboy, as Emery likes to call it.

*Be cool, Cleaton, be cool.*

Ren laughs at what the other man says, mumbling something I don't catch. He looks toward his niece and me—standing on the outskirts of the kitchen, before frowning. "Want to tell me why my niece is showing up with my daughter's boyfriend and not her mother?"

Nori walks over, hugging her uncle as he kisses the top of her head. "Two of the nurses scheduled didn't show up, so mom got called in. She sends her love."

Emery's mom pulls away from the stove long enough to hug Nori and say, "I'm just glad you still came, sweetie. You're too busy and push yourself too hard."

"Please tell me you took today off from training at least. I know your coach doesn't work during the holidays," Ren adds.

Nori looks down at her feet, shyness overcoming her, before looking back up with a smile. "Just don't try and stuff me with food. I'm on a new meal plan."

Ren shakes his head. "You're too skinny. Have you been eating the right amount of calories?"

"I am now. My nutritionist made an error and she now has me on the right track."

"You work too hard for a teenager."

"And here I thought everyone hates on Millennials and their lack of work ethic."

"You're not a normal teenager, Nori," Ren reminds her. I feel like an intruder in this conversation, but I have no idea where else to go. So I guess I'll continue to stand awkwardly on the outskirts, holding gifts that aren't from me and the alcohol that is from me. "Not that there's anything wrong with your generation, because there's not. You're training for the Olympics though, and that takes a certain dedication and discipline that even a lot of adults lack."

She shrugs, looking down again.

Em's mom looks up, coming out of her cooking haze long enough to see that I'm also in the kitchen.

"Oh, Bash!" She rushes over to me, apologizing for her spacey head and saying something about the sweet potatoes not cooperating. She pulls me into a hug that I'm not expecting. "We're so glad you're here!"

"Thank you for having me," I tell her sincerely and hold out the wine and beer as best I can.

"Bash, you didn't have to bring anything!" She grins and takes both from me, putting them in the fridge so they can chill.

I smile sheepishly at her, not bothering to tell her I did, and rub the back of my neck. They're the ones taking this misfit in today. They deserve a lot more than alcohol.

The thought of spending Christmas by myself is sadder than I want to admit. Despite my parents lacking warmth, I've always spent Christmas with them and really didn't want to spend it by myself.

"What about you, Bash?" Ren looks at me and my attention snaps to him. Ren fucking Lawson. "Are you taking the holidays off?"

I shake my head. "No, sir." I rub the back of my neck again with my free hand. "I took today off, but that's it. I'm supposed to be on vacation, but I've been pushing myself harder than I have in years."

I don't mention that his daughter is part of the reason for that. She gives me shit when she feels like I'm slacking.

He nods as footsteps come down the stairs. Emery, Brit, and Geer pop up next to me from a staircase I didn't see.

Emery's dressed in a similar way to Nori, similar crochet ugly Christmas sweater, leggings and fuzzy boots. My girl is beaming.

*Seriously, did no one tell these ladies they live in Florida?*

She bounces on her feet to kiss me on the cheek. "Mistletoe!"

I look up and Brit's holding a small plastic piece of holly above my head, her camera dangling around her neck by a thick strap.

"Merry Christmas, babe!" Still standing on her toes, she wraps me in a hug. One I return one-armed because of the presents.

"Merry Christmas, Firecracker," I whisper in her ear, hoping her parents aren't watching.

"Oh!" Nori comes over, taking the bag out of my hand. "I'll go put these under the tree."

Em pulls away, only to grab my hand to bring me further into the kitchen as more people walk in. Open-mouthed, I stare at one of them.

No fucking way.

What kind of Christmas miracle is this?

"Dude." Emery laughs, drawing my attention onto her. "Close your mouth."

She doesn't wait for me to listen before her hand is under my chin, pushing it up.

"Dude," I parrot in a whisper. "Mick Michaelson just walked into your kitchen."

She laughs, not bothering to whisper back. "That's my Uncle Mick."

She turns to everyone, clapping her hands together while I'm still trying to process her words. "Attention guests of the Lawson household! Introductions are to be made!"

Everyone looks at her, all wearing similar expressions of wariness, but Geer's the only one to ask, "How much of that "water" did you drink upstairs?" He makes air quotes around the word "water."

"A hundred percent just water, Jackson, but thank you for your concern." She nods to him. "We might know everyone here, but sweet, little Bash here doesn't."

Never in my life has anyone referred to me as *sweet* or *little*. Maybe someone did when I was a baby, but that doesn't count. And Emery has some personal knowledge of how not little and sweet I actually am.

I pinch her side, a silent promise to remind her of those

things later tonight when we're alone.

She swats my hand away without looking at me.

"So, yeah. Everyone meet Bash. Bash meet everyone." She points to her mom, who waves her spoon at me, telling Emery we've already hugged. "You already know my dad, Ren, because you were drooling over him last time."

I groan, but she's not entirely off. Ren shakes my hand again. "You sure you want to put up with my daughter?"

"Absolutely." I smile down at her. "She makes life fun."

He nods, like he's digging my answer. I still get the feeling he doesn't like me all that much and I don't know if it's because I'm dating his only child or if it's because I'm a surfer, a bad influence since he thinks Emery doesn't surf.

It's probably a combination of both.

I'm going to corrupt his daughter in more ways than one. *Please fucking Lord, don't have mind reading abilities.* I keep my eyes on Ren for a few moments, waiting to see if he does.

His expression doesn't change and my breathing comes easier.

The next person Emery introduces me to is the man that looks vaguely familiar. "That's Jason, Brit and Geer's dad." Ah, that's why.

Jason shakes my hand, squeezing it a little too firmly. "Be careful with my goddaughter."

I nod. Next, Emery introduces me to Brit's mom, April, who, like Em's mom, hugs me. April looks like a mirror into the future for Brit. Dark hair, soft features, and gray eyes.

And then there is only one more person left to introduce. "Mick, meet Bash, who, as you saw, idolizes you like he does Dad."

"You know, you could at least pretend not to notice when I freak out over surf legends casually chilling in your house," I mumble to her.

"Where's the fun in that?"

Mick steps forward, shaking my hand. He's the most chill of the three men. "I saw your last competition. You got talent, kid."

*What?*

"Mick," Emery groans, but there's a light in her eyes. "We want him social for today. We can't have him frozen like this."

My mind can't process anything aside from Mick Michaelson's words replaying over and over in my head.

*You got talent, kid*

*You got talent, kid*

Along with Ren, Mick is one of my huge influences for getting into surfing. One of my big inspirations. I remember watching documentaries on Ren and Mick and Jason—another reason why Jason looks familiar clicks in my head.

They made and sold a few documentaries. The first was of them surfing up the East and West coasts. The second was chasing waves around the world. I grew up watching them.

My bucket list includes surfing up one of the coasts because of their movie and now I'm in a room with all three of them.

Before I can say anything, Emery pulls on my hand, dragging me out of the kitchen, laughing as she says, "We're headed to the patio. Bash needs some non-oldie surfer air to breathe."

No one follows, but the laughs do.

She pulls me down on one of the patio couches. "You're such a dork."

I don't feel like a dork. I feel like a tool. "You know I'm not with you because of who your dad is, right?"

We've talked about it in the past, but after the way I acted around him and her family friends, I want to make sure. I'm a fucking goober around them.

"I know, Bash." She runs her hand down my arm, putting her palm on the top of my hand, linking our fingers together. "If that was even a question in my mind, you wouldn't be here right now."

"Just making sure." I turn my hand over so our palms connect. "If it helps at all, I'm pretty sure your dad hates me."

"He doesn't hate you," she reassures. I don't believe it. "He's protective, there's a difference. He just doesn't know what to make of us."

I wait for her to explain, even though I have an idea as to what she means.

"The morning I came back from our first date—super awkward, by the way, coming home and having your parents know exactly what happened. Ten out of ten would not recommend." She shakes her head. "They told me that they didn't know how they felt about me being with you, my dad more so than mom, but still. It's not even because of your personality, but because of your job. Because you're a surfer, dad thinks you'll be a trigger for me to start my *hobby* again."

Her voice catches and I pull her closer to me, leaning back, and she tucks her legs under her body. It takes her a few moments before she starts speaking again. "A fucking hobby. Like he wasn't talking about me following in his footsteps when I was growing up. I have to tell them, Bash, but I don't want them to think it's because of you."

"You've been surfing a lot longer than you've known me, Em. How many years has it been?"

"My whole life. You saw who was in my kitchen. I live in a

surfing world. My parents just like to pretend I've never been a part of it."

"Why?"

"After everything that happened, I wasn't Emery Lawson, daughter of surf legend, with her own talent for the sport. I was now Emery Lawson, a fragile and damaged girl. They don't see me as a nineteen-year-old. They still see me as the girl who got attacked by sharks and had a panic attack right when she tried to go back in the water after getting discharged from the hospital."

"Em—" She shakes her head, cutting me off.

"That's why I haven't told them, Bash. A part of me believes them. When they stopped believing I could come back from my accident, so did I. I didn't go in the water for a year." She shakes her head, the movement slow and sad. "A huge part of me missed the water so much that I decided it was time to go back. But it's been so long since I've actually trained that even if I want to try and go pro, I don't know if I can. What if it's too late?"

"You won't know that until you try," I tell her. I'm not one for feeding the ego just because. Any professional sport is hard and challenging to achieve, but Emery has a lot of drive; she has the dedication, and the discipline, to go after her dream. She also has connections, which I know she won't use. She's too independent to rely on others. If she's going to earn this, it'll be because of her own merit.

I want her to make it on her own, too. Without my name having any sway like her dad's will.

"Are your Christmases usually this deep?" She wipes under her eyes, as trickles of tears still pool under her lids. "I swear this wasn't what I planned when I invited you over. I just—well, I just had to tell you all that."

"I'm glad you did." I kiss the top of her head softly as my thumbs wipe away the droplets of tears escaping down her cheeks.

She pulls back and wipes away her tears. "Before I turn sappy, I have something to give you."

*Fuck.* I was so nervous leaving my house I forgot her gift on my kitchen counter. *Fuck.* "Don't."

Emery makes a face at my abrupt, hard tone. I explain, "I forgot your present and I don't want you to give me mine until I can give yours to you."

"Who said it was a gift?"

"Well shit."

Emery starts to smile, but her eyes dart over my shoulder. "We're about to have company within the next fifteen seconds."

I follow her line of sight and see Nori, Brit, Geer, and—"Is that Xavier?"

"I didn't invite him," Emery says, but with a smile, she calls out as the door opens, "What are you doing here and where is your sister? I like her face better."

They all walk closer, taking claim to various pieces of patio furniture.

"Too bad for you, she's traveling with her boyfriend." Xavier sits on one of the chairs. "So, I guess you'll have to settle for me."

"What are you doing here?" Emery asks again, still with a steady smile on her face.

Xavier leans down to hug her, which she returns with a tight vigor. When they pull away, he holds out his knuckles to me and we knuckle touch.

"The lovely Anora invited me," he explains and Emery stiffens under my arm. "Your kindhearted cousin took pity on a friend with no family in the tri-county area since his sister decided to go backpacking. I brought *brigadeiro*. So, Merry Christmas. I got you the gift of food and me. You're welcome."

"Just what I always wanted." Brit grins.

"Except with a bow somewhere on you," Emery adds.

"Do you know where you want the bow, Anora?" He wiggles his eyebrows at her.

Nori blushes, shooting him a look.

Emery makes a sound in the back of her throat, like she's choking.

Xavier winks at her. She glares back.

Brit looks like she wants popcorn as she looks between them.

And Geer's on his phone.

"Over your mouth would be lovely." Nori leans back in her chair. "Then you wouldn't call me by my full name. Especially when you know I hate it."

"But then how can I get you to acknowledge me if I don't anger you?"

"Uh, I invited you," Nori reminds him. "Pretty sure we talk the most."

Emery and Brit are watching Nori and Zay like a tennis match, with rapt attention and intense interest.

I don't get it.

"Dude, what the hell is on your phone?" I ask Geer. Every time I see him, he's glued to the device. I'm starting to think it's surgically attached to his hand.

"Porn," Geer deadpans. But none of us can tell if he's serious. His voice is always monotone.

"Ewww," Brit recoils away, even though she's sitting far from him, next to Nori on the couch. "Don't ask him those questions ever again, Bash. There are some things a sister doesn't need to know."

"Just like a brother doesn't want to listen to you having phone sex with Daimon?" Geer shudders, as if reliving the horror.

"We were not having phone sex," Brit protests, a slight blush creeps across her cheeks as her hands white-knuckle her camera. "He was simply calling to wish me a Merry Christmas Eve."

"Since when do you moan Dez's name as a thank you to that?"

"You had phone sex with Dez and didn't tell me?" Emery pulls away, turning her back towards me to face her friend.

"You hate Dez."

"Noooo," Emery protests, dragging out the word. "We're not friends and I hate what he puts you through, but as long as he's what you want, I support you. Only you. Okay, maybe I hate him," she concedes. "I still need to be updated about this, though!"

"What? Like telling me you had sex with Bash this morning when I came over instead of when it happened?" Brit challenges and all of us are watching with rapt attention. Except for Geer, who's tinkering on his phone, probably wanting to cut off his ears right now. "You didn't even send me a snap of that one song after it happened."

"I was a little busy passing out after it happened. Excuse me for being exhausted."

Is it wrong to take some pride in that? Because I totally do.

"Wait," Nori jumps in. "You had sex with Bash? Were you ever going to tell *me*, your cousin?"

"Of course," Emery tells her. "But I know you, and you'd ask for details and I didn't want to tell you all the kinky stuff we did. I want you to forever look at me as the pure, angelic older cousin."

"I've never looked at you like that, cousin."

"Shhh, don't ruin it for me." Emery juts out her lips dramatically, putting her index finger in front of them.

Where's that damn mistletoe now?

Xavier leans forward in his seat, his elbows resting on his thighs. "I don't know, Em. Don't discredit Nori. You don't know what kind of shit she could be into."

"Can you talking about sex and my cousin just not go together?" Emery's body shakes. "It's unnatural."

"Actually," he points out, "It's completely natural. Animalistic, if you will."

"How about we talk about something else?" I suggest. I foresee this conversation ending one of two ways. Either Emery jabs her thumb into Xavier's eye to make him stop talking about Nori. Or Nori melts into her chair from blushing so hard.

For an athlete who is training for the Olympics, she turns shy when the spotlight or topic of discussion revolves around her.

I get Emery's protective side, you just want to wrap Nori up in bubble wrap and keep her in your pocket.

Is that weird or have I been hanging out with Emery for too long and am starting to sound like her?

I thought that wasn't supposed to happen for another few years.

Or maybe that's looking like her.

"Geer," Emery calls, but the surly guy doesn't pick up his head. "Distract me from Xavier's weird flirting with Nori."

"Like how my phone is blowing up with articles of The Return of Lawson's Legacy and the Hotshot Surfer has been found in the Sunshine State?" Geer holds his phone screen out toward us.

Emery and I both freeze and my heartbeat skips. Brit looks panicked, while Nori and Xavier look confused.

"What does that mean?" Nori asks. It might be rhetorical, but I answer.

At least, I think I do. My mouth is moving, words are coming out, but I can barely hear them as I say, "It means my vacation is about to be over and Emery's secret just got shared way before she was ready to tell any of you."

# CHAPTER TWENTY-FIVE

## Emery

THERE'S THIS FEELING OF SUFFOCATION WHEN YOU drown. Your lungs are depleted from lack of oxygen— crushing under the pressure like a soda can and there's this feeling of knowing how to swim, but with limbs that have forgotten movements; there's nothing you can do to stop that feeling of helplessness as the world crumbles around you.

That's how I feel now.

Sitting on my bed I'm staring at a small fleck of chipped paint on the wall, focusing on it so hard my vision goes blurry. My mom leans against my closed door while my dad paces on my carpet. After Geer told us what headlines were appearing and what websites were posting them, none of us moved.

Frozen in the moment, waiting for the bubble to pop and the reality to crash down around us.

Bash and I didn't even touch.

We all just sat there. Waiting.

And the first ones to poke at the bubble were my parents. They had come outside, their focus on me, and told me to follow them upstairs.

All the adults, including my grandparents, who I didn't know had arrived, wouldn't look me in the eye.

My fate was set. Alone, by myself, left to drown.

Bash was the only one that stood with me, looked at me, and started to follow until Dad shot him a look that warned him not to intervene. Bash watched on helplessly as I disappeared into the house.

Part of me wishes Bash hadn't listened—that he had refused, pushing away my parents' wants and sticking by my side. The other part is glad he didn't. Not only for respecting my parents—can't have them hating my boyfriend on top of everything else—but also because this is a moment for the three of us.

One that has been years in the making.

One that continues to simmer as Dad paces along the floor, rutting a path in the fluffy carpet.

He stops, looking at me before shaking his head and resuming his pacing. I nibble on my thumbnail as my heart races. It feels like time has sped up and slowed down at the same time. It feels like I've been sitting in this spot for a while, when really it's only been a few minutes.

I should feel dread, I should feel anxious, but just like with drowning, there comes a point when fighting doesn't help, tiredness sets in, and everything just stops.

I feel numb.

A shield is around me, blocking any emotion.

"Dad." My voice is small when I can't take the silence anymore. Mom looks like she's going to cry. "Say something, please."

My voice begs at the last word.

He stops walking in front of me. "What do you want me to say, Emery? How disappointed I am? How angry I feel?" He shakes his head. "You already know those things. What you want for me to say is that I forgive you. But I can't." My heart sinks, drops to the bottom of my stomach, shattering as it crashes. "Not yet. Not after this shit just dropped."

He tilts his head in thought before asking, "How long has Bash been here?"

He's trying to figure out how long I've been surfing. He thinks it's Bash's fault. And that almost hurts worse than him finding out in the first place. Not only because he's blaming Bash, a completely innocent guy in this, but because he thinks I don't love the sport enough to fight for it.

He thinks that I've been influenced by a guy and not by my desires. Not by my heart.

Maybe I went about it in a passive, deceitful way, but that doesn't take away how much I love the sport. A sport my dad still participates in, occasionally, with Mick and Jason.

I don't call him a hypocrite. As much as I want to, I bite my tongue, locking the words up. Right now, it's easier to let him simmer in his anger.

"Mom?" I look at her, the silent, still one of the two. She hasn't said anything and she looks like if she tries to speak, a sob will break free.

"Emery," is all she says and a lone tear falls. A knife lodges in my chest. "What were you thinking?"

It's not what she really wants to ask; she wants other answers to questions she refuses to speak. She's trying to keep it together; we still have guests downstairs. Guests I don't want leaving. When they do, the real drama will start. The words will fly and the hurt will be unleashed.

At least from Mom.

Dad looks ready to explode at this moment.

"I tried to stop." That's not what they want to hear. "I didn't go back in the water for a year after the attack. But I missed it. I missed it so much. We always used to joke about how the Lawson's were born with water in our veins and I believed it during that year, but I felt off-balanced. So I went back. I didn't tell anyone. No one knew. For years, I wanted to tell you, but I didn't want for this—" I gesture to the three of us "—to happen. I know you're both pissed, but I'm almost twenty. I can do what I want. And I want to surf."

"You're almost twenty," my dad sneers as he parrots my words. "So that makes you an adult? Not in this house. You've never worked a day in your life. You live off a small stipend from your trust fund. You don't understand what it's like to be an adult. You're in college, but you only have a small taste of what the real world is really like. You don't know what it was like for us to watch our daughter go through that and see you in the hospital after."

"I do know, Dad! I was the one in that hospital bed. I was living your nightmare. But you tried to keep me from my dream. You tried to lock me up in a box to avoid the ocean. You didn't care that it was killing me to not be in the water. Have you even asked me what I want to do for a career?" I don't give him time to answer. "You haven't. Not once have you asked me. You might be hurt that I lied to you for years, but I'm hurt that my future stopped existing for you after what happened."

I have tears in my eyes, collecting on the edges, overflowing and waiting to spill over.

He doesn't say anything. He shakes his head one last time, driving the knife in me deeper, hitting its final target, before he walks out of my room with my mother right behind him.

It isn't until I hear their retreating steps down the hallway that I fall on my side, curling into a ball on my mattress, letting the tears break free.

I sob until I see nothing.

At some point Brit comes into my room and pulls my head onto her lap. She runs her hand over my hair as I continue to cry these deep, gut-wrenching sobs. She doesn't say anything.

I cry until I pass out.

You have ten minutes to say hi to everyone at the party before we go back to my place.

I laugh at Bash's text on my phone. It's been six days since we've seen each other. Since Christmas, my parents haven't let me leave the house unsupervised.

While my parents and I have barely talked since, Bash and I have been texting constantly. Which, surprisingly, isn't as annoying as I always thought it was.

You have five minutes to get me out of there before I jump you.

Promises, promises, Firecracker.

He thinks I'm kidding, but he's not the only one that misses the other. And as much as I want all the time alone with him, I make myself text him:

We have to stay for a while. Like an hour. After that, I'm all yours.

It's a miracle that I'm even going to this party to begin with. Nori was able to convince my parents when she brought me gifts from the outside world, i.e. donuts and iced coffee, two days ago.

Bless.

My parents were so shocked that Nori—the one in bed by 8:30 if I don't force her to stay out longer—is attending a bonfire on the beach. And staying until midnight.

My aunt is working at the hospital again and my parents are going out, so they told me I'm allowed to go. Not to have fun, mind you, but to "watch" Nori. Like she's a child.

But hey, I get to go out and see my friends and boyfriend for the night. I only waited about one second after they said it before I agreed to their terms.

*Freeeeeeeeedom!* rang through my head and I had to physically stop myself from jumping and dancing on the kitchen counter.

My parents gave me a look, seeing into my very being, seeing the plan in my head, and looked ready to shut it down until Nori stepped in. Again, she was able to sway my parents, deflecting their attention from their problem child. They even agreed to let me spend the night at her house since she'd be home alone.

When my parents weren't looking, Nori shot me a look and I could have squished her. She gave me the excuse I needed to spend New Year's with Bash and not have to rush our time together.

Really, I should have gotten her more gifts for Christmas.

My sweet, young cousin is a devious little mastermind.

I've taught her well.

My parents haven't officially said it, but it's pretty damn clear I'm grounded. Under house arrest. I feel like I'm back in high school, standing two feet tall on the ground, being protected from my parents' worries.

I tried to play the "I'm an adult" card again, the day after

Christmas, which was a big mistake. They told me, after they had *slightly* calmed down, that they were punishing me for the years I lied to them as a "child" and they would possibly continue to do so until I leave for college in a week.

Yeah, still haven't told them about *that* yet, either.

When did my life become such a mess that I can't even be honest with my parents? All the whys in the world could be asked and the answer would still be the same.

It all started with my shark attack, and that's something unchangeable. Set in stone and sealed in the history of my life. I fucked up by lying for years.

I should have talked to them about surfing instead of spending years going behind their backs.

And for what?

As much as I practice, go out every day, I'm no better than when I was fifteen.

Hindsight really is a bitch.

"You're frowning. Why aren't you happy?" Nori asks when she walks out of my bathroom and sees me sitting on my bed. "I got you out of house arrest for a night."

She plops down next to me.

"I'm fine. Just thinking," I tell her. "Ya know, Bash told me a few days ago that reporters are camped outside the rental he's staying at and that he had to get a bodyguard to keep them off the lawn."

"What? Is he okay?" She looks concerned and I nod. "That seems a little extreme, right? Surfers don't usually get that kind of press. At least, that's what it seems like to me."

"They do when they're in one of those articles for sexiest athletes of the year. And then bachelor of the season or something." I sigh. "Why couldn't he be universally unattractive?"

Nori doesn't respond, not buying what I'm saying. It's all

true, though. There really were swarms of reporters trying to get the story about why he left and what he was doing with me, or more specifically, "Ren Lawson's daughter," which is how the media refers to me.

Can't say if I prefer that over "Surfer Princess." Both are totally degrading—I'm not even worthy of my actual name.

Nori knows I'm stalling, waiting until I'm ready.

It takes me a few minutes to get there. "My parents still don't know about me dropping out," I tell her. "They've always talked about how important higher education is, which I totally agree with, if you're the right person. But how do I tell them that I'm not meant for a classroom? My mom's a fucking scientist. I've never done great in school, though. My teachers in high school always said how I was smart, but lacked the focus when it came to assignments. Did I tell you how I had to leave one of my classes because I felt like I was suffocating? The room had no windows." I shudder, remembering the awful aftershave of the professor in that small, rancid room.

"Tell them you're not leaving forever, just shutting the door for now. Do you ever plan on going back?" Nori's an overachiever. On top of being in the top ten percent of her class, she's going to graduate with her AA degree before she gets her high school diploma. All of that on top of her intense diving schedule.

I shrug. "I don't even have a major." No one knows that. Not even Brit. Brit's known what she's wanted to major in since she first held a camera. Photography calls to her like the sea does to me. "They don't offer surfing as a respectable degree track."

Nori laughs, but it sounds sad. She knows I struggled when I first moved up to school. The first week in the dorm freshman year I had two panic attacks. I spent a year and half at a college I hated when I finally decided I was done.

My phone beeps, a text message from Bash asking where we are.

Taking a deep breath, I look at my cousin with a smile, ready to go.

New year, fresh start.

# CHAPTER TWENTY-SIX

## Emery

"TO THE NEW YEAR AND NEW ADVENTURES!" XAVIER shouts to the crowd. He's standing on a log near the bonfire, his blue plastic cup raised to the starry sky. Everyone cheers to his toast.

We have thirty minutes until midnight, but my sweet friend is already thoroughly drunk and isn't waiting for time to catch up with him.

He's surround by people and I can't help watching him with a grin. A drunk Xavier is my favorite Xavier.

Bash hands me a beer before wrapping his arms around my waist from behind. As he presses a kiss to my neck, Dez coughs. I send him a glare and Bash digs his fingers into my skin.

Our friends have been watching us since I got here, making sure we don't duck out too soon. It might have something to do with me jumping on Bash and planting a kiss on him, that caused catcalls and cheers, as soon as I got close to him. Brit and Xavier pulled us apart after that.

Friends over fucking and all that, Brit had said earlier.

I just really missed him, and instead of letting that attachment scare me, I'm embracing it.

Nori is standing awkwardly next to us, one arm wrapped around her stomach, holding her opposite elbow.

"You okay?" She's been quiet all night, looking as far out of her skin as a person can be.

She startles before looking over. "Yeah, I'm fine."

I squint at her, trying to see inside her mind. She's not fine, but Nori won't talk about things she doesn't want to, even if I try to coax them out of her.

"Do you want a drink?"

"I have that." She points to her feet where an unopened water bottle chills in the sand.

I sigh. It's New Year's Eve and my cousin can't even spoil herself with a soda.

Brit is on the other side of the fire, flirting with some guy that came with one of the dudes we went to high school with, his name I've long forgotten. But what isn't forgotten is how Dez is glaring at them from Bash's side.

His eyes have been glued on them since the forgotten one came and introduced himself to Brit, coaxing her over to join their little group for a while.

She walked away with a smile on her face while Dez's face collapsed into a surly expression that not even a happy drunk buzz has been able to shake.

I fight the urge to smack him on the head, refraining from telling him he shouldn't have been such a fuckboy.

Tonight I'm exuding self-control. With the banes of my existence, with me groping my boyfriend.

Movement in the corner of my eye has me turning my head to see Xavier stumbling over with glassy eyes and flushed cheeks. His grin has me laughing. Nori frowns. She's been watching him with concern for a good part of the night.

"Shotgun!" Xavier shouts, earning a few stares from the people around us.

"What?" Dez tears his eyes away from Brit and her flirting to give Zay a look. "No one is driving anywhere, dude."

"Shotgun," he repeats, ignoring what Dez says. "Let's shotgun beers."

Before any of us can answer, Xavier is walking to one of the coolers and collecting the goods.

I scrunch my face, mumbling to Bash, "I can't shotgun beer."

"Scared you'll come in last?" he teases and I pull away from him. I'm about to tell him where he can shove that sentence when Xavier shoves a can in my face. I jerk back, taking it from him as he finishes passing out the chilled cans to our group.

I groan at my own can. Xavier fucking grabbed the tall-boys. I'm going to die.

Dez pulls out a pocketknife, puncturing a hole in his can before handing it off to me. I make another face, taking it between the tips of my pinched fingers.

"I don't have any diseases. Jesus, Emery." He shakes his head.

"When was the last time you got tested?" I ask him, eyeing the knife.

Bash chokes on a laugh.

Dez flips me off and I grin before noticing my cousin is beer-less.

"You don't want one, Nori?" I ask her, even though she's

already shot me down. She looks sad and uncomfortable as her eyes are trained on her toes, her big one drawing in the sand.

Xavier is already in motion, handing her a can when she shakes her head, saying, "I'll time ya."

"You don't want to do it?" Zay asks, not accepting her answer.

"I can't stomach beer," Nori says, not mentioning that she's not a drinker. Very rarely will she drink. If ever. The last time was probably at a family wedding two years ago when they served champagne for the toasts. I always offer, though. "Can't stomach the hops, it makes me sick in the morning."

Xavier doesn't look ready to accept her answer, staring at her, as his mind searches for the right words to persuade her.

He doesn't register the finality of her tone. She's not doing it. A part of me wonders if she only came here tonight for me and a stab of guilt settles in my stomach.

Nori looks at me, wanting me to throw her a life raft or something to save her from the attention. So I do what I must.

I jab the knife into the can, some beer spilling onto my hand. They all look at me and I see Nori relax, slightly.

I try to give the knife to Bash, but he already used his car keys and is ready to go.

"Dude, you're about to lose," Bash tells Xavier, who hasn't even prepped his tallboy.

Nori gets her phone out, readying the timer, as we wait for Xavier to get on it. When the four of us are all ready, standing shoulder to shoulder in a line, Nori yells, "Drink!" and taps a button on the screen.

A crescendo of cans opening fill the air around us as I tilt my head back, chugging the beer. The liquid flows into my mouth, going down so fast I don't even taste it. For the first two seconds it's going smoothly, until my throat closes and I can't breathe.

Without even downing half the can, I throw it on the ground, and crouch over with my elbows digging into my thighs and hands holding back my hair as I cough at the sand.

The three dudes all finish around the same time. Blink and you might have missed the winner, but Bash crushes his can first, wiping his mouth with the back of his hand. I glare at all of them.

Nori calls time.

Four seconds flat for Bash.

I lost and that's what pisses me off more.

Not because I convinced myself I was choking.

He whoops and moves to hug me when I step away. He grins. "Don't be such a sore loser, babe."

"Don't be such an obnoxious winner, *babe.*" I cross my arms over my chest, mumbling, "I told you I didn't want to play."

"What was that?" Bash turns his ear toward me. "That sounds like a sore loser complaint."

I take a step toward him, hands balled in fists, when Nori says, "She doesn't do well with swallowing."

The glare is wiped away as my mouth drops open. Equal parts anger and shock show on my face at my cousin's words. I mean, *what the hell?*

Xavier dissolves into laughter and has to bend over as he clutches his stomach. Dez laughs, more composed than Xavier, but laughing nonetheless as he clasps Bash on the shoulder. "Bro."

His words shake with humor.

Bash's mouth mimics mine, hanging open at Nori's words. Okay, so maybe my anger at him has receded slightly.

He recovers more quickly than I do and says, "She didn't have a problem the other night."

His words are thick with meaning and he looks away from Nori to find me smiling smugly at him. He gives me one back. A secret memory that runs through both our heads.

Nori finally understands the impact of her words. Her face rapidly turns red, as she sputters to recover. "That's not what I meant! I just mean she can't swallow pills or chug water because she has herself convinced she will choke."

Oh, great. Since the hospital, pills are just something I can't do. Thank you so much for that, Nori. That sobers up all the men.

"Dude," Dez says.

Xavier is staring at my stomach.

Bash has gone white.

Idiots. All of them. I roll my eyes. "I get the birth control shot, okay guys?" My hand runs down the light sweater I'm wearing. "No little surfers are currently growing inside of me."

As one, all three sigh. I roll my eyes. As a unit, the three of them are ridiculous. I'm about to tell them that when a scream, distinctly sounding like my best friend, directs our attention to the other side of the fire.

The guy she went over to talk to has her thrown over his shoulder and she's laughing hard. One of his hands is resting on her butt. I relax when I see she's having fun, but next to me Dez shouts, "HEY!"

Everyone near us turns to look over, but Dez has on his tunnel vision goggles. And they are focused on the scene before him.

Brit picks up her head to stare at Dez as he stalks toward them. She's shaking her head, silently begging him not to come over, not to ruin her night. Her voiceless pleas go ignored.

I shuffle to Bash's side, slipping my arm around his waist. "Should we stop him?"

"Nah," He constricts his arm around my shoulders, pulling me closer to him. "They need this."

"Brit doesn't need Dez disrupting her happiness."

"No, but she needs to yell at him. She needs to let her hurt out. Making him jealous isn't going to get her anywhere."

Hmph.

"I'm still mad at you."

"We really need to work on your losing face."

"It's not that I lost." Even though it is. But there's a bigger part to it. "It's because I lost to a bunch of guys. I feel like I let my gender down."

He squeezes my shoulder. "You didn't let down your gender. I've been beat by a bunch of girls at drinking games. You just need to find the one you dominate at."

"It's quarters." I did learn some things at college. "And I don't think shotgunning a beer is a drinking game."

Bash shrugs as we hear Brit scream, "What the *fuck* is wrong with you?"

She's in Dez's face now and the guy from earlier is standing off to the side. He watches her verbally spar with someone else and doesn't even look all that interested or concerned. Asshole.

Dez, on the other hand, looks like he's ready to explode. "What the fuck is your problem? You want my attention, come to me, not some fucking preppy douche!"

I take in the other guy's attire and can confirm he is dressed in a preppy way. White button down, pink shorts stopping above the knee, and boat shoes.

On the beach. He's wearing boat shoes on the beach.

Bash is barefoot. The proper foot attire for the beach.

"Maybe I like him. Did you think of that, Dez?" Brit stands on her toes, she is also barefoot, and is now eye level to Dez's nose. "Not everything is about you."

"It is when it concerns you."

"You're not my keeper! You shouldn't care what I do."

"Yeah, well I fucking do!" he screams, his voice cracking at the end. Silence follows. Brit blinks and Dez takes a deep breath. "I know you don't want me to, but I fucking do. I care, Brittany. I care so fucking much."

Brit blinks a few times and my heart catches at her full name.

She shakes her head at him, mouthing something I don't catch before she's sprinting down the beach. Dez goes after her, closing the distance between them. I pull away from Bash, ready to chase after her, after Dez, but Bash stops me. "They need to do this, Em," he reminds me and I nod, allowing him to pull me back into his embrace. He pulls me in front of him, locking both arms around my neck, his stance wide.

Nori is shaking her head at Xavier, who is sitting on the ground against her legs. "C'mon. Let's get you home." She rocks on her feet, knocking her knees into his back. He mumbles something incoherent.

"You're not taking him home," I tell her. I sound like a parent and I hate it. But it's Nori. Nori, who's like my little sister and who I have to protect from the world. My precious baby.

"Yes, I am," Nori says. "No one else is good enough to drive and he can't stay on the beach all night."

Her words make sense, so much sense I find myself nodding in agreement, not even attempting to persuade her to go in a different direction. I don't have the want to try otherwise. My time is limited and I have to make the most of it. Feeling iffy about Nori and Xavier's friendship is not how I want to spend my freedom.

I roll my head onto Bash's chest, looking up at him. "I think I'm drunk."

His chuckling chest vibrates my body.

"Not too drunk," his voice is in my ear. As soft as silk and as deep as the ocean. I shiver against him when he continues. "I have plans for us."

"Want to get started on those plans now?" It's like fifteen minutes until midnight.

He grabs ahold of my hips, holding them still as he rolls his against me and I get a good sense of how ready he is. My mouth goes dry as a tightness settles between my legs.

"Are you good if we take off?" I ask my cousin, my gaze jumping from her to Xavier.

She waves me away, rolling her eyes. "This was my idea, remember? Now go."

Bash is leading me away from them and down the beach before Nori can finish speaking.

Bash presses me against the side of his truck when we get to his house, kissing me with lips that taste like beer and gelatin shots. I'm getting drunk on his touch as his hands grip my thighs and my legs wrap around his waist.

He's kissing me like it's the last time. He always kisses me like it's our last time. I don't want to think about why, I just return with the same vigor. Enjoying the taste of freedom for the night as my boyfriend works his hands under my shirt and creeps the fabric farther up my body until he pulls away and my shirt flies off.

My lacey black bralette follows and I'm left wearing

nothing from the waist up as Bash presses me against the side of his truck.

My pulse races as I feel the cool air caress my skin. My face heats with excitement. Wherever Bash is taking this, I'm following. No matter the adventure, I think I'll always follow him.

# CHAPTER TWENTY-SEVEN

*Bash*

I CAN COUNT THE NUMBER OF TIMES I'VE SEEN EMERY BLUSH on one hand, including tonight. Her wide eyes look around us as she moves her arms to cover herself. I grab her wrists, pinning them to her sides. Leaving her exposed for me to bend down and flick one of her puckered nipples with my tongue.

"Sebastian!" she hisses and I smile into her skin. *Oooo,* I'm in trouble. "What about reporters?"

*Shit.* I forgot. I've become so used to the freedom of being here, it's hard remembering that the peace has been disturbed. I haven't seen any today or yesterday, the story of where I am, has hopefully run its course.

I wind my arms around Emery's back, pressing her as close to my chest as our bodies allow. I start walking us toward the direction of the house, but as my feet move, my brain coaxes. Veering off toward the left, Emery gives me a look as I take us toward the gated backyard.

"That's not the direction of your room," she points out as the gate clicks shut behind us.

"It's not." I lean my neck back to get a better look at her face. "Do you trust me?"

"Yeah?" It sounds like a question. "Should I not? What are you thinking?"

Most of the yard isn't fenced in, but leading back to my pool and the path out to the beach, it's lined with trees and bushes, creating more privacy out here than in the front yard. Perfect for what's been churning in my head. On replay.

I set Emery down and she eyes my shirt-clad chest while crossing her arms, hiding her perky breasts from me. I frown and she smirks. "I don't think it's fair that only one of us is shirtless."

Without looking away from her smirking lips, I reach behind me, fisting at my shirt and pulling it off. I toss it to the side, aiming it a little too far, and hear the soggy sound of the fabric smacking into the water.

Internally, I shrug; it's just as well. Now neither of us can cover back up since I left Emery's shirt in my truck bed.

My fingers slip into the belt loop of Emery's jeans and reel her into me. She comes willingly, wearing the look she gets when she's down for whatever.

Behind me, I hear the fireworks going off, signifying the New Year. My hands move from Emery's belt loops to undo her pants. She holds onto my shoulders as I roll the tight denim and lace fabric of her thong off her body, sand flaking off her ankles and feet as I pull the jeans completely off.

My clothes quickly follow and I'm picking Emery back up, tossing her over my shoulder. She laughs as her hands go to my ass, slapping both cheeks in a silent order to put her down. Her laugh quickly turns into screams as I comply with her demand, tossing her into my pool. I jump in right behind her.

As my head is breaking the water's surface, I'm being pushed back down by a set of hands on top of my head. I open my eyes and the water distorts and stings my vision as I grab Emery's waist, sinking us both down to the bottom.

Emery wiggles around until she breaks free, planting her foot on my chest, and pushes herself back to the surface. Tiny bubbles follow her. She splashes me with water once my head pops up a few paces from her.

"Happy New Year, babe." My grin lures Emery closer to me until she's wrapping her arms around my neck.

"I thought we were going to celebrate in a different way." To further her point, her thigh brushes against my dick.

Emery wraps her legs around my waist and my throbbing erection rubs against her. I swear as I grit my teeth to say, "I wanted to try something."

"You've never skinny dipped before?" The sass shines through her words. "Poor you. Your twenty-two years sound so sad."

"Hush, you. I was just trying to get the sand off of you so it didn't wind up in my ass crack."

I slide my hand down until I cup her, my middle finger teasing her folds. She shudders a breath. "You have my attention."

"Good." I kiss her hard and quick, swimming us to the steps. Keeping her wrapped around me, I stand up. Water races down our bodies as I walk us to where I've wanted us to end up all night.

My outdoor shower.

Emery raises a brow as I push her against the wall, but there's excitement lighting her eyes as I turn on the water and kiss her. My body grinds against hers as it rains between us.

Our kisses mix with the water.

Her hands roam my back, nails digging in every time my erection rubs against her entrance. She arches into me as she tries to pull us closer. I press her harder into the wall as one of my hands moves to grip the base of my shaft and circle her clit with the head.

"Bash," she breathes and there's never been a better sound.

"Tell me what you want, babe." I grin a wicked grin as her heels dig into my ass.

"You know what I want," she whines and I stand corrected. Emery frustrated is my favorite sound.

I continue my ministrations and Emery lets out a small sound, soft and wanting. "Damn you, Cleaton." Her frustration is growing and I grin, loving every word. "If you don't get inside me in five seconds I am going to—"

Not daring to find out where her sentence is heading, I kiss her hard again and am about to give her what we both want, when I freeze.

*Fuck. Shit. Fucking shit. Nononono.*

"What's wrong?" Emery asks, her eyes searching my face. "Why did you stop? Bash?"

"Condoms."

"We don't need one."

I blink. And blink some more. "Is this my Christmas gift?"

Emery laughs, actually laughs. Unbelievable. "No, you'll get that after you give me a few orgasms."

"Emery." Now is not the time for her humor. "Are you serious?"

Her face is clear and doubt-free when she nods. "I'm on the shot, remember? And it's only for right now. After this shower we're using them again."

I nod along, agreeing to all the words she's saying, and I waste no time as I slide in, groaning at the warmth and tightness that engulfs me. My body shudders and I've never felt anything as good as going bare. I push in until all of me is inside her. Filling her.

God, we both have labored breaths and erratic beating hearts. If it wasn't for the shower we're under, our bodies would be coated with sweat.

For several moments, I don't move. I soak up this feeling. Nothing has ever felt better. And it's not just the lack of latex, but because I'm doing this with Emery.

Emery, who is growing more impatient with every passing heartbeat. She begins to roll her hips, moving against me, riding me like she owns me.

And she does. She fucking owns me.

"Fuck, Emery," I growl, squeezing her hips.

I let her set the pace, moving with her, until she pulls me in and tangles her tongue with mine. I grunt, pulling her higher, taking her from a new angle. Her breath hitches and her hips buck up.

Taking both of her arms, I raise them above her head until she grabs onto the showerhead. "Don't let go. You do and I stop." My voice isn't my own. It's too deep and heavy.

Emery nods as her body stretches and I tilt her hips. Her noises of approval spur me on. There's no time for talking as I drive into her and my tongue chases the water falling onto her body.

She screams as I thumb her clit and I feel her body loosen, her hands slipping. I cease moving. I smack her ass for disobeying.

Emery makes a sound of protest, tightening her grip, and

once she's back in position I begin to move again. Thrusting faster and rougher, all sense of rhythm lost as I bring us closer and closer to the edge. Not stopping until we both spill over, our names on each other's lips. I pull out and shoot my load on her stomach, the water washing it away.

I kiss Emery's forehead as more fireworks begin to shoot off from behind me. Exploding and expanding in the night sky. Some people are getting drunk, partying into a new beginning, but as I turn off the water and hold Emery close, I know that my New Year started off the way it was meant to.

With Emery screaming my name.

Emery walks out the back door and onto the patio, a towel wrapped around her shoulders and my phone hanging from her fingertips.

I finish running my towel through my hair and give her a look.

She's supposed to be inside, sleeping. Like she said she would be.

"Your mom has called ten times within five minutes, Bash." She walks closer, pressing her body against mine. Under the towel, her naked body teases me.

I feel hungover and it's because of her.

So far, the New Year has been treating me pretty damn good. Emery and I have barely slept, rotating between sex and surfing—her parents think she's staying at Nori's until noon and I'm trying to not waste any time. And none of that time revolves around my mother.

Especially when my girlfriend is naked and I only have a towel wrapped around my waist.

"I don't want to talk to her." I bring my mouth to hers; each word brushes our lips together. I take the phone from her, putting it on the railing behind me, and move my hands to her body, slipping into the towel and cupping her sex. "I want to keep doing what we've been doing."

She arches into me, her eyes going glassy. "You just don't want me to walk." She moans and I chase it with my tongue.

"'Course, you won't be able to leave then." I run a finger between her folds.

"That sounds very kidnapper-esque." Her voice is breathy and choppy, coming out in gasps.

My mouth moves over her throat, following the path to her ear. Sucking the lobe between my teeth, I tug. Through the fog of lust, I'm barely able to register the sound of my phone going off.

I'm apparently doing a shit job with Em because she pushes away and reaches around me to grab the phone. She shoves it into my bare chest.

"Talk to her."

"I'd rather be doing something else." The phone stops ringing, only to start ringing again when I pull her back into me.

"She's going to keep calling until you answer," she reminds me.

"It's going to be a shit conversation." I hug her to my body. I've been ignoring their calls since Christmas, since they found out where I am.

The source of the photo hasn't been revealed and I've been too distracted by other shit to hire a P.I. or hacker or whoever's job it is to find answers to this shit.

I'm actually surprised my parents haven't rolled into town. It's been a whole week. The only person I've talked to from California since then has been my sister.

Rachel was the only one to check on how I'm handling everything.

Emery kisses my chest. "I'll be here when it's over. You're not alone anymore, Bash. You've got me. And I'm pretty annoying once I get attached to someone. Besides, I haven't had all my sexual demands satisfied by you yet."

I groan and my fucking phone rings again. "We'll get back to that after this call." I bring the phone to my ear. "Mother."

The greeting is forced and Emery can feel how tense I am. She squeezes my hand and walks me toward one of the deck chairs.

I pull her onto my lap as I sit. My free hand rests on her thigh, the one with the scars. She's grown more comfortable with me touching the sensitive area and she doesn't flinch when our skin makes contact.

She still wears her wetsuit out in the water and jeans or long skirts when going out, but she has to do this at her own pace. When she's ready to show her scars, I'll be here for her.

The heat and weight of her body acts as my anchor, the balm to keep me calm through this conversation.

No doubt the same fucking conversation I've been having with my mother since I came out here.

I make sure the towel is covering all of her distracting parts. I have to keep my focus for this talk. I could also use a shot of whiskey, but it's not even nine in the morning and I refuse to move.

"Sebastian." The icy tone of my mother's voice has not changed even though the year has. "It's time to stop being a child. You've proven your point and have had more than enough fun over there." I don't let the slight dig at Emery get to me. She's looking for a fight I refuse to give. "Isn't this temper tantrum of yours over? You've dragged it out long enough."

I repress a sigh, attempting to bite my tongue. I will not give her what she is hoping for. "Happy New Year to you too, Mom."

Not one for holidays, she only called me on Christmas because of the picture that was going around the tabloids.

Emery shakes her head, not having the highest opinion of my mom. Not that I blame her after the verbal lashing she went through the first and only time she'd spoken to the woman who birthed me.

Emery can't wrap her head around the coldness that I grew up with, not when her family is so warm and loving.

Maybe that's why I fell in love with surfing. The heat from the sun warmed the coldness I got from being at home.

"I'm twenty-two," I say into the phone. My hand is clutched around it so tight, the skin around my knuckles is white. "I make my own choices." The words are wasted; trying to remind her is pointless.

"You have surf competitions coming up." As if I don't know that.

My next one is in two months, in March. In Hawaii. It's crazy to think that at twenty-two, I'm capable of remembering shit without my parents there to remind me. "And you have that meet and greet you promised to attend." The meet and greet that was taking place before said competition in March.

She presses on, not waiting for my comments. "Your father and I get it. Your point has been proven."

"I'm not trying to prove anything. You still think I've been doing all of this for attention when all I've ever wanted is a break." *I've wanted to breathe.* "Not everything I do is about you. It probably shocks you to hear that, I'm sure, but very little of my decision-making revolves around you and Dad. I'm my own person and not some drone for you to control."

I don't look at Emery, even though I can feel her stare burning the side of my face. I keep my eyes on the ocean, on the waves crashing onto shore, and continue to run my hand up and down her thigh, tracing unidentifiable patterns along her leg. "I'll put some money into your accounts, since I know that's your main objective." In her mind, I'm easier to control in California. Where I can't say no to her face. "And as far as I'm concerned, I am home."

Emery tenses at my words.

*Shit.*

I hang up, cutting off my mother's retort, and turn Emery's body around to straddle me.

Her eyes have gone wide, her body frozen. She doesn't even blink.

My beautiful, loud, and exuberant girl who will say the dirtiest and crudest things in a crowd of people without a twinge of embarrassment, gets freaked out with intimacy.

Not so much the physical form; she's been more open about me seeing her physical scars. It's emotional intimacy that triggers her flight instincts.

The kind where she gets attached and invested and winds up broken and alone. I've tried to soothe those fears away, that I'm not going to hurt her, but words to Emery are empty and actions are where her truths are.

"Hey," I say softly, stroking my thumb along her cheek. "Come back to me."

"You said you're home." Her voice doesn't hold the panic that reflects in her eyes.

"I did." I grab her waist, holding her in place, to stop her retreat before it begins. "Don't get freaked out by this. I didn't say it because of you, Em." Some people would get offended by that statement, but Emery slowly relaxes into me.

She's so independent and so used to being on her own that the idea of someone tying themselves to her is practically a nightmare. She still hasn't figured out that I'm as much of a realist as she is. She's actually the one that has more aspirations in her dreams than I do. We've barely begun to get to know each other, so I go on to explain.

"I've lived in California my entire life; the only travel I've done is for surfing. I've never gone anywhere for me. Never done something purely selfish. I've wanted a change for a while. To go on a new adventure. I picked Florida because of the beaches and it was on the opposite side of the country. So why not have it be here? I have this cheesy as hell bucket list I made when I was fifteen that I want to complete before I'm twenty-five. I'm also closer to my grandparents." They live in Georgia. They were the ones to show me and Rachel warmth and love growing up. I miss spending a few weeks of my summers as a kid with them on Jekyll Island.

"You're here, yes, but so is Dez." She makes a face and I chuckle. "You don't have to like him, but he is the realest friend I've had. So, don't think I'm staying just for you. I'm staying for me." She relaxes more.

"How long have you thought about this?"

"The idea has been in the back of my mind since I moved out here. Testing the waters and shit. But I don't want to leave now that I'm here. I want to see what the East Coast can offer me. Aside from your orgasms."

"My boyfriend, the romantic."

"I'm the perfect amount of romantic for you," I reminder her, tweaking her nipple as I move in to kiss her, my tongue sliding against hers for a moment before pulling away. "I'm happier here, healthier." So much healthier. "If you should be freaked out about anything, it's by how much you've helped me reconnect with surfing."

"I'll never be freaked over that. That's how we bonded."

"And thank God for that." I stand up, keeping her legs wrapped around me, and walk into the living room. "Now let's go see how well we've bonded before you go talk to your parents."

# CHAPTER TWENTY-EIGHT

## Emery

'M SITTING AT THE KITCHEN BAR WITH THREE CUPS OF coffee in front of me as I wait for my parents to come downstairs.

Bash dropped me off about twenty minutes ago, wishing me luck before he drove back home. He didn't wait around to see if I'd ask him to stay. Just like on Christmas, he knows this is something I need to do alone and knowing he supports me makes facing Mom and Dad a little easier.

I've been actively avoiding my parents since Christmas, only talking to them when necessary. Like when Nori was here and convinced them to let me go out.

No one has ever given me an award for being mature.

They're so shocked to see me as they come down the stairs, they pause at the base of them.

"I'm ready to talk if you are."

They share a look before walking toward me and accepting

the peace offering of coffee that I've made for them.

Coffee holds magic in this household.

After letting them take a couple of sips, I begin. "First, I want to say that I never did this to intentionally hurt you or spite you."

My parents are watching me intently, letting my words fill the kitchen. They stand across from me and I shift around in my seat.

"And I didn't realize how affected you two were over this until I saw your reactions. We haven't talked about it since that year." It's always been a topic we've slid under the rug, brushed by, and stepped around, but never picked up.

And it's not from being shameful. It's from fear. We've all been living, pretending to be fine, that what happened never changed our lives. We've tried to live the same when everything around us is different, when the secrets become the realities we choose to hide.

"Do you know I've never shown anyone my scars since then?" I don't mention showing them to Bash recently, it's probably better they don't know. Or the context in which he's been seeing them. "I haven't worn shorts—haven't bought shorts in years. I never got to play with the crop top trend. I've practically lived in a wetsuit."

"Em, we've noticed, but when we used to bring it up, you'd brush us off. Get angry and yell that you were fine or wanted to be left alone," Mom reminds me, gently.

That entire year I didn't surf, I was a different person. A changed person. Someone who was learning how to become whole again after losing the one constant in their life.

"Yeah, but after that year you just stopped talking about it. We still haven't talked about it." We've yelled about it. We've ignored it.

"We've been waiting for you to be ready," Dad says. "We honestly had no idea you've still been surfing for this long. Em, I've seen what shark attacks can do to people, and while they're rare, you got lucky. And despite my anger, I'm so proud of you for not letting it control your life. But that still doesn't make what you did okay."

"Ren," Mom says, but Dad shakes his head.

"I need to say this—"

"I don't want to hear it." I stand from the chair, my hands braced against the cool counter top. The tiny, logical part of me screamed to sit back down, but again, no award for maturity. "Unless you want to say you forgive me, I'll wait. I don't—I *can't* listen to you say how disappointed you are in me. There's nothing I can do to change that. You said you're proud of me. Don't take that away right now."

I thought I wanted to talk, but what I really want, my parents aren't ready to give me.

I leave the kitchen, walking through the house and slipping out the back door.

I'm a coward, but at least I'm starting to feel whole.

Leaving my house, I have my comfort in mind. Walking to the ocean is quick enough. It's a short trip along the side of Ocean Avenue until I'm able to cut through the trees where the grass yields to sand. A soft surface to meet my bare feet.

This morning the waves were constant, set after set. Now the ocean is calm, a contrast to my wild heart.

Telling the truth doesn't mean it's easy to escape the lies. And I'm still fighting my way out of the ones I've told.

I plant my ass in the sand, close enough to the water that

the froth can kiss my toes. I wrap my arms around my knees and squint out to the horizon.

Emotionally, I see where my dad is coming from.

Objectively, I do not.

What happened to me is no different than someone getting in a car accident, or someone getting bucked off a horse. All very different circumstances, but all could end with a similar result.

But you don't tell a cowboy not to get back in the saddle after falling off a horse. You tell them to suck it up and keep getting on until they aren't afraid of falling anymore.

I was five when my dad started teaching me how to surf on my own, no more riding the board with him. At first I didn't stand up. Dad wouldn't let me. Instead, he had me on my stomach, riding the waves like a boogie board.

He said it was to help me get a feel for the waves. How the board rides with them. I didn't learn how to paddle and pop up in the sand. I learned in the water.

It's not the only method; most people learn the fundamentals on the sand, but it's how dad taught me.

So, I practiced and practiced until I told him I was bored with that. I wanted to start standing. He told me I wasn't ready, but I begged and pleaded. Adamant that I was ready. Dad fell victim to the younger Emery's manipulative charms and caved. Kind of. Instead of having me snap up on my feet, he made me ride a wave on my knees.

That was disastrous.

The board nose-dived into the water, flipping me over.

It didn't get bad until I broke the surface and another wave swallowed me, pushing me back under.

One of the board's fins knocked into the back of my head and kelp wrapped around my legs and went into my mouth, almost choking me.

I stayed down long enough that my lungs started to scream in agony.

I surfaced a few seconds later, gulping as much crisp air into my little body as I could, never getting quite enough to calm the panic inside.

Grabbing my board, the traitor, I marched my feet to shore and threw the board onto the sand.

Sitting next to it, I cried as my dad came to sit next to me. I threw him a baby-glare—one I would grow and improve. "I'm never surfing again! That was awful! I hate you."

"Oh, Em, don't say that when you don't mean it." He tried to pull me into a hug, but I moved out of his reach. "C'mon, try one more time. For me?"

It was awful and terrifying, but I bit my lip and mumbled, "Okay."

He didn't let me quit when I was younger, but he tried to force me to stop when I was older.

As I stare out into the ocean, I feel someone sit beside me.

"When did you figure out I'd come here?"

"Before you were even out the door," my dad admits. "I followed you here."

I don't say anything. I don't look at him.

"Sometimes I don't like admitting we're so much alike. When you were born I always wanted you to be better than me, do better than I did in life. But the more you grew up, the more I saw I was in a deep level of hell. You were worse than I was. Grandpa always used to say—"

"That I had your stubbornness and impulses, but got lucky with Mom's smarts," I finish, an almost smile on my face at the mention of Grandpa.

"Yeah." His voice sounds far away. "You don't know how

scared that made me. I was always so worried about bad things happening to you. When you were attacked and I was on the beach, my heart stopped. It was like I was frozen." His voice cracks.

"When Geer came back with you and I saw how bad it was, I cried. I had only cried one other time. And that was when the doctors put you in my arms after you were born."

"Dad." I look at him and suck in a breath. He looks trapped—reliving the memory through red-rimmed eyes. "You can't always protect me. Life is a game of risk."

"As a dad, I'm supposed to protect you."

I lean on his arm to comfort him, to show I understand. I'm not just his only child, but also his baby girl. "You have. And you still do."

"You hardly ever did what you were told. I don't know why I thought you'd give up surfing." He pinched the bridge of his nose. "I sure as hell wouldn't."

He's quiet. I'm quiet. Until he says, "You were right, Em. Saltwater runs deep in our veins."

"We belong to the ocean."

He nods. "We belong to the ocean."

Dad pulls me into his side and we sit on the beach, staring out at the horizon. It's been a while since we've been at the beach together, another thing we avoided for years, and it's nice to have the little moments back.

Or it is until Ren Lawson starts the conversation I've been dreading since he told me I wasn't allowed to date until thirty-five. "So about the boy."

"Yes?" Inwardly I groan, but physically keep my face blank.

"He's too old for you."

I can't stop the rolling of my eyes. "He's not even five years older than me."

He grunts. "He doesn't have a stable career."

"They say he's a better surfer than you were."

"Emery." He narrows his eyes.

"Dad." I narrow mine back.

"Shit," he mumbles. "He likes you and I hate him for it. He symbolizes everything I've been trying to ignore."

"And what's that?" Curiosity is a cat of mine.

"That you're no longer my baby girl. You're a woman."

I grimace at his words. "Please don't ever say that again." I shudder again before telling him, "I'll always be your baby girl."

"Remember that when you get married and you're dancing an arm's length away from your husband and you're shaking his hand after the priest pronounces you man and wife."

"Whatever helps you sleep at night, Daddy-O." I bump my shoulder into his before he stands up and helps me to my feet.

We're walking up the beach, back toward the house, when my phone goes off in my pocket.

Bash's name is on the screen.

"Hey, babe." There's a smile in my voice and I feel lighter than I did when he dropped me off earlier this morning. "Do you have a sixth sense for—"

"Emery."

I stop walking and Dad gives me a look. I don't give him a glance. Bash doesn't sound like himself. He sounds tense and anxious. My name quivers on his lips.

"I need you to come back to my place." There's a pause before he whispers, "I need you."

# CHAPTER TWENTY-NINE

*Bash*

THE PLAN AFTER DROPPING EMERY OFF IS TO PASS OUT.

The sexfest from earlier really drained most of my energy. All I want to do is sleep for the rest of the day. If I could be a professional napper instead of a surfer, I'd change careers in seconds.

Turning onto my street and nearing the house, I see an unfamiliar car parked in front of the garage.

Black paint, tinted windows, and a woman next to it.

I slam on the brakes in the middle of the street and look in the rearview mirror, wondering if I could reverse down it and get the hell away. I hesitate too long and another car heads in my direction.

I have no choice now but to go home.

The house I'm renting is on a dead-end street, naturally. Just my luck.

Standing in the driveway, with her arms crossed over

her chest and a foot rhythmically tapping the cement, is my mother.

Behind her is my father, looking down at the ground.

Typical.

My thoughts are muddled as I pull into the drive. The front end of the truck stops within a few inches of my mother. I'd never, ever hurt the woman, but the driveway is a half-circle and she isn't moving.

We stare at each other, both pairs of eyes hiding behind sunglasses. My fists clench around the wheel and I grit my teeth. Molars grind.

Without getting out of the truck, I reach for the phone in the cup holder. It feels as if someone else is in control of my body as the screen unlocks and I open my text messages, opening to the name on the top of the list and hitting the small phone symbol.

Slowly, the device rises to my ear.

And rings, rings, *rings*, until it doesn't and the voice on the other end is the comfort I need to soothe the burning anger in my chest.

"I need you to come back to my place—I need *you*." I can hardly tell if I'm actually speaking or if I'm just making noises.

"I'll be right there," she promises. "What's going on?"

I don't want to talk, but I don't want to be alone. My parents are watching me through the window. The hand that isn't holding the phone is white-knuckling the steering wheel to the point of no circulation.

On the other end, I hear an engine starting.

"Bash!" Emery sounds as frantic as I feel.

"I'm here. Where are you?"

"Five minutes, babe. Five minutes. Tell me what's going on."

My parents haven't moved. My mother keeps tapping her foot, refusing to concede first. Her stance is a message. She's not going to leave here until she gets what she wants.

And what she wants is my money.

"My parents."

Emery curses and I hope she's speeding now. If she gets a ticket, I'll pay for it.

She stays on the phone with me even though no words are being exchanged. It's enough though, to not feel so alone as I refuse to leave the truck.

I'm a grown-ass man who doesn't want to face his parents by himself. Pathetic.

But my mom likes to remind me she's in charge of controlling my whole career and can destroy me just as easily as she created me.

A car parks on the side of the road and I'm out the door before Emery can whisper that she's here.

My mother calls my name, but I ignore it as Emery steps out of her car.

She hasn't changed out of the clothes I dropped her off in, my t-shirt pooling around her thighs and over her leggings. Her arms wrap around my waist and she places her head on my chest. "You're shaking."

I run my hand down her hair before wrapping my arm around her neck. "I'm angry." The basic definition for the complicated mess that is me.

"Bash." Emery tries to pull back, but I don't let her go. I hold her tighter to me. She sighs. "You're her boss, remember? You make the rules. They can't make you do anything you don't want to do."

I know. I *know*. But when I try to do that, the guilt sets in. My parents gave up their dreams and sacrificed so much when I was younger and just getting started. And when I try to stand firmer with them, I'm reminded of that. Every. Single. Time.

Emery sees it all on my face.

"I'm not leaving," I reassure her as she looks around me with unease. "That's not why they're here, anyway. They don't care where I live as long as they keep getting money." I grab her hand, pulling her toward the house. "Let's just get this over with."

With Emery's hand in mine, we walk past my parents and into the house. Without looking to confirm, I know they're behind us.

I lead everyone into the living room and stand in front of the TV with my arms crossed over my chest. I tilt my chin at Emery, letting her know I'm okay for now, and she settles into the corner of the couch, curling her legs under her butt. No matter where she is in the room, she's on my side.

My parents stand on the opposite end of the couch and my mother looks ready for a fight.

She barely spares Emery a glance before her laser-focused eyes target me. "Sebastian."

"Mother," I say, nodding toward my father. He's like my mother's bodyguard, not saying anything, not engaging in anything. His presence is to be seen and not heard.

"When are you going to be done with this fit of yours?" Her arms cross over her chest.

"I'm not having a fit." It takes all the control I have, but I don't roll my eyes or throw in a curse word.

"You have commitments—"

"Commitments I can do from wherever I live." Airplanes and cars are such nifty little inventions.

"The waves here are not going to be enough to keep up at

your level. They're nothing."

This time I do roll my eyes. "Then I'll go back to California or Hawaii and train there every other month. It's not like I'm living in the desert. I have an ocean."

She wants to fight me more. I can see it in the way she presses her lips together. And she probably would've if Emery didn't jump up and offer to order some lunch.

I watch as my mother moves her attention away from me and finds her new target. I move closer to my girlfriend.

"Are you staying because of her?"

Lunch is forgotten.

I don't get a chance to answer before Emery says, "So what if he is? Don't you want your son to be happy?"

"Of course, but I also want him successful and that's not going to happen living here."

"He's already more successful than a lot of people his age. While some are just graduating college, up to their necks in student loans, your son is one of the best surfers in the world." *The* best, but now isn't the time for interruption. My girl is on a roll. "He has a ton of sponsors who throw enough money his way. He can retire from surfing before he has to."

They both stare at Emery in silence, no doubt trying to figure out why she's speaking. Mom's used to being the loudest voice in the room. But she can roar as much as she wants—Emery's words will still be more powerful.

"His entire life is in California," Mom tries to argue, but right now she's pulling at strings. Emery has her caught in a place she's not used to being—against a corner. She's used to doing the backing.

Emery leaves my side and moves closer to Mom, and lowers her voice. Dad and I watch frozen, but tightly coiled, ready to jump in to pull away the claws. "He's happier here. Can't you see that? Don't you want him to be happy?"

I should step in, handle my mom myself, but I hear something in Emery's words that she might not even be aware of. This is how she's wanted to talk to her parents, but Emery likes being the shield for other people rather than a sword for her own battles.

Mom doesn't answer. Her mouth is twisted to the side as she looks lost in thought. But I know that look. She's trying to keep herself from saying shit she doesn't want other people to hear.

She should care that I'm happier here, but she doesn't.

Knowing what needs to be done, I brace for the outcome as I step behind Emery.

She's the silent reassurance that I can do this. She's the support beam holding me in place. My hands rest on Emery's shoulders. She crosses her arms over her chest and we both stare at my parents.

Standing in a room shrouded in silence, the cold, narrow gaze of my mother becomes even harder. As if she can see into my mind, knowing the path it's traveling down.

She starts to warn me, but I'm quicker. "You're fired."

Not the most eloquently put or how I wanted to handle it, but Carpe fucking Diem and all that shit. Why put off something that can be solved with two little words?

Two words that go over as smoothly as chipped glass being dragged down a mirror.

Mom moves closer and I make sure Emery's out of the way before Mom's palm collides with my cheek. I don't look away from my mother. The only reaction she gets out of me is the lock in my jaw and the fire in my brown eyes.

I don't touch the mark that feels like fire as it wells up on my cheek. Emery stands where I pushed her, to the side, looking at the scene that just unfolded. Her green eyes wide and hands pressed over her mouth.

Mom looks stunned. Dad closes his eyes.

This isn't the first time I've been smacked by her. This is just the first time that she's done it in front of someone she's not married to.

The first time she hit me, I was fourteen and she smacked my cheek so hard my head jerked to the side as tears burned, unshed, in my eyes. Now, my body is numb to the touch. The only reaction is from the physical mark of her fingers on my skin.

There's a slight ringing in my ear, and Emery yells, but I can't hear the words as she tries to move in front of me. I grab her and bring her to my side.

"Leave," I growl. "You can't stay here."

My parents left with little resistance, especially after I handed them a check.

If they spend wisely, it should last a long time.

And it better 'cause that's all they're getting from me. Every cent was worth it to be done with them. Maybe one day we can try to rebuild our relationship, but I don't know how much time will pass until any of us will want to attempt to be a family.

After I shut the door on their retreating forms, I walk up the stairs to find Emery sitting on my bed with her legs crossed. She's changed from earlier, now wearing the one and only sweatshirt I brought with me. Her bare legs stick out from the material.

I stalk toward her, placing my hands on her upper thighs.

"You're amazing."

"Duh." She smiles, cupping my struck cheek, leaning in for a kiss. "You should let me fight all your battles for you."

"Only if you let me help you fight yours." I squeeze her thighs.

"This should be iced," she says softly as the pad of her thumbs brushes against the red mark. There's a heartbeat pounding in my cheek. Her hand stills when mine covers hers.

"Later." I kiss her palm before putting both her arms around my neck. She kisses my neck and I push her down on the bed, placing my body on top of hers. Her breath hitches when I put more weight on her. "I'm sorry you had to meet them."

The tips of her fingers brush the back of my neck. "I'm glad you called me."

"It went well with your parents?" I smooth some fallen hair out of her face. I don't want my problems to distract from what she needs to work on with her parents. She doesn't need to be focusing on mine.

She nods before shaking her head. "I ran from them." She gives me a look to not interrupt and I stay quiet as she explains. "But then my dad followed me out to the beach. I feel better after talking to him. He's starting to get it. It's just going to take some time for all of us. I haven't asked them yet, but I'm going to see if they'll help me find a new therapist."

"Good." She needs to address all the issues that she's been repressing, but at a speed she's comfortable with. "Maybe I'll go see one here as well."

With the move that I'll be doing soon, I'll need to find someone more local to talk to. Until then, I can still video chat with my current one.

"You should." Her hands move up and down my arms.

"You should look into them when you get back from packing up your stuff in Cali."

My arms dig into the mattress on either side of her head, caging her in. "Given any thought about coming with me?"

"What?" She laughs. "You mean between your invitation that got lost in the mail and when your mother shed light on who she really is? No, I haven't thought about it. Especially since this is the first you've offered."

I want to show her a sliver of my life in Cali before I pack it all up in boxes. It'll be a quick trip. One that will probably only take a few days. I'm not selling my place there, instead keeping it to rent out. According to Dez's mom, it's a good investment move.

She's already looking to find me a place here to buy.

"I want you there with me." I rest my forehead against Emery's. "Let me show you my world before I completely join yours."

Emery's hands go to my shoulders, pushing on them and I roll over onto my back, her body covering mine. With her head resting on my chest, I feel her nod before she agrees.

My arms drape over her back, keeping her close.

"You sure you want to do this?" she asks, and I hear the hesitation in her voice. She's afraid I'm not ready, that this is going to blow up and we're going to implode, but what Emery still hasn't realized is that this is where I'm supposed to be. In this town. With her. Finding a new life.

Her weight is the security, holding me together as my foundation shifts, realigning to a new path, one that leads to many roads unknown. I hold her tighter. "I'm sure, Firecracker."

# CHAPTER THIRTY

## Emery

A FEW DAYS AFTER NEW YEAR'S, WE'RE AT BASH'S HOUSE in California. Officially moving him out. He hasn't said it, but Bash is ready to cut ties with a lot of things here on the West Coast.

"OHMYGOD, BASH!" I scream.

We're in separate rooms of his house. He's packing his bedroom while I'm in one of the guest rooms. Which really is just a trophy room with a bed.

You know, for when he's feeling braggy and wants his guests to know how talented he is. But in a subtle, décor way.

He also doesn't have any kind of organizational packing methods. His exact words were, "Just throw shit in boxes."

I try to be organized. I like order, but that takes a backseat to being lazy most days, and today happens to be one of them.

I'm exhausted. And sore.

So fucking sore.

*Someone* thought that it was a fun idea to give me a tour of his home by taking my naked body on at least two hard surfaces in each room. Fun in the moment, but oh does my body hate me now.

Anyway, Bash's packing method is making the process easier, except when things need to be organized. Like breakables.

His trophies, for example.

This isn't the only room storing his prizes. They are in every room and I can't help but cringe as I hear him throwing items into the cardboard boxes we picked up last night.

The noises stop as Bash comes running into the room, looking around frantically. A shoe in hand. "What? What is it?"

I'm standing near the built-in shelving. One that is full of trophies, shot glasses from his travels, and other knick-knacks. In the midst of packing all of it, I find something that has me laughing at the weird kismet energy of the universe.

When he sees I'm fine, laughing instead of crying or panicking, he stalks further into the room, leaving the entryway and shaking his head. "Damn it, Emery. I thought I had to kill a spider again."

"Excuse me, that was a big-ass spider that fell from the ceiling. I don't think it was asking too much of you to kill it while I freaked out." I shudder at the memory.

"You took off your shirt in the process." His lips twitch at the memory of events earlier today.

"I had to make sure nothing got in the actual shirt."

"Uh-huh," he chuckles, crossing his arms over his chest. His bare chest. "So, what had you screaming this time?"

I hold out the framed photo in my hands.

He takes it, features pinched in confusion as he studies it. "It's me at a surf competition years ago. I don't get why you screamed though." He holds it out for me, not sure why he has it. "Is it because I'm shirtless? Does younger me do something to you?"

"Look closer, in the background." I laugh, because really, while he looks good in the picture, really good, I'm not freaking out to stroke his ego. The background is the real prize.

"I don't get—" he pauses, squinting his eyes and pulling the picture closer to his face. Nose to frame. "Is that *you?*"

I nod, not even bothering to stop my grin. "Don't I look cute?"

"How old were you?" He looks at me briefly before going back to the picture.

I move closer to look at the picture. I vaguely remember the event. It was here in California. "Thirteen or fourteen. I don't remember exactly."

In the picture, Bash is standing with his surfboard and trophy, smiling at the camera. It's not a magazine photo; it looks like it was taken on an old, crappy cell phone camera.

Maybe his mom took it. Before she became a momster.

Behind him, a little to the left, stands a little me. My hair is a tangled, wet mess from the saltwater and my body is facing directly toward the camera. But I'm not smiling. Instead, the photo catches me mid-sneeze. My face is all scrunched up with my nose pulled back like a pug's while my mouth looks like invisible hooks are pulling at my skin.

Really, I couldn't look any better.

"I could say something cheesy right now, but I'm resisting." I lean into him, looking at the picture with a smile. "But, aw, look at our first picture together."

He hooks his arm over my shoulders, pulling me into his side and nuzzling my neck. "I love it. I wonder if we can blow it up bigger."

I hold onto him, closing my eyes when I feel his lips brush the side of my head. His chest bounces off my cheek as he chuckles.

"You're ridiculous," I tell him, hoping he's not serious. That picture should stay the size it is.

"You appreciate it," he reminds me.

I do and wouldn't have him any other way—look at me being all cheesy.

I have to get out of California.

# CHAPTER THIRTY-ONE

*Bash*

"I DON'T WANT TO DO IT." EMERY MOANS, HER HEAD falling back and hitting my shoulder. "Why are you making me?"

I'm kneading into her shoulders, massaging her stiff muscles. We've been back in Florida for a few days. Only staying in California long enough to pack up my stuff so the movers could bring everything here.

I thought I was going to feel a little something about leaving, but after the boxes were cleared and my place was barren, I felt as empty as the house looked. As we were leaving, almost out the door, I turned off the light in the foyer and when the room went dark, my time there was over.

Since coming back, I've upped my workout routine in the mornings, logging in countless hours, more than I had been, staying in the water until my skin prunes.

And Emery, since she wants to get back on the scene and

truly be ready for it, has been working out with me. No more surfing in secret for her.

Unfortunately, she wasn't as in shape as we thought.

She's been sore and aching and doesn't stop complaining until I get to work on her muscles. An activity she takes great pleasure in.

My girl likes having me at her mercy.

"I'm not making you do anything, I'm just telling you that it's probably better if you told your parents today, you know, since they think you're going back to school tomorrow."

"They've been out of town since the day after New Year's. I can't ruin their first day back in town," she argues. Her mom had a conference to go to and Ren went along now that Emery isn't on lock-down.

Things still aren't the best between them, but she's been talking to them every day and that's been an improvement.

"Emery," I say, digging my elbow into one of the tighter muscles on her back.

She's been using the same excuse all day, hiding behind it and pushing the issue away. But since she's not going back to college, she'll be living with her parents and they're going to notice that their daughter is at home and not in Orlando like her best friend. They're not dense. So she's going to have to suck it up and stop with her avoidance.

"I know, I know, Surfer Boy." Her sigh quickly turns into a moan from my elbow. "I just don't want them to be mad at me."

"They'll be more mad at you tomorrow when you don't actually go to school."

"What if I tell them I'm doing online classes?"

Now it's my turn to sigh, shaking my head down at her. "Do I need to remind you of Christmas? When you didn't tell them about surfing and they grounded you?"

She grumbles something I can't hear before saying, "I still can't believe they grounded me at nineteen."

I can't either, but then again, having parents who care and worry about their child is such a strange concept to me.

But that's the kind of parent I want to be. A parent who gives a double damn about his children.

You know, one day in the far, far, way far off untouchable future.

Looking down at Emery, I see my exhaustion reflected in her. These past few weeks have been hard and I can't help but push her to face one more hardship.

"Sure you don't want me to go with you?" I ask for the third or fourth time. So far, her answer hasn't changed.

She needs to do it by herself. Just like with her surfing, this conversation is between her and her parents.

Em shakes her head, confirming what I already know. "I'm sure."

Conceding, I remind her. "You can come back over after and I'll have sushi waiting for you."

She pulls away, peering up at me, interest showing on her face.

I smile. She'll agree to pretty much anything for food, especially if it's one of her favorites.

"And a movie?"

"All the movies you added to my movie queue." There's over ten that she added on the flight home from California. She gave me shit for not seeing any of them. God forbid I haven't seen any cheesy romantic movies from the early 2000s.

"Will you drop me off?" she concedes.

"Nah," I tell her. "Since your car's not here I thought I'd just let you walk."

She backhands my chest, softly. "Ass."

I laugh, squeezing one of her ass cheeks.

She pulls away from me with a glare. "No, no, no!" Her glare is coupled with head shaking. "You don't get to go from talking me into telling my parents to feeling me up. Do you want me to get this done or not?"

"I'd rather be doing *you* right now, but sometimes we have to be adults."

"Ha-ha, aren't you funny," she deadpans.

"You think I'm pretty funny." I try to reach for her, but she moves further away and out of my reach.

"*You* think you're funny. I provide pity laughs." She folds her arms over her chest as she stands above me, her glare firmly in place.

"Did you also give me a pity orgasm this morning?" I grin.

She's not amused as she turns around, walking down the hallway to the garage. As she goes, she calls over her shoulder, "Grab your keys, Bash. And I want sushi on your naked body when I come back."

# CHAPTER THIRTY-TWO

## Emery

SADLY, I DO NOT GET SERVED SUSHI ON MY BOYFRIEND when I get back to his place later that night.

Instead, I'm greeted with a frazzled Bash. I'm barely up the driveway when his door swings open and he says, "We have a problem."

"Damn right we do. You're supposed to be completely naked covered in artfully prepared fish rolls." I eye his naked chest before putting my palms on his abs. They slide over the ridges and tight muscle as they make their way down to his athletic shorts' waistline. "These need to come off."

"Not that kind of problem." He smiles at me, but it's defensive. "Dez is here."

I'm not seeing the connection between company and his weird attitude. Dez is with Bash most of the time.

Dez being here doesn't really scream *problem*, ignoring the fact that I'm not his biggest fan. Or a fan of his at all.

"What's he doing?" I raise a brow. "Streaking in the backyard?"

"Negative. He's being a drunken mess on my couch." Bash comes outside, easing the door closed behind him. "How did things go with your parents?"

I narrow my eyes. I can smell a subject change like a bloodhound.

He's hiding something.

If it's about Dez that means it's probably about Brit.

A surge of protectiveness toward my best friend surfaces and I try to move past Bash to storm into the house with fire in my eyes and nails as knives.

Bash catches the murder on my face and grabs me around my waist. He brings our bodies together, my back to his chest, and I squirm in the embrace. Legs leaving the ground and flailing about.

"Oh no," he tells me. "You're not going in there until you calm down."

"I am calm." My tone is anything but calm and I'm struggling in Bash's hold even more. Wiggling isn't getting me anywhere, so I aim my heel for his knee. He barely flinches.

"Calm as an angered bumble bee," he deadpans.

I'm squirming like a crazed animal and he doesn't sound like he's struggling at all. Holding onto me with ease.

The bastard.

"Put me down, Sebastian." I try a new form of attack, digging my nails into his skin.

Bash hisses in pain the deeper I go, but he still holds on, keeping my feet from touching the ground.

"Not until you're calm and you tell me how it went with your parents."

"I refuse to talk to you rationally while you hold me like

a monkey."

"You're the one flinging your limbs around like one," he argues, lips brushing the shell of my ear. The kiss contrasts with the strength of his hold.

"Bash," I say.

"Emery," he counters.

"If you put me back on my feet, I'll tell you what happened."

He does, only to keep his hands on my waist. His grip is tight, anchoring me to the spot.

He's a good friend for trying to protect Dez, but he's only delaying what will happen. I'm imagining nails to the eyeballs or suffocation by a pillow over his face.

I need a release after what went down with my parents.

"What happened, Em?" Bash pulls me from my torture plans.

"They weren't mad," I whisper, hoping the wind, which is barely at a breeze, catches my words, blowing them away before he hears. But he does and I watch as his face compresses into confusion.

"Isn't that a good thing?"

I nod, shake my head, and nod again. Confusing not only him, but also myself.

I've been confused since I left my house though, so it's not really saying much.

"I thought that they would be pissed, like they were on Christmas, but they got really quiet instead," I tell him, remembering the looks on my parents' faces. It was like masks were being placed over them, covering their real feelings and hiding them behind something fake.

"At least I'm not grounded, right?" I shake my head again, laughing without humor. "Do you want to know what they said to me?" Pressing on without waiting for his reply, I tell him,

"That they aren't surprised. College isn't for everyone. And it's not. That's what I've always said, but hearing it from my parents? It hurt."

The pain is still present in my chest from their words. They didn't believe in me. At least, that's what I first thought.

Closing my eyes and taking a deep breath, I finish telling Bash what happened.

The condensed version, anyway.

"So, yeah." I stall for a few more seconds. "We talked a little more and decided that I'm going to take this semester off since classes are probably full anyway, if I find that I miss it, I can just go back and start taking online classes in the summer."

He stares at me for a while after I finish explaining. I shift nervously from one foot to the other, waiting for him to say something.

It's a little awkward since Bash is still holding me by the waist.

Finally, his face breaks out in a smile.

He pulls me close, burying one of his hands into my hair so he can cradle the back of my head. "That's great, Em." His voice matches the excitement of his words. "Now we can get you ready for your comeback."

Like my mind isn't in the water twenty-four seven already.

"Yeah." I nod, but pull away slightly so he'll see my face for the next part. "On two conditions." Well, just one condition that applies to two people. "I don't want you or Dad to help me. Outside of training, that is."

I want to do this on my own. Achieve this on my own. I want to know if the track I was on when I was younger, before my accident, had anything to do with my dad or not. If I have the talent that I think I do. But there is only one way to tell.

My way.

"Deal, but you do know that once your name is out there it's going to be associated with your dad and me."

I do know that and I hate that my success will be seen as a reflection of the men in my life. That my talent will be questioned because of who I go to bed with or who I'm related to. But I also know that if anyone tries to accuse me of skipping dues they had to pay and not working as hard, I can say that they're wrong.

That I climbed and fought to the top all on my own.

No matter what men I associate with.

"I'd like to see them try." I push up on my toes, kissing his lips. He kisses me back, opening my mouth against his as he pushes his tongue to mine.

As his hand leaves my waist, moving a little further down, I push away from him so fast I stumble backward.

"What the fuck?" He looks at me, but I quickly turn around and run for the door. One problem taken care of and now it's on to the main attraction of the night.

"Never let your guard down, suckaaa!" I yell as I go into the house.

"Emery, fucking don't!" Bash moves to come after me, but I'm already through the door and slamming it closed.

Right in my boyfriend's face.

Oops.

I hear noises coming from the living room, groans and bottles hitting the floor.

"What the fuck is wrong with you?" I yell as I walk into the room.

I see the backside of Dez's body as he leans forward. Hunched shoulders that are folding into his body and his elbows are digging into his sweatpants-clad thighs.

Dez doesn't react to my words. He doesn't even

acknowledge that I spoke or that I've moved further into the room and am now standing in front of him.

He looks miserable and smells like stale beer that's been left in the sun for too long. And his hazel eyes are tinged with red with dark circles dragging down his cheekbones, making his tanned skin look a shade or two lighter. He mumbles something in Spanish, the word harsh as it leaves his mouth. Probably something about me being here.

I don't care. I keep my glare firm as Bash comes into the room, looking at me standing over his miserable friend, who is clutching the bottleneck of a beer.

Several empty bottles litter the floor around his feet.

"Em, don't," Bash warns as he moves further into the room. No doubt to pull me away from Dez.

Yeah, not happening, Surfer Boy.

"I'm not doing anything," I defend, looking at him with what I hope are innocent eyes. Hoping that he can't read minds and see that I was, moments ago, thinking about taking one of the empty beer bottles that decorate the floor and smashing it over Dez's head.

"Leave him alone." Bash walks toward me, carefully, like I'm a feral cat he's trying not to spook. "You don't know what happened."

"Yes, I do." My voice rises, bordering on a shout, and I try to reign in. Try to focus on the calm. Except there is no fucking calm in my body at the moment. "Dez did what he's always done and he fucked up. He did something to hurt my best friend and now he's here feeling sorry for himself."

My words are cold and I don't care. Because if he's like this, then Brit is ten times worse. I know my best friend and she feels every single emotion, every fiber of feeling.

Dez has had the power to destroy my best friend since we

were growing up and he's finally done it. Destroyed one of the sweetest people in our town.

But Bash shakes his head at me. "That's not what—"

"I told her I didn't want us to stop seeing each other after she goes back to school and she broke things off with me."

My brain does not compute. I hear his words, I understand what Dez is saying, but I refuse to accept the truth behind them. "Was there even anything to break up, Dez?" My tone isn't any nicer than it was when I first came in. "You didn't even want to date her."

"But we were," he argues back, his voice soft. Like a blanket in the cold. "We were dating since two days before Christmas. We weren't telling anyone because we both thought I'd fuck it up. But I didn't. I didn't," he argues louder. "She ruined us. Ruined me."

"Dez, why would she trust you after only a few weeks?" Bash looks at me strangely. I ignore it. "You've played her emotions too many times. You've never acted like you wanted anything serious."

Dez looks up at me. His face flushed from all the alcohol, eyes bloodshot, and hair all a mess. Despite all of that, he's angry with me. So angry that even the amount of booze he's consumed cannot disguise how much rage is in him.

Only his body does.

Dez tries to stand up, but he ends up wobbling on his feet and falling ass first back onto the couch. "I've been in love with her since we were in middle school!"

It's a rare time when I get stunned into silence, so much so that there is absolutely nothing running through my head. It's just empty.

One of those rare occurrences is now.

Until the first word that returns to me flies out of my

mouth. "Bullshit."

Middle school wasn't that long ago and if he loves her like he says, then he should've done something about that in high school. But my memories conjure up a different history, one that shows he barely acknowledged her.

His bloodshot eyes glare at me. "Fuck you and your bull-shit, Lawson. You don't know shit about me and her."

*Oh yeah, drunk guy?* "She's my best friend."

"And she's the girl I lost my virginity to."

Within the span of countable seconds, Dez again steals my words and thoughts.

Oh my God. What did he just say?

Bash is now behind me, bracing his hands on my shoulders like he's trying to steady me. Am I swaying? Lightheaded? Woozy?

What am I feeling?

Like I got dunked into a bathtub with water from the arctic.

Dez, either too drunk or numb to care, doesn't address my frozen look. No, now that I got him talking, he's on a roll. "Her freshman year, my sophomore. It was after a football game, during a party I was having at my parents'. We snuck up to my room, locked my door, and took each other's virginities." His head falls into the hands, muffling his next words slightly. "She avoided me for the rest of the season after that. I was going to ask her to homecoming the following week, too. I thought that's what I wanted. To date me. But after that she acted weird when I came around, I didn't want to make her uncomfortable, so I left her alone."

He roughly runs his hands up and down his face, pulling skin as he goes on. "I don't know how to do relationships any-more. I don't think I ever did, but when I finally got her? I had to ask her, but then she fucking freaks out and tries to throw a shoe at my head." He glares at me. "You make her mean, Emery. You're a mean bitch who's hated me for years, but guess who's always treated who like shit, hmmm?"

Bash digs his hands deeper into my shoulders. I don't know if he's trying to hold me back or himself. "Dude. I know you're having a shit day, but call Emery a bitch one more time for any fucking reason and your ass will be outside. If I'm feeling nice about it. If not, it's going to be a hell of a lot worse."

"Thank you, Bash." I grin up at him and he glances at me briefly before going back to stare at his friend. I don't mention that I didn't get angry when Dez called me a bitch because to him, I'm nothing but mean.

Not saying it's okay to be called that, because it's not, but Dez only knows that side of me now.

"I fucked up," Dez moans as his head flops back into his cradling hands. "No," he amends. "She fucked up. She's going back to college tomorrow, right?" He doesn't wait for an answer. "She's pushing me away. Why is she pushing me away?"

Dez isn't my favorite person, not in the slightest, but as I stand in front of him, watching the man break down as he forgets other people are in the room with him, my heart breaks.

Stepping away from Bash, I sit on the couch next to Dez, wrapping the blanket that's chilling on the couch across his back and around his shoulders. My arm curls across his shoulders as I hold him to my side for a few minutes. It's awkward, but I don't pull away.

Not until Dez does and sprawls out on the cushions.

I get up as Bash places some medicine and a bottle of water on the table next to the couch. He grabs my hand and pulls me out of the living room to his room and pushes me down on the bed.

My mind is reeling, going around and around Dez's words,

trying to piece them with my high school memories and they don't fit.

Brit is my person. I know her. Or…at least I thought I did.

"Why wouldn't she tell me?" I whisper to my hands in my lap. I don't feel betrayed. Just hurt that she thought she had to keep this from me. We were all friends once, but it seems I was the only one left behind by Dez. Brit always had him.

Bash crouches in front of me, his finger goes under my chin, and raises my head to meet his eyes.

"Hey," he whispers back. "Don't overthink it. Don't dwell on it. Just ask her about it later."

"But—"

"She's not going to tell you right now, Em. She's not going to tell you over a text or a phone call. If you go over there right now, she's not going to open the door."

Damn him. He's right. And damn him for knowing my best friend. Brit doesn't let anyone in when she's hurting, and if what Dez looks like is any indication, she's not going to let me in yet.

"I just—I just don't know how to feel right now. I feel alone," I admit, hugging my elbows.

"Hey," he repeats. "You're not. I'm here. And Brit's never left you. You'll work this out, Firecracker. You know better than anyone that people keeping secrets think they're protecting the people they're hiding it from."

Did he have to go and throw that argument at me? Have to get all philosophical and rational when I don't know what's happening?

"Fine," I concede, not having the energy to think. To dwell. There's another important issue tonight. "You still owe me your body covered in sushi."

Bash gives me a look. "I think we can arrange that for another night."

# CHAPTER THIRTY-THREE

## Emery

"YOU HAVE FIVE SECONDS TO START TALKING," I TELL Brit as she walks into my room. She raises an eyebrow, but walks further in.

As she does, I assess her appearance. Her dark hair looks washed, even having a nice shine that reflects the ceiling lights. Her metal-gray eyes look well rested with no red outlines and no swollen purple bags weighing her face down. Even her makeup is put together, with the perfect shaping and shading of her drawn brows.

Brit doesn't look like she's going through any emotional turmoil. The only distress she's projecting is with her steps as she walks to my desk. Her footing is as unsure as her facial expression.

Pretty sure I'm scaring her—which is appropriate retribution for how scared she's making me.

Brit never puts in extra time when she comes over,

especially when we're doing movie night. The only time she really does is when she's masking the pain on the inside with an allusion of perfection on the outside.

She's hurting. A lot, judging by the winged liner she has going on.

Her reaction parallels Dez's. They're both aching, but one wears their pain while the other numbs it. So what the fuck actually happened?

"What are you on today?" Brit asks.

"I want to know what happened between you and Dez."

Her eyes widen slightly, but other than that she doesn't give any reaction. Not until she says, "How did you know—"

"Because he woke Bash and me up in the middle of the night last night puking every little thing in his stomach." I shudder at the memory. "And because he told me."

My least favorite person told me because my favorite one didn't.

Now guilt settles in her features, as Brit looks away.

"He wants to actually be with you and you kick him to the curb?" My head aches from trying to think as she does, trying to understand this push and pull that goes on with Brit and Dez.

"He doesn't mean it," she whispers and her voice cracks on the last word. "I think a part of him wants to mean it, but I'm leaving today so he's trying to keep me tied to him. He wants to use me."

"He said you were dating."

"Code for fucking," she clarifies. "That's all we do."

I don't think so. I saw Dez and that is not the reaction of a person who wants to keep a girl only to ride his dick. Especially one that is going back to school two hours away. "What aren't you telling me?"

Brit bites her lip and she looks down at her lap, where she's wringing her hands together. "He's done a lot and I keep wanting him to change, but that's unfair to everyone involved. He is who he is, but he's not who I want him to be."

"Who do you want him to be?"

"Someone who doesn't hide behind the lies on their tongue and tells the truths in their heart." She adds, "I don't want easy words to make me happy, saying what he thinks I want to hear. I want hard and difficult, I want to know that what we have is real."

"And it's not with Dez?"

She bites her lip and shakes her head. "I can't stay away from him, because I want it to be him. I *want* him, but he's not for me."

"He also told me that you two took—"

"I can't talk about this anymore," Brit says, not giving me any time to answer before asking a question of her own. "How's Bash settling in since officially moving to Florida?"

I concede to her. For now. But she and I will be talking about what Dez told me.

"Good." I glance at my phone seeing a text from Bash and do a double take.

So, I did a thing.

*Oh God.* I stare at the text from my boyfriend.

Oh God.

I text back. Immediately sending another.

What did you do?

"What's going on?" Brit asks.

I hold up a finger for her to wait as I stare at the texting bubble. When my phone vibrates with his response, my mouth drops open. Not at his words, because there are none. Instead, Bash sent a picture.

"Oh God." I cover my gaping mouth with a hand.

"What the hell is going on?" Brit tries to grab my phone, but I swat her hands away.

"Shhhh!" I yell, looking down at the picture filling my screen. Staring back at me are the biggest brown eyes I've ever seen. I press a hand to my mouth as I make a call.

"Emery—" Bash starts, but he's not getting the chance to finish.

"You got a puppy?" I ask and Brit mouths back, *a puppy?* Excitement is growing in both our eyes.

"Yeaaaah." He drags out the word, like he's stalling. "It kind of just happened."

"Bringing home a puppy *kind of just happened?*"

"Well—"

"Bash," I interrupt as he starts laughing. In the background, I hear the puppy give a high-pitched bark. My heart soars at the sound.

"Sorry, but come over here. He's barking at his reflection in this mirror." His voice sounds soft and distracted. "I want you to come meet him."

I'm already out my door with Brit close behind before he even starts to ask.

They're on the porch when I pull my car into the driveway. Bash's back is leaning against the railing. His blue shirt is tight, just enough to see his muscles, but not tight enough to look like a douche. I don't see a pup at first, but I do notice they're not alone.

Xavier is standing with them. His face is bent down at the bundle he has in his arms.

He's holding the puppy! A sense of giddiness takes over and I try to take my keys out of the ignition before I even have the car in park. Brit gives me a look as my hand slaps down on the gearshift.

"Em." Her voice is full of caution, as if my behavior is scaring her. "You have this look in your eyes that's freaking me out."

"It's a puppy!" I look at her, blinking. As if that would clear the glossy glaze of the craze.

Brit nods, slowly. "Yes, yes it is. And you don't want to scare it."

No, I don't. I want to hold it.

I realize I'm acting a little irrationally. Even for me. But here's the thing. I love dogs. Like *lovelovelove* them. If one walks by me, I'll get all teary-eyed. This might not be a healthy kind of love, but it's the purest form I know. Dogs give so much, do so much for people, and no matter what, no matter how much you screw up or fail or fall down, they will always be there to pick you up and love you.

Bash has never had a dog. His life has not known pure light until this moment. His momster took so much away from him during his childhood. Now he's grasping at the fraying straws of memories he missed out on.

Bash meets me on the steps of his porch while Xavier is still hogging the puppy, making it hard to get a clear look at him.

"When did you decide this?" He's never mentioned wanting a dog, only that he missed out on having one growing up.

"When I saw him," Bash explains. "We went to lunch by the beach and they were doing this event. One of the booths had adoptions." Xavier puts the pup on the floor and my eyes bulge as the small white and tan creature runs toward us.

I crouch down and his wet little black nose bumps mine before his tongue hits my cheek.

My heart melts as I scoop him into my arms. He licks my face again and Bash grins at him before finishing his story. "We were walking past and this sucker," he rubs the puppy's head in my arms, "starts crying as we go. So we stopped and he licked my fingers and I got him."

"Just like that?" I raise a brow.

"I'm a very impulsive person," he defends.

That he is. If he wasn't, he would've never come here and we'd both be in different places in our lives. It's crazy how some choices require no thought, only action and how those decisions can turn into some of the best of your life.

They open new doors and opportunities. New adventures with new people.

Sometimes life will open up a door you long since closed, where you open your heart to another person.

*Or animal*, I think as I look at the furball in my arms.

The risks in life might be scary in the moment, but in the end they take you where you need to be.

Later that night, after dinner with Xavier, Bash and I are sprawled out on the bed. Today has been exhausting. Between not sleeping because of Dez, Brit's weirdness, and spending all day outside playing with the new puppy, this girl is exhausted and ready to sleep. The puppy is between us, sleeping away.

He doesn't have a name yet. Bash can't decide on one, so we've been calling him Puppy or Pup. Brit and Xavier kept throwing out names as we tossed a tennis ball around in the front yard. The last name Brit suggested, before Geer came to pick her up, was Muffin, which Bash gave a firm no to. Brit left after that, hugging me and promising to let me know when she makes it back to school safely.

As she drove away, I had a few tears prick my eyes, the watery bastards threatening to fall. This is the first time Brit and I aren't going to be attached at the hip for the chapters we're about to begin. She's finishing up her sophomore year of college and I'm about to try for a career in my sport.

I'm getting all teary-eyed thinking about it now. It's always been Brit and me against the world, tackling challenges and hardships together. We've always been there for a shoulder to cry on or for someone to toss confetti with in celebration.

She's only going to be two hours away, but that distance feels tripled. No more best friend Sunday movie dates. No more walking down the dorm hall with a bottle of wine and cheap plastic cups.

My best friend and I are growing up and finding our places in life without the other beside them. It's sad and nerve-wracking, but most of all, it's exciting.

A little wet nose bumps my chin before yawning in my face as the pup snuggles into the bed. His head rubs against one of the pillows as he gets comfortable between Bash and me.

Bash has his elbow on the mattress and his head propped on his hand as he watches the both of us.

I play with one of the pup's soft ears as I nod. "What breed is he again?"

"Pit-lab mix."

I grab one of his paws and spread the toes apart. Pit bulls aren't water dogs. Most of them don't swim well, often sinking. All the muscle mass doesn't do well with water, but labs are pretty much the definition of a water dog. So I check the puppy for webbing between his toes, the classic trait of a water dog. Sure enough, he has them.

The puppy tries to bite my hand. Bash pulls him away from me, cuddling the critter to his chest. The furball wiggles around, trying to turn his body around as his head is against Bash's chest, looking up at him.

"He needs a name." Bash's hand rubs his little pink belly.

Now, there are some things a woman can't deny. One happens to be when men hold babies and another is when they're holding a puppy that does something to their insides.

Bash is an attractive man, a quality that isn't just recognized by me, but also the internet, yet when he's holding the puppy, I feel my face flame and my temperature tip towards feverish.

"What are you thinking?" I scratch at the base of my neck, pulling away the collar of Bash's shirt I stole earlier. Guy t-shirts are so much comfier than women's.

"I was kind of hoping you could help me." He looks at me with puppy dog eyes that are mirrored by the wide, brown eyes of the pup.

As much as I love the dog, because this is the kind of love at first sight I'm on board with, he's not mine. "He's yours."

Bash just rolls with what I said, not even letting the statement faze him. "Yeah, but you're going to be here with him. And I can't think of a name for him. So help me."

"Well, when you ask so nicely." I drawl out the words as I sit up on the bed. The pup pulls away from Bash and runs straight to me. I pick up his little three-month-old body and ask, "What's your name, little bean?"

He tilts his head to the side in that cute dog way, like he's trying to understand me.

"What about Hurlee?" I ask. "It means the sea tide."

Silence. My answer is greeted with silence.

"Or, you know, we can go with another—" I try to back-track, but Bash puts his hand against my mouth, shutting me up.

"I love it," he says. "That's his name."

I try to respond, but it comes out muffled by the palm that is still pressed to my mouth. I run my tongue, slowly, up the calloused hand.

"Is that supposed to make me want to remove my hand?" Bash raises an eyebrow. Despite the cocky brow lift, I see the emotion behind his eyes.

Since I can't speak coherently, I nod my head, his hand following the motions.

Hurlee watches us before he tries to bite Bash's wrist. I grin as his hand falls away. The dog is on my side. Things around here are definitely about to get more interesting.

Hurlee starts barking, trying to get attention from either of us, even though I'm still holding him. Bash pats the bed in front of him and the pup jumps out of my arms and darts off, putting his oversized paws over Bash's hand.

Hurlee tries to nip one of his fingers and Bash wiggles it in his face while laughing.

"Welcome home, Hurlee," Bash says with a huge grin on his face.

Today has been the happiest I've seen Bash since meeting him. In over a month his smiles have become less sad; the out of practice awkwardness has faded away.

He still has rough days, where he doesn't want to do any-thing or be around anyone, and no doubt will continue to have them. But his laughs aren't broken, his smiles are brighter, and his life is fresher.

Like me, Bash is starting over. Finding his footing on a new path full of awaiting adventures.

But for right now, for today, he's found his point zero. He's found his base.

"Welcome home, Bash," I whisper to him.

# CHAPTER THIRTY-FOUR

## Emery

*Two Months Later*

**I**'M SORRY, *WHAT*?" I SAY INTO MY PHONE.

"Dez is driving up to see me," Brit says and I have to check the connection. Because being in Hawaii has to have something to do with what I'm hearing.

"You and him are giving me whiplash." Seriously, I can't keep up.

She loves him, she doesn't. He loves her, it's a joke. They're casual, they're dating. They're not talking, he's driving up to see her. It's all very confusing.

"I know," she sighs. "But things are going to change after this."

"Brit?" I don't like the tone of her voice. She sounds detached and monotone.

"Don't worry, Em," she tries to reassure me, but the words fall flat like her tone.

"Brit—"

"Hey, I gotta go, bye!" She hangs up as I hear a knock on her dorm room door.

I sit on the edge of the hotel bed as Bash comes out of the bathroom. He's only wearing baggy athletic shorts while rubbing a towel over his hair, which is shaggier than it was when we first met. Little droplets of water run down his neck and onto his bare sculpted chest.

*Hello.*

I'll never tell him this because magazines do enough to feed his ego, but Bash is the most attractive man I've ever seen. Sometimes when he walks into the room, my breath will catch and my heart will race. The feeling takes me by surprise every time and it's one that I hope will never go away.

Bash makes my life better, makes me laugh harder. He also banters with me better than anyone else I know. I'll spar against him any day of the week.

Being on this trip has been fun, but I miss Hurlee. He's Bash's dog, but he secretly likes me better. The five-month-old pit-mix is staying at Dez's. He almost went to my parents', but I've been around Dez a lot these past two months, have seen him with his niece and nephew, and know that despite his flaws, he truly is responsible. But if one hair is out of place on that dog's body, there will be words—

Wait. Brit's dorm isn't dog friendly.

"Hey," I say. Bash looks at me, towel still in hand as droplets race down his chest. My tongue pokes out of the corner of my mouth. He raises a brow, a smirk growing on his face, and I blink. *Right. Focus, Emery.* "Dez isn't watching Hurlee. He's on his way to see Brit."

Bash doesn't look shocked. Doesn't even blink or looked phased.

"You *knew!*" I jump to my feet and march over to him. A finger presses between his pecs. "And you didn't tell me?"

My neck stretches out like a turtle's as I try to get in Bash's face. His lips twitch as he tries to keep from laughing.

"Calm down, Firecracker." He grabs both my wrists and brings them over my head, backing me up until I hit the wall. "He's with your parents."

"That's a better option for him anyway," I grumble as my body stretches up on the tips of my toes. "He doesn't need all of Dez's partying in his life. He's very impressionable in these early months." When we dropped him off at Dez's, I told him that we better not come back to the pup doing keg stands.

Dez made no promises.

"Be nice," he whispers, his voice much closer than before as he presses his body into mine.

"You don't want me nice," I remind him as he pulls at my earlobe with his teeth.

Since January, between my decision to get back on the circuit, Bash firing his mom, and having a new puppy to take care of, our lives have been crazy.

Things haven't settled, a lot of details are still swirling in the air around us, but for right now we're where we want to be. We're focusing on the now instead of what's going to happen in the tomorrow.

My dad has been helping both of us in the water, with assistance from Jason and Mick. All three of them even became Bash's replacement for his mom. Managing and training, basically helping my man outside of the water as much as in.

For me? It's my mom. Despite her insane hours at the lab, she's working her ass off with me.

I think she's using Dad to help, going to him for tips, but as upset as he was when I told him I didn't want his help, this is the least I can do.

I still don't trust the water and I never will. But I love it with all my heart. It's where my discomfort and comfort meet in the middle and despite never knowing what's swimming with me, I feel at home.

I feel at home in the ever-changing scenery of the sea.

It's on land that I'd rather not be.

Bash pulls away and I chase after him, my body a magnet to his.

"Hey, Em?" His voice gives me pause.

The rushing heat that consumes my body freezes. "Yeah?"

"I love you."

Three simple words, *I* and *love* and *you,* strung together to mean something so much grander than the basic function of the individual words.

My heart stops and my breathing slows, my pulse rate drops dramatically as the words crash over me again and again and again.

*I love you*

*I love you*

*I love you*

"I love you too," I say, or I think I do. Maybe I thought it. Everything feels discombobulated. Feeling as if I'm observing things from the outside, I taste the words as they leave my lips. I've always thought they would taste like ash.

Yet, they don't. They taste natural, sweet and sugary. Like chocolate chip cookies fresh out of the oven. Or maybe that's because I'm hungry.

I love yous have always scared me. I've spent almost twenty years avoiding saying the words to anyone who isn't family. And then this Hawaiian-born Californian crashes into my life and throws that entire belief out the window.

Bash chases my words with his mouth as he kisses me with a new kind of hunger. One I've never felt from him. One I've never felt myself.

Soon my clothes are gone and his shorts are at his ankles.

I'm trying to branch out with my clothes, wearing more shorts on the occasion, shorts that are now on the floor next to his, but blogs and online articles haven't been kind to me, saying shit that has made me want to hide behind the denim and cotton and neoprene. Even the girl with the thickest skin as her armor can crumble with the right hit.

Bash is always there though. He gives me strength when it's too hard to stand on my own.

And it's because I love him and he loves me that I know whatever we face we'll have each other for the highs and lows. Plus, we'll have Hurlee, and that makes everything better.

He pushes me against the wall, rolling his hips into mine.

My head falls back against the wall as I arch against him.

Bash slips on a condom and slides into me. My nails dig into his back as he slams my back into the wall, thrusting up. He grabs my chin, bringing my mouth to his. His lips, his tongue, are as frantic as his thrusts. Dirty, sloppy, *hungry*.

A hunger building toward satisfaction as he moves us to the bed, covering my body with his. Sweat and sex fill the air around us and he bites my neck, my shoulder, growling for me to let go.

And I do; I let go and scream his name. His moans follow, muffled by his face buried in my neck.

Heavy breathing and pounding hearts fill my ears as I hold onto him.

After a while, Bash pulls back, licking my neck as he does. He gets up to dispose of the condom before climbing back into bed and pulling me on top of his chest.

I smile down at him, tired and sleepy, as his fingers drum over the scars.

"I hope you know that you're stuck with me now."

His hands still. "I don't remember agreeing to that."

I pinch his nipple as my lip fishhooks into a snarl. His hissing in pain quickly turns into a laugh as he slaps my ass. "Kidding, Firecracker. I wouldn't have it any other way."

"*Woooo!*" I cheer with the crowd around me as Bash comes in from his set. Cameras are flashing, catching my every reaction. Some lenses have been trained on me the entire day.

I'm wearing a slouchy tank and midi shorts. The shirt covers my scars, but the shorts don't. The denim cuts off as the raised fleshed carries down my leg and to the top of my knee. My cross-body bag, thankfully, has a long strap and is wide enough that, from certain angles, they can't be seen.

Or, what I truly fear, having them on camera. I can see the taglines now for online news articles if they do get a shot of them. Using my story for clickbait ratings.

A part of me wanted to wear jeans. It is the safer option, but I'm in Hawaii, on a beach, at a surf competition. Having legs that are clad in denim would've made me stand out more.

So here I am, standing in a crowd of people with a huge smile on my face as Bash walks my way. He just killed it out there, some announcers even commenting on how that's the best he's surfed in years.

Feeling proud and giddy, my feet start to move in place. Waiting with a bundle of excitement. As Bash comes closer, I'm unable to stop them from racing to him and jumping into his arms.

He's still holding his board, but catches me around the waist with his free arm. With my arms around his neck and my feet off the ground, bent at the knee, I hear cameras clicking and capturing this moment. And despite my reservations, I'm glad. I want him to remember this moment. I want us to remember the feeling of triumph while surrounded by chaos.

"You did it," I whisper in his ear. "You're back."

Bash doesn't say anything. He only squeezes my waist until I look at him and his mouth claims mine. The kiss is hard and drawn out. The kind of kiss that takes over the senses, that blocks the world out.

We kiss as they announce the scores, missing the numbers entirely. But it doesn't matter because Bash did it. He's made his comeback.

And in two months I'll be making mine.

Want more Bash and Emery? They're coming, but first Brit and Dez have their story to tell.

Coming soon!

# ACKNOWLEDGEMENTS

To Mom and Dad, you never let me give up on my dreams. You never told me I couldn't do what I loved. You only asked me when I was going to do it. You have always supported me, even if you didn't know what the outcome would be, you'd be there to either catch me if I fall or watch me soar. There are no words to describe how much you both mean to me, how much I love you, and how much I look up to you both.

To Matt, Zach, and Josh. You didn't ask for a fabulous older sister, but you got one anyway. And I never asked for three people who brighten up my days like y'all do. From the laughs to the pranks to ganging up on the parents, I have so many memories with you three that I cherish daily (aside from Z brainwashing my cat to love him more). We bicker and fight as siblings do, but you three are always my number ones. I love you, you crazy fools.

To my grandparents, two of you are here to see this moment and the other two are watching from above, but I hope that I've made you proud. So many of my favorite memories and stories to tell are about you. I know everyone probably says this about their grandparents, but I have the best. Thank you for never letting me go a day without your love.

To my Aunt Jenny and cousin Nikki, for all the tireless hours of editing and proofing, helping me whip this book into shape. No words can express how thankful I am for all the time you've put in. And to the rest of my fam, some of you might not get my obsession with books but you've supported me anyways.

To Grandma Dee, who stepped up when everything became too much, assured me of this story when I was feeling lost and helped me polish off the document after I made changes after changes. You might not be family by blood, but the fam and I love you dearly.

To Allison Riddles, thank you for being you. For being the best creative writing teacher I've ever had. Spring 2014, in your class, was the first time I ever shared my writing with other people. Thank you for seeing potential in my writing and helping me grow. The three semesters I spent with you taught me so much, expanded my writing, and gave me more confidence than I can ever thank you for. So, I'll just thank you for all the time you've put in to help your students, to help *me,* be a better writer then I was yesterday.

To my BFF Jessica, my lemon Morelia, and my book-twin Lacey. For being the first readers of *Break Line,* for seeing the potential and loving the story from the very beginning. You put up with my questions, my freak-outs, my hang-ups without complaining, even as I blew up your phones. You put so much time, did so many read throughs, that I think you know the story better than I do at this point. I'll forever be grateful for the book community, for many reasons, but the biggest three are y'all. Three of my best friends who know me better than anyone and are always willing to fangirl (and fight) over our book boyfriends.

To my forever friend, Julia, from writing self-insert fanfiction in your dad's computer room to workshopping in Riddles' class together. You've been with me since day one, the girl who

I share all my best memories with growing up. From the cumquat fights to baseball games to just riding in the car together and having every song that played be your favorite (we won't talk about the van you swear you didn't see). You're the sister I've never had, but the one I've never let go of. Thank you for reading and helping get BL to this point. For always being honest, not just with this book, but in life. You're the day to my night and the loud to my sarcasm. Thanks for always being weird with me.

To R. Scarlett, my dear sweet friend! I am so thankful you came into my life. Not only did I get Tensley, but I got you too. One of my closest friends whom I badger on a daily basis, bless you for putting up with me! I have so many things to thank you for. From all our convos (you're my long lost cousin!), your endless encouragement, all our word sprints, and all the guidance you provided for me along this journey—I honestly don't think I would've gotten this far without you. But most of all, thank you for your friendship. I'd be a mess without ya!

To my squad, Breezy, Dani, Alicia, and Aidan. For all the times we've sung musical numbers, to our beach days, our food dates, trivia nights and all of our random adventures, my life would be dull without y'all. You four are my backbone when I need someone to lean on, when my days are hard and I just need someone to talk to. When I said I was writing a book, that I finished said book, and wanted to publish it, y'all rallied behind me, keeping my head up when I felt discouraged and always being an ear to vent to.

To Alex, for calling me an author at the start of our friendship, long before *Break Line* was ever finished. For always asking me about my book, asking when it's getting published. For all your excitement, even when doped up in the hospital you'd ask me about BL, what the book cover was going to look like, and asking to see who the cover artist was going to be. I don't think I've ever told you, but your questions, your genuine interest gave me the push to get this book published. So, thank you for helping get to this point. Thanks for all the laughs and ridiculous looks you've given me, for showing me how frat boys shotgun beer under three seconds in my shower before screaming like a girl when you turned the shower head on. I think I still have that video somewhere. For all the FSU and football talk, I'm still amazed you didn't know bae's mascot—I've failed you. But most of all, thank you for our friendship. You'll always be my favorite frat boy.

To the friends I've met through blogging, especially my HWTB '18 girls! My days aren't the same without group chats or y'all laughing at me for whatever random shit I decide to freak out about that day. You girls are always there for me and your enthusiasm and support for this book have truly blown me away! (And a special thanks to all those who helped me polish BL off!)

To Bex Harper for being a godsend, swooping in at the last minute, and helping me when I felt like I was falling apart. Your time and dedication to help make this book as perfect as possible, on top of your enthusiasm for this book and the characters have been a ray of light I've needed! You rock my fuzzy socks ;)

To Autumn Grey, for messaging me on Facebook that one day and offering me so much advice and wisdom, and always being there to answer my questions. You are one of the sweetest people I know. Thank you so much for taking time out of your day to answer my questions and help me find solutions, and I'm so glad to have you in my life.

To Letitia Hasser and Stacey Blake, for all your hard work making my book as pretty as can be! I'm in awe of your talent. *Break Line* wouldn't stand out without you both!

To Enticing Journey, for blowing me away with all the hard work you put into making this book get into the hands of bloggers and getting my work out there. Your patience, kindness, and support mean everything to me!

To my reader group, thank you for your support of *Break Line* from the beginning. You all have blown me away with your excitement and support, and I hope you enjoy BL as much, or more, than you thought you would!

To all the bloggers, reviewers, and readers who pick up this book. Thank you from the bottom of my heart for picking up my baby. I know what it's like to be in your shoes and know how many books are out there to read, so I'm honored you took a chance on a new author and BL!

# *CONNECT WITH THE AUTHOR*

You can find her on:

Facebook Page:
www.facebook.com/authorsarahegreen

Reader Group:
www.facebook.com/groups/695086787351048/?ref=bookmarks

Instagram:
@wordswithsarah
www.instagram.com/wordswithsarah

Made in the USA
San Bernardino, CA
07 January 2020

62752712R00191